BY THE BAY 2:

MORE EAST BEACH STORIES

BY THE BAY 2:
More East Beach Stories

Written by members of the
East Beach Writers Guild:

Gina Warren Buzby
Patrick Clark
Michelle Davenport
Karen Harris
Will Hopkins
Elizabeth Kimball
Jamie McAllister
L. W. "Skip" McLamb
Mary-Jac O'Daniel
Jayne Ormerod
Mike Owens
Jenny F. Sparks

*Foreword by: Mary Ann Fussell
and Gayle Greene*

All characters in this book are fictitious, and any resemblance to actual persons, living or dead, is purely coincidental. Furthermore, all incidents, descriptions, dialogue and opinions expressed are the products of the authors' imagination and are not to be construed as real.

Copyright 2017 by:
Gina Warren Buzby; Patrick Clark; Michelle Davenport; Karen Harris; Will Hopkins; Elizabeth Kimball; Jamie McAllister; L. W. "Skip" McLamb; Mary Jaq O'Daniel; Jayne Ormerod; Mike Owens; and Jenny F. Sparks

All rights reserved. No part of this publication may be reproduced, stored in a retrieval system, or transmitted in any form or by any means—electronic, mechanical, photocopy, recording or any other—except for brief quotations in printed reviews, without the prior written permission of the author.

Cover art scene: East Beach Oak
Medium: Oil on Canvas
By Gina Warren Buzby, Professional Artist
Permission licensed to Bay Breeze Publishing, LLC
for book cover and marketing materials
related to *By the Bay 2: More East Beach Stories*.
All other rights reserved.

Back cover photo by Jessie Wilkens

ISBN-13: 978-1543151398
ISBN-10: 1543151396

Published by
Bay Breeze Publishing, LLC
Norfolk, VA

ABOUT THE BOOK

The East Beach writers are at it again, this time offering fourteen new fictional tales about life along the Chesapeake Bay. The neighborhood of East Beach in Norfolk, Virginia is the setting for these vignettes of family, friendship, mystery, history, adventure, love, and light-hearted fun. Join the characters as they walk the tree-lined streets, stroll the sandy shores, or relax on a rocking chair on one of the deep front porches that define this community. *By the Bay 2: More East Beach Stories* is the perfect beach read, whether you've got your toes in the sand or simply wished you did.

All proceeds from the sale of this book are donated to local non-profit groups dedicated to improving literacy. For more information on the designated charities, please visit our website, www.bythebaystories.blogspot.com and click on the Charities tab.

ACKNOWLEDGEMENTS

"Editing might be a bloody trade, but knives aren't the exclusive property of butchers. Surgeons use them too."
~Blake Morrison

The members of the East Beach Writers' Guild would like to thank independent editors C.B. Lane and Mike Owens for their expert eyes and honest feedback, which made all of our stories stronger.

When it comes to the t-crossing/i-dotting review, it took a village. Thanks to all first readers who caught spelling and grammar issues. Special thanks to contributing authors Karen Harris and Jamie McAllister, whose efforts went above and beyond the call of duty.

TABLE OF CONTENTS

FOREWORD
   by Mary Ann Fussell and Gayle Greene i

THE BEST OF FRIENDS
   by Jenny F. Sparks..1

COMINGS AND GOINGS
   by Karen Harris...13

THE DANCE LESSON
   by L.W. "Skip" Mclamb...................................25

DEAD DROP
   by Patrick Clark 43

FIRST LANDING
   by Will Hopkins..69

FORAYS INTO SAILING
   by Mary Jac O'Daniel....................................87

THE GATLINS COME TO EAST BEACH
   by Elizabeth Kimball 97

THE MERMAID
   by Jamie McAllister....................................115

MULE'S BIG DAY
   by Will Hopkins..127

PLEIN BLACKMAIL
   by Gina Warren Buzby 147

THE PRODIGAL
   by Mike Owens...165

TABLE OF CONTENTS

THE PROPOSAL
   by G. Buzby, J. Ormerod, and J. Sparks 179
TAG! YOU'RE DEAD
   by Michelle Davenport 195
WRITE BY THE BAY
   by Jayne Ormerod 207
ABOUT THE AUTHORS 225

FOREWORD

By Mary Ann Fussell and Gayle Greene

Here's a writer's mystery for you to solve. Which comes first: location or inspiration? Located on the Chesapeake Bay, near the first landing of ships ultimately headed to Jamestown in 1606, our locale has a rich history of gastronomically fabulous oysters, pirate's lore, Indians, sailors' shanties, and the famed Ocean View Roller Coaster.

Do writers move to East Beach because they know this epicenter of lighthouses, the shipping industry, and Doumar's Drive-in will lubricate their creativity? Or is East Beach—with its pristine beach, beautiful dunes, unique byways and new urbanism architectural design—so alluring that those who live here start to write stories they did not even know they had in their heads or hearts?

One way or the other, location is a significant factor that has inspired twelve members of the East Beach Writers Guild to create their second anthology of short stories. There are other elements, as well, that keep this group writing.

One is their ability to imagine themselves living out of their comfort zone, as evidenced in "The Dance Lesson" and "Tag! You're Dead." These stories bring readers to a point where they are more than a little uncomfortable.

Another aspect is these authors' unquenchable thirst for

adventure. "The Gatlins Come to East Beach" and "The Proposal" will make readers wonder why they are sitting on the beach reading and not out involved in their own adventures!

Perhaps it is their unique ability to transport the reader to a specific historical period with just a word or phrase. When you see the words "butch wax," you know "Mule's Big Day" is taking you back to the 1960s. When you are "marooned upon the desert strand of the great Chesepeook Sea" in "First Landing," you know immediately you are in the 1600s.

Or could it be from that special bonding that only comes with shared loss? "Breast of Friends," "The Mermaid," "Comings and Goings" and "The Prodigal" touch us deeply and make us thankful for friends and support.

Our East Beach Writers Guild is famous—or infamous—for its ability to draw us into the intrigue of a well-crafted mystery. With "Dead Drop," "*Plein* Blackmail" and "Write by the Bay," our unique group of neighborhood writers has perfected the craft of presenting a good mystery and solving the crime.

So what is it that pulls twelve skilled writers together to produce an entertaining, well-written anthology? Perhaps it is a well-bonded group with a keen sense of adventure, coupled with a love of writing and having a story to share. Or is it location? Or is it inspiration? It hardly matters! *By the Bay 2: More East Beach Stories* is an amazing anthology.

About the authors: Mary Ann Fussell and Gayle Greene are long-time East Beach residents. Both are avid readers and gifted writers. The members of the East Beach Writers' Guild thank them for sharing their time and talents to write this foreword, setting the perfect tone for the anthology.

THE BREAST OF FRIENDS
BY JENNY F. SPARKS

    Some people gravitate toward the city. The anonymity of walking down a busy street with skyscrapers towering over them is where they feel alive and at home. Others find their way to the mountains. Peace comes to them on a path strewn with pine needles, the tree branches swaying in the cool mountain breeze. Me, I need the ocean. There is nothing more soothing than the sound of waves lapping at the shore while gulls squawk overhead. I love the feel of the sand between my toes as I walk and ponder whatever might be troubling me. The beach is my happy place.
    It made sense that I would marry a Navy man. Most assuredly the water would always be a part of my life. It also made sense that as we were planning our final tour in the Navy we would settle in coastal Virginia. We searched and found the quiet shore-side community of East Beach in Norfolk. It's a quaint neighborhood with pastel-colored houses wrapped with welcoming front porches. Most of those porches are furnished with rocking chairs and dogs. Boston ferns hang from the rafters in front of many houses while beach towels hang from the railings in back. No one lives more than a few blocks away from the shore of the Chesapeake Bay. An easy walk when you need some peace.
    But today my walk down 26th Bay was not as easy as most

of them had been since we'd moved here nine months ago. My mind kept going back to the words I'd heard at the doctor's office that morning. I'd been in for a follow-up appointment after a biopsy. My mammogram had shown a mass. I go religiously every year and every year I get an "all clear." Until today.

"There isn't an easy way to tell you this, so I'll just come out and say it. The results of your biopsy show cancer. We need to remove the mass and then follow up with treatment."

I couldn't help but wonder what it must be like to tell someone this kind of news. Worry and concern had shown in the doctor's gray eyes.

A dull roar had begun in my ears and I'd had to shake my head to make it go away. Breast cancer. Every woman's worst fear had just become personal for me. There is a history of it in my family. I shouldn't have been surprised, but I was. For all of my fifty-three years I had done my best to live a good life. I do admit to two vices. One, I swear. Like a sailor. I blame it on my husband. After all, he is a professional sailor. A captain in the Navy, to be specific.

Of course, he was deployed overseas when I got the news.

My other vice is wine. I drink it. Daily. This I take complete blame for. I always justify this by drinking red wine. It's supposed to be healthy. I guess it isn't healthy enough.

I'd shaken my head again and came back to what the doctor was saying to me.

"We caught it early. I believe with the proper treatment you will be fine."

"And what is the proper treatment?"

"A combination of therapies has proven to be most effective. After we remove the mass you will need to have radiation and chemotherapy."

"I want to start as soon as possible."

We'd gone on to discuss treatment schedules, side effects and support groups. By the time I'd left, I had more questions than answers. I'd need to go home and google everything the doctor told me. But not before I spent a few restorative hours on the beach.

❖❖❖

I found a spot to settle in near the Bay Front Club. I stretched my five-foot-three-inch frame out on my blanket and waited for the sun and surf to work their magic. My mind swirled with thoughts and questions. How would I tell my husband, who was thousands of miles away? For that matter, how would I tell my children, my mother, and my friends? There were details to work out. Who would be willing to take me to my treatments? Visions of me without hair floated through my mind. For certain, I wouldn't be the prettiest girl on the pier when the ship returned.

"Are you all right, dear?" A strange voice woke me from my nap beside the Chesapeake Bay. "It's getting dark. I really don't think you should stay out here by yourself."

"Goodness. I must have drifted off. Thank you for checking on me." I rubbed the sleep from my eyes and tried to stretch myself awake.

"It's all right. If you were my daughter I would hope someone would do the same for her."

Standing, I reached my hand out to her. "My name is Grace. Grace Tucker. Are you new to the neighborhood?"

"I'm Judy Williams. I just moved into my daughter and son-in-law's carriage house."

"Well, welcome to the neighborhood. I think you'll like it here. Everyone is quite friendly. I hope you like dogs. It seems like everyone has one. Where did you live before you moved here?"

"Charlotte, North Carolina. After my husband died, my children thought it would be best if I lived near one of them. I chose here because the carriage house offers me a little independence and a lot of privacy."

"Sounds like a good plan to me." I folded my favorite faded blue beach blanket.

"It works. How long have you lived here?"

"My husband Sam and I moved here a little less than a

year ago. He's captain of one of the ships here in Norfolk."

As we walked back over the dunes, we continued to get to know one another. I learned that her husband had been a pediatric cardiologist at Levine Children's hospital in Charlotte. They'd moved there after he'd finished medical school.

Before I knew it we were in front of Judy's house on Pleasant Avenue.

"Well, I so enjoyed our visit, Grace."

"I did too, Judy. Would you be interested in lunch one day? Have you tried East Beach Sandwich Company here in the neighborhood?"

"That sounds lovely. Are you sure I'm not too old for you?"

"Not at all. How about day after tomorrow?"

"I'll see you then."

Navy wives aren't picky about making friends. It doesn't matter how old they are or what color their skin is. We take them when we can get them. I've been blessed to make friends from all walks of life all over this country and overseas as well. Something in me was telling me that I had just made a new friend in Judy.

❖❖❖

The next morning, coffee cup in hand and our golden doodle, Twyla, at my feet, I settled into a rocking chair on my own front porch to call my husband. One of the perks of being the commanding officer is having a regular telephone line in his stateroom. After years of only snail mail and email contact during deployments, I was enjoying the ability to hear his voice when I needed to. I tried to time my call to coincide with the end of his day on the other side of the world. I didn't want him to have to go through a workday and worry about me at the same time. We'd made a promise many years ago to never keep things from one another when we were forced to live apart. He knew about the biopsy. He wouldn't be completely shell-shocked when I told him I had cancer.

❖❖❖

My phone call with Sam had been emotional. I knew it would be. The sound of his voice always made me weepy when we were apart. He did his best to reassure me. And I did my best to reassure him. I knew he felt guilty that I had to face this new challenge alone. After the call was over I let myself rock and cry. Then, a wet nose intruded my thoughts. It was time for Twyla and my morning ritual.

Blue skies and warm sunshine accompanied Twyla and me as we took our daily walk. Someone just driving through East Beach would think it a cookie-cutter community, all pastel houses with front porches. But take a stroll through it and you will see the details and the charm.

To get my mind off my worries that morning I made a game of paying close attention to the houses and their personalities. College allegiances were vast and varied. We had fans from Clemson to Ohio State to, not surprisingly, the Naval Academy. Evidence of military service was all around us here in the form of flags, military base stickers and anchors. Whimsy showed its head as well. One house had a large mermaid in the front yard. I was falling in love with this neighborhood.

For Twyla, the best part of our walks was when she met a canine friend. She had become particularly fond of an older golden doodle named Millie. Whenever they see one another, they run around and wrestle. I didn't mind because it gave me a chance to chat with her owner, Jenny.

❖❖❖

The East Beach Sandwich Company is on the southern edge of East Beach on Pretty Lake Avenue. It's a charming little restaurant with brightly colored chairs and stools and beach décor all around. Samples of the artwork produced by the patrons of the monthly Van Gogh and Vino painting classes adorn the walls. I arrived a little before noon and found a spot in the corner and settled in to wait for Judy. I was gazing out at the sailboats in the marina across the street when Judy walked in. I caught her eye and waved her over to me.

"Hi! I'm so glad you could make it," I said.

"Wouldn't have missed it."

We went to the counter and placed our orders for a sandwich and a glass of pinot grigio each. Wine in hand, we settled in and started to chat. Conversation flowed as we continued to get to know one another. I told her about all of the places we had lived while moving with the Navy. When she asked me which my favorite was, I told her I didn't have a favorite. Each place has a charm to it if you look hard enough. Charleston has the beach and the wonderful southern way of life. San Diego also has beach charm in a different laid-back way. Newport is so full of history and gorgeous mansions to tour. Memphis has the best barbeque I've ever eaten. The prettiest place we ever lived was Seattle with its lush green mountains in the distance and the water at your feet. I admitted to missing the bustle and culture of Washington, D.C.

Judy told me about life in Charlotte as a doctor's wife and how her husband could be called at any time if a sick child needed his help. I told her that was much like a naval officer always being attached to his BlackBerry. We found we both had a huge background of volunteering. My experiences were all related to military wives and my children; mentoring or PTA projects. Judy had been a member of the Junior League in Charlotte as well as the hospital ladies auxiliary group. She also would go and read to children in the hospital to give their parents some much needed respite.

All of a sudden she said, "If you don't mind my asking, is something bothering you? You seem to be a little sad."

I was taken aback as I thought I had been hiding it quite well. I decided to be honest. "You're very astute. The day before yesterday I found out that I have breast cancer."

"Oh my, I'm so sorry to hear that. I know how you feel. You have a breast-cancer survivor sitting in front of you."

It was as if the weight of the world had been lifted off my shoulders. I was glad to have someone to talk to who knew firsthand what I was going through. "How long ago was your diagnosis?"

"It was about ten years ago. Back then the treatment was radical mastectomy and lots of harsh radiation. I understand things have changed since then."

"It sounds like it. My doctor is recommending a lumpectomy, radiation, and chemotherapy. It's all so scary."

"Of course it is. I know your husband is away right now. Who will take you for your surgery and treatments?"

"I'm sure my mother will come for the surgery. I haven't gotten as far as the treatments yet."

"I know we just met, but I'm happy to take you to your treatments. Obviously hospitals don't scare me at all. And I know my way around an oncology ward."

"You're very kind to offer. I think I'll take you up on it."

❖❖❖

As I predicted, my mother did come for my surgery and stayed for a few days to get me on my feet. Judy dropped by the day after to check on us and to meet Mom. They hit it off immediately and had a long visit while I napped upstairs. By the time Judy left they were fast friends and had exchanged phone numbers and email addresses. Judy promised to be back to take me to my post-operation checkup, as I wasn't allowed to drive until I went back to the surgeon.

On the way to the hospital several days later, Judy asked how my husband was doing being so far away. I told her in all honesty I wasn't sure. It's difficult to gauge someone's mood via emails. The few actual conversations we were able to have were spent giving medical updates and talking about treatment. We were never able to get to how he was doing. Suddenly I felt quite selfish. Judy was quick to reassure me that was not the case.

"I don't think you're being selfish. You need to concentrate on yourself and healing right now." She paused, then continued, "My husband was always very strong for me while I was in chemotherapy. It wasn't until long after I had finished my treatments that he confessed to me how hard it was to watch me go through such a difficult process, knowing there was nothing he could do to help."

"My husband has said the same things to me, but I'm used to hearing those comments after all of these years about so many things. He is sorry if he can't help when the car is broken or the children are fighting. I think I have become immune to the sentiment. I know that's not fair to him."

"Challenges are hard enough when you're in the same room. I can't imagine what it's like to deal with them when you're so far away."

I looked out the window and pictured my husband's face. "Thanks for bringing it up, Judy. I think I need to send an email when we get back home."

❖❖❖

As the weeks and the treatment progressed, Judy and I became closer and closer. When I felt up to it, I introduced her to East Beach life. We played Mahjongg and Bunco. Judy's green thumb made her a natural fit in the garden club. She even gave me a few pointers on my front garden. She particularly seemed to enjoy listening to music at Friday Nights in the park with bands like the Tiki Bar Band. We had a particularly fun night at the East Beach Sandwich Company when we got to witness a proposal at a Van Gogh and Vino class. Mary and Keith, Judy's daughter and son-in-law, turned out to be good friends as well. They were very gracious and included me in their activities. Keith took it upon himself to make sure our cars stayed in working order and that my grass was mowed. I was certain he and Sam would become friends when Sam got back from deployment.

❖❖❖

Breast cancer patients all fear the day they begin to lose their hair. So often a woman's self-esteem stems from how she looks, particularly her hair. I was no exception. I melted when the first fistful of hair came out in the shower. Sinking to the

floor, I hugged my knees to my chest and sobbed. When the water ran cold, I dried off, wrapped myself in Sam's robe, and crawled into bed. My phone rang several times but I let it go to voice mail. I just wanted to sleep and not think about anything.
Ding dong.
Ding dong.
Ding dong.
The insistent ringing of my doorbell woke me. I got out of bed and grumpily went down the stairs. I would shoot the person on the other side of the door if they were selling anything. Even if it were a Girl Scout. I caught a glimpse of myself in the hall mirror on the way to the door. What was left of my hair was frizzy and sticking out in all directions. My eyes were red and puffy and my nose looked like Rudolph's. Good! Now I wouldn't have to shoot them. I could just scare them to death.

With a scowl on my face, I opened the door.

"My! You look like death on a Triscuit." The only person who could get away with that comment was Judy.

"I feel like death on a Triscuit. Enter at your own risk," I said as I stepped back to let her in. No front porch sitting for me today.

"What's wrong? Are you having a bad chemo day?"

"A bad hair day." I ran my fingers through my hair and showed her my hand full of hair.

"Oh, Grace, I'm sorry. I've been dreading this day for you."

Like any good mother and friend, she had a ready supply of tissue and hugs. She sat quietly with me on the couch and let me cry. Once the tears and the tissue were exhausted she said, "Let's go shopping."

"I don't think I can handle being out in public."

"We'll go to Chesapeake. No one knows us there."

I rolled my eyes and let out a sigh. "Death on a Triscuit?"

"I learned that watching TV a few days ago. I've been dying to try it."

"So glad I could help."

Thirty minutes later, I had made myself as presentable as I could. We were both outfitted with ball caps and sunglasses to make sure we weren't recognized. We pulled into the TJ Maxx parking lot and Judy said, "All right, look around. Do you see anybody you know? Are there any familiar cars?"

"I think you are taking this too seriously."

"Nope, you are. Let's go." She got out of the car and pulled her ball cap low over her eyes. Then, walking as if she were a spy trying to avoid detection, Judy made her way into the store.

I finally caught up with her inside the store. "You know, for a grandma you move pretty fast. Why are we here?"

"We're buying scarves and hats. They will get you through until your hair starts to grow back. Do you want a wig, too?"

I know that some women wear their chemo head proudly as a sign of fighting the good fight. They wear all manner of pink clothing to bring about awareness of the disease. While I was more than willing to find a pink shirt to wear, I was not willing to show my scalp. Maybe that would come later.

For the next hour, Judy showed me all of the ways she had learned to hide her own bald head. She told me about the time she and her husband had attended the symphony and her scarf had fallen off. It was springtime and Charlotte was in bloom. There were pink azaleas, white dogwood and yellow forsythia all over. But, with the beauty of the flowers came the pain of the pollen. Judy had worn a light pink sheath with pearls on her neck and ears. She had found a coordinating scarf for her head. They were standing in the foyer of the Belk Theater enjoying some wine with some of the bigwigs at the hospital where her husband worked. Before she could do anything to stop it, her allergies overtook her, and she sneezed. Her wine slopped out of her glass and her silk scarf fell from her head, landing in a heap at the feet of the chief of staff from the hospital. Being a good southern gentleman, he continued his conversation as if nothing had happened while a waiter cleaned the mess and handed Judy her scarf. It ended up being her first outing with her bald head. Ever the optimist, she concluded her story by saying, "At least the lights were dim for the rest of the night."

❖❖❖

Sam was able to arrange a Skype session for us that night. I was anxious to see his face and hear his voice. But I was nervous as well. He had no idea about the trauma I had suffered that day. I hadn't the heart or the strength to email him about it. I chose to wear one of the scarves we had bought earlier. After we exchanged our greetings he said, "I like that color. It makes your beautiful eyes that much bluer." That was all that he said about my hair loss. And I was thankful.

❖❖❖

I finished chemotherapy in four months. I had lost all of my hair and a little bit of weight. Summer had left East Beach and fall had arrived with cooler days and even cooler nights. Judy, Twyla and I took long walks on the beach and watched the sailboats on the bay dance in the fall breeze. I told Judy about the excitement and anticipation of a Navy homecoming. "There's nothing like it. The pier and wharf both crawl with family members dressed in their most patriotic outfits. There are American flags and yellow ribbons everywhere."

"It sounds wonderful and chaotic at the same time. How do you ever find your husband?"

"Most couples have set up some kind of rendezvous plan ahead of time. As the captain's wife I'll be lucky enough to be one of the spouses allowed on board to greet their sailor first."

"Others are allowed on the ship too?"

"Yes. For morale, the night before they come home we raffle off the first kiss and the first hug. The lucky winners are also let on board the ship. It's a lot of fun."

❖❖❖

The big day arrived a few days later. I made my way through a sea of red, white and blue to stand on the pier. I knew that it would be way too windy on the pier to keep a hat or a scarf on my head. So, for the first time, I went without a head cover. My hair had begun to slowly grow back. That day I looked like a new recruit with a very short crew cut. The families had all heard of my illness and had been good to me during deployment. No one said a word to me about my hair. But I felt some kind of secret in the air. I passed it off as homecoming jitters.

It wasn't long before the ship came into view. The tugboats were tooting back and forth to one another as they maneuvered the ship into place alongside the pier. As the lines were being secured, I caught the command master chief's eye. He was alternating between hugging himself and kissing the back of his hand. I realized he wanted the first kiss and first hug winners out front. The two spouses who had won the raffle stepped forward and up the brow to the deck of the ship. Then it was my turn to go aboard. I ran into my husband's arms with such force that I knocked his hat off. When I pulled back from our kiss I saw that he had shaved his head. As I laughed and rubbed his head I looked around to see that most of the officers and sailors had also shaved their heads.

We were able to leave for home soon after that. Sam knew that the sooner he left, the sooner his sailors would feel comfortable to go home to their families, too.

We rounded the corner on Coventry Lane to see our front porch covered in balloons and streamers. Judy, Mary, and Keith had gone all out. They had even put a red, white and blue ribbon around Twyla's neck.

We popped the cork on a bottle of champagne to celebrate homecoming and the end of chemotherapy. Sam told us stories of his visits to foreign ports. We told him about the summer here in East Beach and some of the neighborhood gossip.

Finally, our friends realized we wanted to be alone and began to say their goodbyes. As Sam hugged Judy that afternoon, he said, "Thank you for taking care of my girl."

My friendship with Judy continues to this day. We have started our own team for the area Relay for Life, aptly named The Breast of Friends.

COMINGS AND GOINGS
BY KAREN HARRIS

One Last Night

They sat in silence on the side porch swing. The supper dishes sat cold and unwanted on the table behind them. Only their wine glasses were empty, but even those looked bereft, not sipped from with pleasure, but consumed purposefully. A few cars slid by, their headlights strafing the couple's faces, the night darker once they were gone. A party on the beach, only a block away, echoed off the intervening houses, a shout, bottles hitting each other in the recycle bin, hoots of laughter. The evening grew shorter, longer, frantic. She gripped his hand more tightly, wishing she could keep him there forever.

His fingers were slack. He hadn't looked at her since before dinner. He was already gone. Gone on that damned ship, gone from Coventry Lane, gone from Virginia, gone from her. They had only this last night, and now, they didn't even have that. Nine months. A woman could have a baby, a whole pregnancy, without her husband home, in that amount of time. A kid could finish nearly a year of school. Thank God, they were past the era of numbered letters, and MARS calls, she thought. But, if he Skyped the way he was sitting here now, what would be the point of keeping in touch?

Her heart was in her sandal, where it could slip through the wooden deck to the ground below. Only the call of

"Underway" would make the next twenty-four hours any worse. That could wait until tomorrow.

He shifted on the cushion. She found she was holding her breath, but he didn't say anything. Didn't look her way, just stared out into the darkness, maybe seeing the next day's schedule. Another car passed by, full of happy teenagers, some calling a cheery goodnight as they spotted the pair. She raised her hand to respond, and let it fall into her lap. He rose and went into the house.

❖❖❖

Arriving

"Maybe we need to put the Persian rugs in here," Scott said, turning the knob on the Bang-Olufsen turntable. "You know, to deaden the sound a little?"

Marisa looked up from the music stand where her score lay open to the solo lines of Verdi's "*Libera me.*" The Requiem was to be her swan song, and she needed it to be perfect. In her self-focused drive to study other singers to learn from their musical decisions, she had forgotten how far the sound would carry from their nearly empty house.

The furniture and furnishings were coming in the morning, but for tonight, and the last three nights, they were campers in their new home in East Beach. This was to be one last move, until the undertakers or their adult children, concerned that dementia had overcome them, took them away. Scott was over seventy, and she was his trophy wife of a mere sixty-four. Their fortieth anniversary was on the horizon, and this house was a gift to themselves. Once the Verdi was in her rearview mirror Marisa would throw herself into party planning. This house was made for large and lavish entertaining, with its expansive hardwood floors for dancing the night away, the large kitchen clearly planned for the crowds that somehow always gathered there, and the open layout meant for mingling.

"Are you worried about tomorrow, 'cause I sure am," she said, closing the book on the evening's rehearsal. "The movers were better last time, don't you think?"

"Everything will be fine. You say the same thing every time we make a big change. Come and sit on our 'divan', my dear." He patted the pair of camp chaises. "We can swap foot rubs and listen to something else for a while. I put something more modern than the four Verdi albums in the record box. How about some jazz?"

"Is there any wine left in the cooler?" She pulled off her old cowboy boots and padded over to the chair as Scott eased an album out of its cover.

"Nothing sounds as good as analog." Marisa mouthed the words as he spoke them. She knew this speech by heart. Catching her eye, he grinned unabashedly.

"Do you mind if I turn off the big light? I know the one on the stand is small, but the house seems too open and naked in this brightness." Marisa clicked off the overhead fixture. The room did seem cozier in the semidarkness. The music stand had a glorified book light clipped to its frame. It cast a blue glow on the music and the surrounding floor. With Jae Sinnett softly playing, a sip of Fumé Blanc in her plastic cup, and Scott's hands expertly massaging her right foot, she realized she could get used to his retirement quite easily.

"Look over there." Scott indicated the house next door with his head. "Looks like the neighbors are home."

Marisa glanced over her shoulder as casually as possible, not certain if she and Scott could be seen in the semi-darkened room. Like a mirror image, the neighbors' porch lay only a short distance away. At first, only a pacing figure on the porch was visible; then the seated man came into view as he made a small gesture. They, too, were in the dark, but even a cursory look revealed their tension. Simultaneously, Scott and Marisa looked away from the apparently unhappy couple and turned their chairs back toward each other.

Scott took her hand. "Are you going to be happy here?" he asked. "I know you're worried about my being underfoot, and the concert coming up, and the move." He dropped her foot and jumped up abruptly. "Shoot!"

"What's up?"

"I forgot to give you something at dinner." He rummaged through the debris from their beach picnic, then through the towels and other beach detritus.

"Did you lose something?" Marisa asked, not sure whether to grin or worry.

"No, it's here somewhere." He had run his fingers through his hair, leaving some of it on end, a white halo in the light from the stand. "I put it somewhere so I wouldn't forget. You know where that leads."

"Like all good intentions," She smiled slightly at his discomfiture. "Usually, I'm the one digging through everything."

"Ta-da!" An envelope fell to the floor as he shook it loose from a magazine. "I wasn't going to tell you until the real thing arrived, but you know me and surprises."

Throughout the years, she had teased Scott for being unable to keep a present in his pocket until the appropriate milestone. The gifts were lovely, thoughtful, sometimes expensive, and nearly always a day, or even a week, early. On the other hand, Marisa loved the suspense of Christmas, birthdays, and anniversaries almost more than the presents they occasioned. Scott had been known to shake his gifts, weigh them in his hands, even try to bribe family members into spilling the beans. Whatever the envelope held would not be unknown for more than another minute.

"It isn't anything big. I just can't wait to show you. You know me." He smiled sheepishly, handing her a photograph.

"You are so hopeless. Guess that's why I love you," she replied, returning his goofy grin.

Peering down, Marisa gasped. Her own face looked up at her: one final appearance on a concert advertisement. Scott, who had lovingly guided her minor career, had worked some kind of magic to cajole his artist sister into creating a flattering portrait of his wife. The silver streak in her hair had the look of a salon-created highlight to complement the pale blue eyes below. No lines creased the face, confident and content, that smiled back. The rich-hued azure gown, off the shoulder but demure enough for her age, the diamonds that graced her ears and throat, and the swept-up hairstyle, were reminiscent of divas past. Marisa knew this portrait would grace some room in the new home very soon. It was such a lovely gift; she hardly knew what to say.

"Oh, Scott," was all she could manage, tears springing to her eyes.

"You will always be my star," he said, taking her hand. "I know you gave up a lot to marry an ole knucklehead like me. All those Navy moves didn't do your career any favors."

Putting a finger to his lips, she shook her head. "We sure saw a lot of the world back then. I wouldn't trade our adventures for a lifetime at the Met. No regrets, no what ifs. You can put that on my tombstone."

❖❖❖

Pleasant Avenue, 10:45 a.m.

The cat was minding her own business, having a nap on the cushion. It was a large, square pillow meant for a tatami-matted floor, but it had seen better days. Now it served as a cat-rest atop a wooden chest under the sunroom windows. Athena, a velvet panther in her own mind, graced this part of the house most mornings, once the sun had warmed her spot. As she slept, a brilliant-hued goldfinch eyed the thistle seeds in the feeder that adhered to the glass outside and above her pillow. A cocky little fellow, he hesitated only a moment before alighting and eating his fill. Sated, and full of himself, he flitted to the edge of the windowsill and tapped at the glass. Athena's head shot up and her eyes widened in surprise as she came face to face with the goldfinch. Her teeth chattered and she ever so slowly rose to her feet. The bird eyed her, the glass between them, and the length of the window. He raised a wing and shook it at her. A slight meow escaped her lips and she gingerly touched the cool pane.

The bird hopped along the window, now fully confident of his position. Athena began to hunt in earnest, lowering her profile and then popping up, ineffectually hitting the window, biting at the glass and then retreating, only to try again at his next provocation. The goldfinch strutted back and forth, raising and lowering his wings, his tiny talons clicking as he went. Several minutes elapsed, with Athena's frustration growing ever greater. The commotion drew the Siamese cat from beneath the television in the den. Kumquat slunk from his warm hidey-hole and skulked into the sunroom. One silent leap onto the second square cushion and he was in the fray. His appearance beside Athena discomfited her, but not the bird. The finch continued his dance without missing a beat. Athena hissed and huffed, and then left her perch and prey to the larger cat. The bird waved his wing a few times, and as inexplicably as he had begun his taunting, he abandoned his audience, flying off into the midmorning.

❖❖❖

Coming and Going

"It's crooked," she said, stepping further back. "Raise the right corner a little. No, too far. That's it."

Jeff let go of the wooden frame and scowled up at the woman he saw there. She had a ridiculous pointed hat, lopsided features, and had been painted in vivid colors. The signature said Picasso, but that seemed unlikely.

"Why do you keep moving this hideous print from pillar to post? Why not put it in the Goodwill bag and get a real painting at the art show this weekend?" He brushed dust from his otherwise immaculate trousers. "You don't even like this ratty old thing."

"It was my mom's favorite, and I just can't let it go yet. Maybe when we pack out from this duty station." Diana slashed at the tape on yet another box, sighing over the collection of them that occupied the guest room. "No one will even see it unless they come in here. It's not like we have lots of visitors. Anyway, you'll be gone a lot, so you won't have to look at it much."

Her anger was palpable. Jeff opened his mouth to argue, and then seemed to think better of it. He picked up three flattened boxes and headed out of the room. Diana heard him stomp down the stairs, through the foyer, and out the front door. She stepped to the window, but he had stopped on the wide front porch directly beneath her, out of view. She strained to hear his mutterings, but the words were unintelligible.

Diana turned back to her work, but found her attention straying. Why did she keep that picture? Truthfully, it had not been one her mother loved; rather, she used its bold colors to draw attention away from a drab wall-to-wall carpet, and to unify the pinks, olives and tangerines of her mid-century modern furnishings. Some of those pieces were now in this guest room, temporarily buried beneath the boxes, papers and strands of packing tape. The teak side table and the tall cork lamp, the pink velvet chair, once one of a pair, and the throw pillows from her mother's sofa, now resting on the double bed, gave her a sense of continuity. She and Jeff needed a little stability, she thought, at least until this rental felt more like home.

A small missile darted past the window, casting a fleeting shadow, causing her to look up and out. Diana saw the flick of a tail as the bird alit in the neighbor's leafless tree. Spring buds, tiny and tightly coiled, adorned each branch, giving her hope that the chilly mornings were nearly over. If only the warmer weather could defrost their marriage, she thought ruefully. In her heart, she knew this was just one of their usual stress-induced spats. By the week's end, the boxes would be gone, the house would look like their own, and they would have found twenty reasons to love their new neighborhood. They would sit on that big front porch in the chairs Jeff had ordered this morning and laugh at this silly fight. He would apologize, and tell her the picture wasn't half-bad, and she would admit it was her mother she wanted to hold onto, not that print. They would walk hand-in-hand to the art festival, just a few blocks away. She would agree to really look for something new, something they could decide on together. It would all work out fine in a few days. Just not today.

❖❖❖

Driving with Dad

"What kind of tree is that?" my father asked as we drove away from The Atria, the assisted living home he never remembered.

"Crape myrtle, Dad," I replied, relieved that he was finally in the car. It had been a prolonged shuffle from his room, through the locked doors, past the dining room and front desk.

We had stopped to chat with the lovely French woman whose name I had never learned. "How do you say bird?" Dad would ask her each time, as if he were a traveling ornithologist. "Oiseau," she would answer, with a kind smile, never scolding him for his forgetfulness.

"Where did you go on the bus today?" I asked, though I had the itinerary at home.

"Aw, you know, they always take us to look at houses in Hillsborough." He scorned the few hours a month he spent on the Atria bus. Perhaps his years of driving for the city of San Mateo, taking elderly folks from one senior center to another, had soured him on the experience.

Mom would have enjoyed today's jaunt to East Beach. The lovely homes, with their wide porches and tasteful landscaping, were more her cup of tea than Dad's. She had always had an eye for design, and would have ooh-ed and ah-ed as the bus turned from one tree-lined street onto another. In years past, Dad had driven her all around the San Francisco Bay Area, attending open houses to peek inside the new developments. Without her, today's tour was just time out of his reclining chair.

"What kind of tree is that one?" He looked so much older, diminished by the dementia that had precipitated the move from his beloved hillside home.

"A crape myrtle. Just a pink crape myrtle." I sighed inwardly. A third summer of this quiz show. The trees lined many of the streets in Virginia Beach. They dotted the entire landscape with their fuchsia, white, pale pink, or lilac blooms.

"Dad, they come in lots of colors, but they are all crape myrtles."

He tapped his fingers on the armrest, then abruptly gripped the edge of the passenger door's window. "You're driving awfully fast," he griped.

"I learned to lean into the curves from you," I said as evenly as possible. "Tell me about the ride today."

"Hillsborough, or Burlingame. You know. Nice, big houses. What's to tell?"

"Dad, I think you went to Norfolk today." I tried to sound helpful, not corrective.

"Yeah, yeah. You keep trying to convince me, but I'm on to your tricks." He was dead certain he was still in California. Anytime anyone asked how he liked living in Virginia, he would tell them he knew they were part of my conspiracy to convince him he was not still living at home.

I looked down the boulevard and sighed deeply. I just had to let it go. We would get to his dental appointment, maybe stop for coffee, then back to Atria for him, and back to some sane conversations at home for me.

We turned onto Mustang Trail, and I waited for the question.

"What kind of tree is that?" asked my father, the orchardist.

❖ ❖ ❖

Elizabeth, Leaving

"Is everything out of the upstairs bathroom?" she asked, peering up and over the hand-rubbed oak railing. She allowed herself a last caress of the handrail, fighting back tears. This was her dream house, their dream house. So many years of saving, so many years of delayed gratification. Was that what psychologists called it? This happy oasis had been theirs for only three years. Esophageal cancer had taken her beloved Christopher so swiftly. Six weeks from the diagnosis to that sad ride in the ambulance, and the quick sale of her home, was just too much for her to bear. Elizabeth turned on her heel and walked into the kitchen.

"What did you say, Mom?" Her son Rodney taped boxes while his wife attached mailing labels to postcards advising friends of Elizabeth's new address. Andrea looked at her expectantly, with a touch of impatience visible on her perfectly made-up face.

"Oh, I just was wondering if everything got picked up from the hall bath." She tried to sound casual to fend off any unpleasant murmurings from Andrea about old age and dithering.

"I'll go check in a minute," said Rodney, as he pulled the last strip of tape over a container marked OLD COOKBOOKS. "You want these in the car, right? These, and Grandma's silver, and the photo boxes."

She nodded, and managed a wan smile. He was such a good son, her Rodney. It was hard to imagine him as the little boy who had thrown tantrums, or the bright but indifferent student, or even the young man who had brought Andrea to meet his parents those twenty-odd years before. His auburn waves had given way to silver on the sides, his broad shoulders were starting to stoop a bit, just like his father's had at that age. Tears welled, and she closed her eyes to quell them.

"Here," Rodney murmured, handing her a handkerchief.

She dabbed at the corners of her eyes, taking a deep breath. "Thanks."

Rodney patted her hand, and then her shoulder as he passed her to go up the staircase.

Andrea kept her eyes on her task, studiously avoiding her mother-in-law, her thin lips pressed together. Elizabeth stood watching her, trying to think of some neutral comment to ease the tension in the kitchen, but words failed her. Whatever it was that Rodney's wife had on her mind, this was not the day for her usual criticisms. Not for the first time, Elizabeth wondered at her son's abiding love for this cool, distant woman.

Rodney clumped down the steps, his face flushed from his dash. "All clear up there. Mom, if you could carry the address cards, Andrea and I can get these last two boxes. I think our work here is done."

Andrea threw her purse over her shoulder and bent to pick up a box. "I'll be in the car." She strode through the house and out the door without a last look.

Elizabeth, on the other hand, was suddenly rooted to the floor. She looked up at her son with a touch of panic in her eyes. She saw concern and a more than little fear dash across his face. Was he worried about losing her so soon after his father's death? She was too weary, too old, suddenly, to reach out to comfort him.

"You look like you need a minute. We don't have to race out of here. Why don't I give you a minute to say your goodbyes?" He hugged her gently before taking up the last box, leaving only the postcards and her handbag on the granite countertop.

Elizabeth reached out to steady herself against the cool surface. She tried to memorize every detail of the kitchen, from its Sub-Zero fridge to the glass-fronted cabinets, to the hardwood floors and even the under-cabinet lighting. Memories of the meals she and Christopher had prepared together, the blue pottery fruit bowl that used to host the winter clementines, and other minute details came flooding back. She spun on her heel to take in the rest of the house, but somehow the kitchen, the heart of this wonderful house, held her in its sway.

"Oh, Chris, I miss you so much. Leaving here feels like I'm leaving you forever." She gripped the counter's beveled edge for a moment. "Oh, God." She whispered a quick prayer for strength.

Then, shaking her head as if to beat back both the memories and worries, Elizabeth picked up the postcards and tucked them into her brown leather purse. She slipped keys from the outer pocket, removed her house key from the ring, and laid it on the counter. One quick look up the stairs, one last glance through the living room, now just a bare space, and she walked out into the crisp afternoon.

Rodney and Andrea sat in the front seats of their Volvo sedan, checking their cell phones, as Elizabeth started down the wide porch steps. They could wait a moment longer. She paused and turned when she reached the bottom. A trick of the afternoon sunlight against an upstairs window cast an odd shadow on its pane. Elizabeth's breath caught in her throat as she imagined, for just a moment, it was Christopher up there, watching her leave.

"Good-bye, my love," she murmured. "Good-bye."

THE DANCE LESSON
BY L.W. "SKIP" MCLAMB

I hate moving, I hate it with a passion. I despise packing up boxes and dislike dealing with moving companies. But, after almost thirty years in the Coast Guard which included eleven moves, I, Master Chief Buddy McCain, am ready to retire. I hope this will be my last time to move. I'm looking for a real home this time, not just a house my wife and I feel like we're borrowing for a couple of years. We want a home where we can enjoy our golden years together.

My wife and I are house hunting in Norfolk, Virginia. She considers our task today an adventure, while I view it as a chore.

"Tell me again why you like this Tidewater area so much," Elke says.

I glance over at my German-born wife who is on her first visit to Virginia and decide to give her my tour guide spiel. "I was stationed in Norfolk for two enjoyable years in the nineties. Norfolk, and this whole Tidewater area, is loaded with local attractions. There are beaches and forests, Broadway shows and peanut festivals, modern military bases and many historic landmarks. You get a taste of big-city life while surrounded by open country. Plus all these features and many more are marinated with a friendly, laid back southern charm."

"That's quite an advertisement. I do like all the water and

natural areas. You're a pretty good salesman, Buddy. I can see why you want to move here."

There are three open houses scheduled this morning in the East Beach community of Norfolk. Several Coast Guard friends recommended Elke and I check out the neighborhood. We turn right off of Shore Drive at Mac's Place on the Bay and pick up East Beach Drive. Our ears are assaulted by the sounds of dump trucks, nail guns and power saws as we pass through a section of new construction. We continue on and drive into a much larger section of established homes.

"This is a very nice neighborhood," Elke says. "It reminds me a little of Germany. The houses are colorful, clustered together, and there's a lot of open space."

"I have to admit I'm impressed. And that new construction we passed is a good sign of positive housing demand. Look on your port side, there's a community center. It looks like a replica of an old Coast Guard Station."

We continue driving and Elke points out a tennis court. "Maybe you can teach me to play. And let's check out the beach later today. I saw a walkway behind the community center."

The first two East Beach homes are definitely out of our price range, but we decide to look just for kicks. Both are two-story, three-bedroom homes with lots of construction upgrades. They're over two-thousand square feet and both have unique features that make them very tempting. After some discussion, we decide that the size and price are more than we can handle.

The third property is smaller; two bedrooms and only seventeen-hundred square feet. Efficient construction and design features take advantage of every inch of space. The open floor plan, large windows, and layout of the kitchen are also impressive. We like that it's centrally located in the community and has more than enough space for the two of us. We leave the showing very interested and decide it's a good time to find a place to sit, sip a glass of wine, and discuss submitting an offer.

Just as we get back in the car my phone buzzes. "Hello."

"Pops, it's your loving daughter. What are you up to today? And, are you ready for some really good news?" Karen says.

Four years ago Karen broke my heart when, after college graduation, she moved to the left coast—Los Angeles, to be specific. It's just too far away. "Let me guess. You've lost another cell phone so you're getting your own phone, and I can finally take you off my plan."

"Nope, no phone issues, Pops."

"You still working on getting yourself centered and finding your Zen? You know I've been looking for my Zen for years and can't find it anywhere."

Elke glares at me then pokes me in the arm. She thinks I tease my daughter too much.

"You're funny, Pops. You need to stop talking and listen now. I have news, really big news. Are you ready? I'm getting married. Pops, are you there? Pops?"

I'm speechless. I've known this day would come, but why is it coming today? It will be best to stay calm and collected. Finding my voice, I ask, "Who the hell are you marrying?" I try to ask politely, but fail.

I peek at Elke. Her eyes grow to the size of silver dollars at the mention of the "M" word.

"You're still so funny, Pops. You know who it is. It's Dean."

"You mean Dean the dancer? You've only been dating him for about a year. Aren't you going a little fast here? And will I have to pick him up on my phone plan, too?"

"Okay Dad, comedy hour is over. Dean makes plenty of money, so he won't be on the phone bill."

I cover my phone with my hand and shoot a look at Elke. "She just called me Dad. She only calls me that when she's mad at me or in trouble."

"Dad, don't talk, just listen very carefully. You'll have two assignments to complete for this upcoming California mission. You have to give away the bride, and you have to be ready to dance. Yes, I said dance, as in the father-daughter dance at the wedding reception. And Dad, we need to look good when we're dancing."

"Damn, girl, I know you're serious now, you just called me Dad. You really know how to shock an old man. When and where will this fateful event take place?"

"Three weeks from today, beside the ocean in Ventura, California. I'm e-mailing you more details about the wedding tomorrow. When you get it, call me if you have any questions. Get someone to teach you East Coast Swing. It's easy, Pops. I learned it in high school."

Elke sits, staring bug-eyed, with hands spread out, palms up, silently begging for more information.

"Just three weeks, sweetie? We're in the middle of moving. It can't happen in three weeks, especially if you want me to dance. Wait, I do remember a little of the Bunny Hop we did when you were three."

"Okay, Pops, no more phone plan jokes, and no more dancing jokes. There will be a wedding in three weeks and you better be here, wearing your dress whites and ready to dance. You're retiring. You've plenty of time to get ready. I have to hang up now and call mom."

"Wait, one more thing. Congratulations, baby girl. I love you."

"Bye, Pops. Love you, too."

I look at my wife. "Holy cow, can you believe that? I'm totally, completely in a state of shock. How can she do that?"

"What are you going on about? Your daughter is twenty-six. She's bright, beautiful and a great catch for any guy. Why does that shock you?" Elke asks.

"That's not what shocks me. How the hell am I going to learn to dance in three weeks? That's what shocks me." I look down, close my eyes, and sit very still for about two minutes. I raise my head slowly and look at Elke. "What's East Coast Swing?"

Elke is laughing so hard she can hardly talk. "That's an awesome question. I suggest we finish up our house hunting business and rush you to the nearest Arthur Murray Studio."

❖❖❖

As we drive west on Pretty Lake Avenue, toward Shore Drive, we pass a little sandwich shop. It's located in a five-story building with shops on the first floor and condos on the upper floors. It looks like a great place to discuss our thoughts on that last house, and my new dance lesson situation. We walk in and look around. The place is perfect—they serve wine.

"This shop is really cute. I like the beach-style furniture and the mellow colors. They even have gifts and souvenirs," Elke says and heads toward a hat rack.

"I like the marina across the street." I nod toward the finger piers filled with all kinds of watercraft. "I can picture a nice twenty-four foot Boston Whaler with my name on it tied up in there. You scout out the shop and I'll order us something to eat." I walk up to the counter and talk with a nice young lady who recommends the chicken wraps and provides a list of craft beers and wine. She brings our meal to the seating area within minutes.

"Hey sweetie, let's grab that table over by the window."

"Sure. This is a great place, very cozy. And the wrap smells delish."

I pull out my notes about the house. "Okay lady, what do you think? It's near the top of our price range, but I—holy crap!"

"What's wrong, Buddy? Are you okay?"

"It has to be an omen. Look out the window. It's got to be fate. Look over there," I say while pointing.

"What in the world are you pointing at?"

"The building next door. Look at the signs on the windows."

"I see the signs but I don't have my glasses."

"It's a dance studio. A dance studio right here. God brought me to a dance studio. Can you believe that?"

"Let's go take a look before you have a heart attack. And if I remember right, I drove you here, not God." We tell the waitress we'll be right back and walk to the adjoining building.

Elke looks through the window toward the large dance studio with beautiful wood floors. "There are no lights on and no people in here."

"Do you see any phone numbers?"

"No, but God has left you another sign, Buddy. Look over here. 'Building for lease.' The place has gone out of business, sweetie. I think God just played a little trick on you. Let's go finish our meal. Oh my God. Wait, Buddy. You better look at this." She points to a small orange sign on the side door. "Someone is offering private dance lessons. Maybe it's fate after all."

"Stand aside, let me see." I read, PRIVATE DANCE LESSONS. FLEXIBLE SCHEDULE. CALL FRANCIS MARION. At the bottom of the sign there are little tear-off slips, each with a phone number. None have been taken yet. "Yeah, maybe God is looking out for me." I take a phone slip. "Francis Marion, I remember that name. That's the Swamp Fox."

"What do you mean, Swamp Fox?" Elke asks.

"Francis Marion was an American general in the Revolutionary War. He was from South Carolina and became famous for his use of sneak attacks and a hit-and-run battle strategy. The British could never catch him because he would hide in the swamps, thus Swamp Fox."

"Thanks for the history lesson, sweetie, but you need to worry about dance lessons not history lessons."

"I know, I know. It's just kind of a strange name. Let's go finish our lunch."

❖ ❖ ❖

After lunch we head to our hotel, a nice, bay-front building on Shore Drive. "Let's divide the duties. Elke, you contact the realtor and let them know we want to meet and possibly bid on that last property we saw. I'll try to set up some dance lessons." It's hard to believe those words just came out of my mouth. I can't believe I'm more worried about dance lessons than buying a new house, but somehow it does seem more important. After all, she's my baby girl. I call the number on the phone slip.

"Hellooooooo," a deep, but sexy voice echoes over the phone.

"Yes, hello, I'm Chief Buddy McCain. I'm calling for Francis Marion to inquire about dance lessons. This is an urgent situation." I try to sound calm and in command.

"Well, this is the right number for dance lessons, urgent or not. Please tell me more, Chief McCain. Are you a fireman?"

"Negative on the fireman. I'm Coast Guard. Here's the deal. My daughter is getting married in three weeks and I need to be prepared for a, uh, father-daughter dance. And, according to her, I've got to look like I know what I'm doing when I'm on the dance floor. She's in California, and we won't have time to practice together. Plus, I can't dance. Can you teach me East Coast Swing?"

"You have called the right place. I agree, your situation sounds urgent, but it's not impossible, actually very doable. Come over tomorrow night at six and we'll get to know each other and get started on a solution to your problem. I'll text you the address."

❖❖❖

It turns out that Francis Marion lives in The Villas at East Beach, located right over the dance studio. As I stand at the door the sound of a golden oldie, "My Girl," by the Temptations, wafts through the air. I knock and the door is opened...by a man.

"Chief McCain, I'm Marion." He firmly shakes my hand. "Come in, come in, and we'll get started right away."

I try to figure out what to say. "Wait. Marion, you're a man," I say as I look at the six-foot-two, middle-aged man built like a marine. His hair is grayish, well styled, and has streaks of purple dye. He's dressed in black from head to toe and sports a small goatee. He looks back at me without speaking.

"Marion, who are you? I'm looking for Francis. Francis Marion. Where is she?"

"I'm so sorry. You saw the orange sign, right? There's a

slight problem with the sign we posted. It's supposed to say Francis *and* Marion, not Francis Marion. But, no worries. Francis is my sister and we both teach dance."

"Maybe no worries for you, but I really prefer a female dance teacher. No offense intended."

"No offense taken. Francis isn't feeling well tonight, and she asked me to fill in for her. Come on in, and we'll get started on some introductory stuff, and I'll teach you the basic dance steps. We'll let Francis take over when the instruction gets more...physical. Please have a seat on the sofa." Marion sits down beside me.

As the background music changes to "You Can't Hurry Love" by the Supremes, I catch Marion up on the wedding information. "Like I told Francis, this isn't just any wedding, it's my daughter's wedding and we have to dance together. She suggested I learn East Coast Swing. She learned the dance while in high school and claims it's so easy to learn that even I can do it."

"Aren't children just the funniest little creatures?" Marion says and pats me on my thigh. "May I call you Buddy? Chief McCain sounds so military. Give me a moment to visit the little boy's room and go put on my dancing shoes. Make yourself at home."

"Wait, how much will this cost?"

"We'll talk money after tonight's session. If you decide not to continue, you owe nothing," Marion says as he walks down the hall.

I sit very still. I'm strangely uncomfortable and not sure why. The guy seems nice enough. I should be excited and happy because I think I've found a solution to my dance problem. But I'm developing an uneasy feeling. The place where he touched my leg still tingles.

I look around the room. Very expensive furniture is perfectly placed throughout and looks brand new. Luxurious, pale-pink drapes cover two walls from ceiling to floor. There is a tall, expensive-looking silver statue of a naked guy in one corner. Two large paintings hang on the other two walls; a San

Francisco sunset and a rainbow over Niagara Falls. The whole place is meticulously neat, and I can see my reflection in the oak floors. Then it hits me. The funky hair and clothes, the neat-freak thing, the stylish furniture; this dance teacher has to be an interior decorator, gay, or both. What is my daughter getting me into?

Marion comes back in the room with new shoes on. "Francis and I talked. We feel your urgent situation will take four to six two-hour classes. I'll teach introductions and basic East Coast steps tonight. Francis will handle closed-stance dance steps, turns, and passes tomorrow night. The third session will focus on additional moves and steps to help build a dance routine. The last class, maybe even the last two classes, will be held at a local dance club. The club experience will prepare you to really kick some dance butt at the big event in California."

Marion sounds very excited about all this, but I'm not so sure. "That sounds pretty intense. I thought we could knock all this out in just a few hours."

Marion laughs loudly, stares into my eyes and explains in a serious tone. "Did you say just a few hours? Buddy, dancing is not just moving to music. It's a form of expression that allows you to share your soul without saying a word. It allows you to communicate in a very personal, private way with your dance partner. It also allows you to send out messages to every person watching you and your partner dance. Dancing is a lot like making love, except you're standing up and fully clothed. Buddy, any woman can watch any man dance and tell if he is a good lover. When Francis and I are done, your daughter will be thrilled. Plus, every woman—and possibly a few men—at this wedding will want to be your partner. Now, if you are an exceptionally hard working dance student with a little natural talent, we may finish in less time."

I'm not sure about the vertical love-making junk, but if I say what I'm thinking Marion might show me the door. Do I stay or do I go? Gee, the things you do for your children.

"Okay, Marion, let lesson one begin, but no stand-up love

making." The music changes and Marvin Gaye sings "Show and Tell" in the background. Marion begins swaying with the music as he talks. "East Coast Swing's a very basic yet very versatile dance. It's not hard to learn and can make you look like a better dancer than you really are. Let's move to the middle of the floor to begin. Okay, face to face, straighten that back, posture is important. Extend your left hand, fingers curled upward like a cup. My hand is curled down and sits lightly in your hand. We'll stand side-by-side to learn the basic step. This is an eight-step dance pattern; three steps left, three steps right, then a two-count back-step with the left foot. Watch my feet and follow me; left, one-two-three, right, one-two-three, and left foot back-step, then return. Good job, Buddy, keep going. You must practice the basic steps over and over. Make your steps a little smaller. At the end of our session tonight you'll be doing these steps without thinking about them at all."

All I can think of right now is that it feels weird holding hands with a man. After dancing for a couple of minutes, I look down and catch a glint of blue. "Marion, do you have blue polish on your nails?"

"Absolutely not, Buddy. It's liquid aqua, a brand-new color."

That doesn't make me feel any less weird, but I keep working on the basic steps. Marion walks to a corner of the room and opens the drapes, revealing a mirrored wall stretching from floor to ceiling and corner to corner. I watch him attach a doorknob with small suction cups to the mirror. "Come over here, Buddy. Your job is to keep practicing the basic step. Remember, it's all muscle memory. You can hold on to the doorknob if it helps. If you pull the knob off the mirror, you're holding too hard. There'll be a performance test before you leave tonight." Marion leaves the room and I'm dancing by myself.

It isn't pretty at first, not pretty at all. The reflection I see in the mirror is a bowlegged, hunchbacked Coast Guard Chief missing steps and tripping over his own feet. As I continue holding onto that doorknob and practicing, doing the basic step over and over again, the footwork actually starts to smooth out a little. I dance with the doorknob for almost thirty minutes before Marion comes back in the room.

"Buddy, that basic step is looking good. Square the shoulders up. Straighten the back. That's very good. Take a quick break. Francis will take over tomorrow night. She wants us to finish up tonight with just a little partner dancing, face-to-face. I hope you are okay with that. Just thirty minutes more and you're out of here. Move to the middle of the room. We'll use a slightly slower song to help you get the beat down."

Marion faces me and extends his right hand. I hesitantly connect with my left hand as the music begins. The new song is "Lady in Red."

"When you dance with your daughter you'll lead, so you decide when to start dancing. Listen to the song, pick a good starting point, and keep the eight-step beat."

We work on the basic step for about fifteen minutes in the one-hand, open position. It's easier dancing with a person than with a doorknob, even if the person is a man with liquid-aqua nails. After a while, we dance doubled-handed. Then, the question is asked.

"Buddy, are you ready to try closed position?"

Marion doesn't wait for me to answer.

"Okay, Buddy, pull in toward me from single-hand position. As the space between us closes, your right arm goes around me and you place your hand on my back between my shoulder blades. My hand will lie on your shoulder. That's very good, Buddy. Remember to maintain good posture and keep enough space between us so our feet don't bump together. Great job. You keep that step going."

My heart rate increases. I feel my face flush. For the first time in my life, as best I can remember, I'm dancing almost cheek-to-cheek with a guy. That item is not on my bucket list.

"Buddy, you look a little pale. Are you uncomfortable dancing in closed position with me?"

"Well, it's a little uncomfortable just because you're a

man. Now if you tell me I'm also dancing with a democrat, I'll really flip out."

Marion laughs. "Your sense of humor is still working fine and your footwork is working ever better. Keep it up, Buddy."

I feel Marion's hand moving up and down my back as if he's trying to comfort me. Then his hand starts moving further south, a little too far south. This is more than a little awkward, and I feel sort of trapped. I remember, in my much younger days, trying the very same move on some of the young ladies. So I know what to do—exactly what Cindy-Lou did to me at my senior prom. I reach down, take his hand, and move it back up north while politely saying, "Please keep your hand on my shoulder, big guy."

Marion laughs so hard he actually misses a step. "Buddy, you're a very, very funny guy. You're one of the few to experience and survive my 'sneak attack move.' This means you pass your first test with flying colors."

"What test? What sneak attack?" I have a flash back to the Swamp Fox.

"While dancing together, you didn't miss a step. You stayed in step when getting a back rub and then, unbelievably, even when I try to get a little fresh with you. You were never out of step and never missed a beat, not even once. Buddy, you're a fast learner and off to a great start. Lesson one is officially over. Now, I'll not be here tomorrow night. Francis will be in charge and she'll work with you on turns, passes, and a couple of new moves. Will you be here tomorrow night, Buddy?"

"I think I'll be here tomorrow. But first, I have to ask you, Marion. Were you putting a move on me or was that back-rubbing stuff really just a test?"

"That was just business, Buddy. It's part of the instruction. You're not my type, not even close. Please close the door on your way out. Francis will be your instructor tomorrow."

As I head down the stairs to my car, strange thoughts run around in my head. Marion's last comments, "just business" and "not my type" were spoken so matter-of-factly. It bothers

me somehow. Why?
 The dance lesson was great. I now believe this dance lesson deal can work. My worries about the wedding dance are almost gone. The thought that bothers me is kind of crazy. I was just shot down by a guy and a part of me wants to know why. What's wrong with me?

❖❖❖

 After some soul searching and a long, late-night talk with Elke, I return for the second dance lesson. As I knock on the apartment door, I hear a familiar Motown tune, "Under the Boardwalk" by the Drifters.
 "Come in, the door is open," a voice sings out. I walk into the living room. The curtain is open, revealing the floor-to-ceiling mirror. The lights are dim and several candles are lit and glowing. Then, she enters the room. Francis is tall, but not as tall as her brother. She has straight, jet-black hair that falls to her waist, ruby-red lips and very long legs. She wears a red, flowing skirt with a long slit up one side. The skirt covers a red, full-body leotard. Now this is a dance teacher. Francis is a knockout.
 "Buddy, I feel bad about not seeing you last night. I had the headache from hell that wouldn't go away. Marion said you did wonderful, and that you are ahead of schedule."
 "It's nice to meet you too, Francis. I'm so glad you feel better. Marion's a great teacher, but I feel much more comfortable with a female dance partner."
 "Tonight we'll build on what you've learned and also try to have some fun. Do you like the room? I tried to create a more romantic setting like you'll probably have at the wedding reception. We've a lot to cover, so get over here. You and I are taking East Coast Swing to a new level."
 Francis and I begin dancing. First, we do a quick review of the basic steps, then she heads into new territory. She teaches me to lead her into turns and quickly introduces inside and outside passes. For a full thirty minutes we dance, stringing together turns and passes. We move from open position to

closed and back to open. It's trickier staying in step with all the added movement.

"Okay, Buddy, this is a new move called the cuddle. You spin me inward and we end up arm-in-arm and facing the same direction."

Our arms wrap around each other in an embrace and Francis passes back and forth in front of me, very close and very slow. I couldn't imagine learning this dance move from Marion.

Francis introduces more moves: the hammerlock, star promenade, toe point, and the sailor shuffle. The steps and moves are arranged into a routine which we practice over and over. We dance nonstop for almost ninety minutes.

"Buddy, you were born to dance. You pick up new steps fast, and you don't forget them. It's a shame you didn't start dancing when you were younger. Let's take a break and decide where to go from here. I think you're about ready for a night at the dance club and your final exam."

"You're a great teacher, Francis. Swing dancing is really fun once you learn a few steps and have the right partner. I think I'm ready for the dance club and the final exam, whatever it is. I do have a question. Will it be you or Marion at the club with me?"

"I'm not yet sure who will be there. I do need to make you aware of something before we talk any more about the club. I know a lot of people at this club, and it'll be better for you to find out now."

"Okay, tell me. I'm pretty sure I'm ready for anything."

I was wrong.

"It'll be easier to show you, Buddy. Stand up. Face me. Assume dance position, left hand extended. Good, now close your eyes, and no peeking. Let the music be your eyes."

Music begins to play and we begin to dance. The song is "What Kind of Fool Am I" by Bill Deal and the Rondells. We move to closed position and execute several turns and passes. I'm dancing with my eyes closed. Francis and I are communicating through our fingertips and with subtle body movements. Elke will never believe this.

"Okay, Buddy. Open your eyes."

When I open my eyes I look at my partner and am now dancing with ... Marion? He's wearing Francis' clothes and holding a long, black wig. This is sneak attack number two, and it's more shocking than the first sneak attack. The amazing thing is, I still don't miss a single step. The music stops and I make a beeline for the door. "Well, times up," I mumble. "See you at the club tomorrow night." I wave without looking back at Francis, or, uh, Marion.

I need to go home.

❖❖❖

I walk into the hotel room and give Elke a long hug. At first, I hesitate to talk about Francis, but then it just pours out. "You will not believe the night I've had. I need advice. Tonight I found out my dance teacher, Francis, is a cross dresser, and my other teacher, Marion, is also Francis. Francis Marion is actually Francis and Marion, two people in one. I'm not sure I can handle this. Do you understand what I'm saying? For two hours, I was romantically dancing with either a man who likes to dress as a woman or a woman who dresses as a man."

Elke's expression is one of total confusion. Then I guess her highly logical German brain kicks in, because she asks me a simple but important question.

"Buddy, how did the dance lesson go tonight?"

"It was super. Francis and I danced all night. I learned new moves and now feel confident about leading my dance partner. I'm really starting to feel the music in my dancing. I can even dance through complex routines with my eyes closed."

"So what's the problem? Listen to yourself. Your dance teachers, oops, I mean teacher, is doing his, or her, job. Buddy, I know it's confusing, but stop whining and worrying about things you can't control. Your best course of action is to do whatever your daughter needs so she can have the best wedding possible. It doesn't matter if the person teaching you to dance is short or tall, Catholic or Baptist, gay or straight or whatever, as long as they can turn you into a dancer. If you have to take lessons from the devil himself, that's what you do."

This time I really listen to my wife because she's right. She's dead right. "Hey, doll, do you want to go to a dance club tomorrow night? I'm not sure what's going to happen, but it's bound to be entertaining."

❖❖❖

The Banque is a well-known Norfolk dance club that has been around for decades. It's located in a shopping center on Little Creek Road. The Janitors, a local beach music band, are playing tonight. When Elke and I walk in around eight o'clock, the place is packed. The music is loud, the people are loud, and the drinks are flowing. We look around and see Marion waving us over to a table.

"Have a seat, Buddy. And you must be Elke. It's wonderful to meet you. Let's order drinks. I wasn't sure if you would come tonight."

Elke's gaze slides over Marion. She whispers in my ear, "This guy does not look like a woman."

"I have to be honest, Marion. That was quite a shock at the end of our lesson last night. At one point I thought about not showing up. A close friend of mine reminded me I'm doing all this for my daughter, not for me, so here we are. Plus, I'm very curious about this final exam."

"The exam is pretty simple, Buddy. All you have to do is get someone here to dance with you so you can demonstrate to me that you can lead them through the East Coast moves Francis and I taught you. And you must look good doing it. I suggest you start with the table to our left. The four ladies seated there look ready to dance."

At the table to the left are four middle-aged ladies who appear to be out for a big night on the town. I walk over to the table knowing exactly what I want to say and speak quickly to each of the potential dance partners. They smile as I walk back to my table alone.

Marion is also all smiles. "Poor boy, did you get shot down? I forgot to tell you that most of the patrons here are very serious dancers. They seldom accept a dance request if they haven't seen you dance."

"I thought it might be something like that. Marion, I want my first dance to be with you. You're my teacher, and you helped me in a time of need. It'll only be right if we dance this first dance together. Plus, those four ladies agreed that if I dance here, tonight, with another guy, all four will dance with me. So, get up and let's go put on a show."

"Buddy, you've almost aced this exam without dancing a step. I think there may be a little Swamp Fox blood in your veins."

❖❖❖

The next two weeks are a blur. In between completing a deal on a new house and arranging to move our possessions to Norfolk, Elke and I fly out to California for the wedding. The Ventura Marina Resort lies about an hour north of Los Angeles and is a beautiful setting for the event. A large crowd gathers on the beach. Over the next twenty minutes the vows are spoken, "I do's" are promised, and rings are exchanged while we stand in the sand beside the Pacific Ocean. Everyone is either laughing, crying, or both. The wedding party then follows a path of tiki torches back to the resort for the reception.

An outdoor patio with a raised dance floor is partially surrounded by a semicircle of white tables facing Ventura Harbor. Accompanied by red, orange, and yellow rays of a perfect Pacific Ocean sunset, the newlyweds join the party and dance their first dance as husband and wife. As their song begins to wind down, I feel little butterflies in my stomach.

"Smile, Buddy, you shouldn't have such a worried look," Elke says.

"That Dean's a pretty good dancer. I guess he should be since he's in the profession. I think I'm up next. I'm not sure how this is going to go."

"Stop that worrying. Just remember everything Francis and Marion taught you. Look, Karen's waving to you."

"Yep, that's my signal." I stand, brush off my dress whites, head to the dance floor and meet my daughter at center stage. I take her right hand in my left hand as the band plays an old Bobby Vee song, "Take Good Care of My Baby." We start slow, in closed position, and get into the rhythm of the song. I spin Karen out and a perfectly executed inside pass is followed by an outside pass. There's a smattering of applause from the crowd.

"Wow, Pops, you really did take some lessons."

"Yes I did, sweetie. I had great teachers. And it turned out to be much more than a dance lesson. But that's a story for another night. Tonight, we dance. Are you ready for a triple turn?" We move to the music, alone on the dance floor. I look in my little girl's eyes. The same eyes and the same look as when she was a two-year old toddler dancing with me while standing on top of my feet. I lead my daughter through almost every move Francis and Marion taught me. The wedding party chatter slows to a stop, and all eyes follow us on the dance floor. We end with a flourish with me sliding to the floor on one knee and Karen completing a double inside turn and sitting pertly on my leg.

I walk off the dance floor elated. My daughter is happy and is now dancing with her new husband. She's very impressed that her old man learned to dance just for her. Also, I guess I looked pretty good on that dance floor. One older lady hits on me as I walk off the dance floor, saying she "loves the way I move." That vertical love-making crap Marion talked about just might be true after all.

DEAD DROP
BY PATRICK CLARK

Friday, June 10th, 6:15 a.m.

A bright orange sun poked above the watery horizon beyond the Chesapeake Bay Bridge and the sky was pink with the light coloring the clouds above. Cole Draper was out for an early morning run on the beaches of Ocean View. His breathing was in tune with the steady thump of his footsteps in the sand on the water's edge.

Wow, what a spectacular morning.

Sweat beaded on his forehead, and as he approached East Beach from the west, he pushed a little harder.

Another hundred yards!

His throat ached for water yet he pushed. And pushed. Finally he passed the Bay Front Club tower, broke stride and began to walk.

Breathing heavily, he walked about fifty steps then stopped, bent over and placed his hands on his knees, and inhaled deeply. He scanned the horizon. Two fishing boats were leaving the Little Creek Inlet. A row of seagulls perched on the breakwater, squawking. A man stood waist deep in the water, net fishing.

This is the best part of the day. He half smiled. *All downhill from here.*

Cole's breathing gradually returned to normal. He stood

and walked slowly, his hands on his hips, back toward the Bay Front Club. It was quiet at this time of the morning. He heard the increasing sound of a small boat's outboard engine, and turned to face the bay. His gaze searched for the source of the noise.

That's strange. There's no boat!

The sound intensified as he continued to scan the horizon. Then he saw an object flying about fifty feet above the water. As the sound moved closer, the object grew larger and began to take shape. It was flat on the top, like wings, with an elongated blue undercarriage. The object quickly closed the distance and Cole saw four rotors spinning rapidly. *It's a quadracopter drone! Pretty cool.*

The drone flew directly over where Cole stood and headed toward the Bay Front Club tower. He saw what he believed was a leather satchel, a man-purse, that hung from what looked like a mechanized arm. Cole watched the drone as it approached the tower, ascended to the tower balcony and hovered.

A second quadracopter approached behind the tower from 25th Bay Street. This one had a white undercarriage and it also carried a satchel. It came around the corner of the tower and maneuvered into a hover next to the blue drone

What the hell is going on here?

After a brief pause with both drones hovering, the white one slowly moved into a position behind the railing on the tower balcony and dropped its satchel on the deck and then moved back to a hover position away from the deposited satchel.

Cole left the beach through the access near the Bay Front Club and walked closer to the tower to get a better look. *Is there anyone else here watching this?* But he was alone.

The blue drone moved over the balcony deck and dropped its satchel a few feet away from the other. The drone then slid over, and with a hook, picked up the satchel that had been left by the white drone.

Whoever is piloting these is being very deliberate—and

very good.
The blue drone lifted away from the tower and sped away on a reverse vector from the direction it had come in on. As it departed, the white drone moved in and picked up the satchel that had been left and then departed on a route parallel to 25th Bay Street.

Cole stood in the corner of the green space next to the clubhouse and tried to assess what he had just witnessed. *I don't know what just happened here, but that was unusual.* He shook his head. *I have a bad feeling about this.*

❖❖❖

8:00 a.m.
Cole returned home, showered, and dressed casually in jeans and a light green safari shirt, a perfect ensemble for running errands all day. The aroma of fresh coffee and toasted bagels lured him to the kitchen. Yet the entire time he could not stop thinking about the drones he had seen.

"Good morning, stud muffin," Diana said from her seat at the solid-pine kitchen table. She turned to face him, head tilted slightly, with glittering blue eyes and a genuine smile.

Cole kissed her gently. "I hate it when you call me that."

"I know." Her eyes blinked with feigned innocence. "The coffee is fresh and the bagels are a day old." She held a half bagel in one hand and a knife with cream cheese in the other.

Before Cole had retired early from his job with the FBI and opened his private investigative consulting business, Diana Shelby had worked with him on an anti-terrorism task force while she was a special agent with the National Security Agency. She was recently divorced, recently resigned from the NSA, and had moved from her apartment in Washington to an East Beach carriage house, an arrangement that seemed increasingly unnecessary based on her affectionate relationship with Cole.

Cole sat at the table across from Diana. While she poured him a cup of coffee, he grabbed a bagel, plunged a knife in the cream cheese and started to spread it. "So Di, I saw something a bit odd this morning and I'd love to hear your take on it."

Diana chewed and nodded.

Cole described what he had seen at the Bay Front Club. How the two drones had been piloted so expertly and how they had come in from different directions. He emphasized the way the satchels were exchanged.

"You think this is foul play, don't you?" she asked.

Cole took a sip of coffee and then placed the cup on the table. "Yeah, I do. What do you think?"

Diana stopped spreading cream cheese on the second half of her bagel and set it and the knife on the table. "I remember this case a few years back involving an active FBI agent up in Reston who was caught clandestinely placing a package containing highly classified information at a pre-arranged, or dead drop, site for pickup by his Russian handlers. What you just described sounds like a pretty clever dead drop." She placed her elbows on the table and rested her head on her hands. "Holy shit, Cole!"

"Yeah. Holy shit."

"What are you gonna do?"

Cole leaned back in his chair and interlocked his hands behind his head. "I guess I'll start by talking to Goodman over at the Bureau."

"Mind if I tag along?" Diana asked.

"I guess that kinda takes care of us getting our errands done today, then."

"Great!" exclaimed Diana. "I'll take a shower and get dressed."

"I'll call Goodman and see if he's available."

❖❖❖

2:00 p.m.

The local field office of the Federal Bureau of Investigation in Chesapeake was a thirty-minute drive from East Beach. Blaine Goodman, the Special Agent in Charge, was there to greet Cole and Diana in the reception area near the visitor parking lot.

"You're a sight for sore eyes," said Goodman, offering his hand. "Good to see you again, Cole." Goodman placed his hand on Cole's shoulder as they turned to face Diana.

"And Diana, it is so good to see you as well." He gave Diana a quick hug. "C'mon, let's get you two processed and then we can talk." The guard perused their identification and typed their names into a computer, then issued yellow visitor badges.

Goodman escorted them to his office in the southwest corner of the third floor in the main building. The afternoon sun was bright so Goodman partially closed the blinds while he invited Cole and Diana to take seats at a round, six-person conference table. Goodman then sat and placed his interlocked hands on the table and smiled. "Okay, so what did you see this morning that was so intriguing?"

Cole explained in detail what he had seen at the Bay Front Club. He used a whiteboard located on Goodman's office wall to show the location of the club in relation to the bay and surrounding neighborhood and depicted the directions the drones had arrived and departed from.

Goodman listened, his gaze fixed on Cole and the whiteboard. He interrupted only one time and asked, "How large were the satchels and how heavy do you think they were?"

Cole answered, "They were about the size of a courier pouch and probably weighed no more than ten pounds."

When Cole completed his spontaneous presentation he remained standing in front of the whiteboard and faced Goodman. "Diana has a theory that this may be high-tech espionage. So what do make of it?"

"Shit, Cole." His gaze lingered over the drawing on the white board. After a pause, he continued, "Well obviously, this could be nothing at all, just some smart kids learning how to play with a new toy. However…" Goodman paused, scratched his cheek and furrowed his brow.

Cole set down the whiteboard marker and took his seat at the table while he waited for Goodman to continue.

"However much I'd like to think that," continued Goodman, "my gut tells me that's not the case. I'm much more inclined to agree with Diana. This looks like a high-tech dead drop. And a pretty sophisticated one at that."

Cole glanced sideways at Diana then turned toward Goodman. He placed his elbows on the table and leaned forward.

Goodman looked fixedly at the tabletop for a few moments. Then he looked directly at Cole and said, "You want to help on this? I can have a sole-source contract approved and ready for execution by tomorrow morning."

"Yes, I would. Definitely. If someone is selling confidential government information, then I would like nothing better than to be a part of taking him down."

Goodman looked at Diana. "And?"

"Count me in."

"Good. Let's meet here at nine o'clock tomorrow and we'll get started."

They all rose together and shook hands.

"If you don't mind, I'll have my assistant escort you out. I need to get started on those contracts."

❖❖❖

Saturday, June 11th, 5:00 a.m.

Cole's iPhone alarm went off and he moved quickly to silence it. He slid out from under the sheet, his legs over the side of the bed just touching the floor.

Behind him, in a soft, sleepy voice, Diana asked, "What time is it?"

Cole turned around. Diana was face down and naked except where the white bed sheet covered her legs. Her head was turned toward Cole. His gaze lingered on her sensuous backside for a moment.

"I thought I would go to the Club and hang around," Cole answered. He reached over and flicked Diana's hair off of her face. "I want to see if there is another drop today."

"Good idea," she mumbled, still half asleep. "I'll get

dressed."

Cole smiled and chuckled. "No need, I'll take Cooper and be back soon."

"I'll make some coffee." She yawned, then fell back to sleep.

Cole stepped out of the bed, pulled open a dresser drawer and removed a blue pair of Hanes briefs, black athletic shorts, and an old Gold's Gym T-shirt. He slipped into the clothes and laced up his black Asics running shoes. Accompanied by Cooper, his Irish Setter, they walked down the stairs. Cole snapped a collar and leash on Cooper, then the two ran to the Bay Front Club.

He returned an hour later and came in the back door then unhooked Cooper's collar. She walked directly to her water dish and enthusiastically lapped up some water.

Cole smelled fresh coffee so he pulled a cup out of the cupboard and stepped over to the counter and poured, mixed in some half and half, then entered the nook in the house that was his home office. Diana was seated at a table with her back to the doorway focused on the screen presentation on the Macbook in front of her. She wore purple yoga pants and a white-laced strap top. Cole walked up behind her and stood over her shoulder. "Hey babe. What are you doin'?" He placed his hand on her shoulder.

She reached up and touched Cole's hand then looked at him and smiled, "Did you see anything at the beach?" she asked.

"Nah, just a few boats heading out for the day."

"Well, I've been doing a little homework while you were at the beach." Diana turned her chair and faced Cole. "Look what I found." She drew her lower lip between her teeth and pointed at an image on the computer screen "These small, battery-operated drones have an air time of only twelve to fifteen minutes before the energy dies."

Cole set his coffee cup on the table and pulled another chair alongside Diana. He placed his hand on his chin and his forefinger tapped his lips. "If you subtract the four to five minutes that it took to make the exchange, that leaves eight to ten minutes total air time. So the operators can't be more than four or five minutes away from the Clubhouse."

Diana's smile grew wider and her eyes flickered.

"Do you know how fast these things go?" asked Cole.

"Max speed is twenty knots."

Twenty knots is twenty-three miles an hour. Five minutes at that speed is one point nine miles. "So the operators are less than two miles away." Cole sat back in his chair and rubbed his forehead.

"There's more," added Diana. Her lips pressed together smugly.

"Okay, smarty," coaxed Cole. "What else ya got?"

"Drones are controlled by radio waves and apparently most operators also use Wi-Fi hot spots to receive a video downlink. So the operators are probably using a tablet or a laptop to control them."

"Yeah, how is that helpful?"

"Radio waves, Bucky." Diana leaned toward Cole. "Before I left NSA we were working with the FAA on a system that can track radio waves in a five-square-mile area and triangulate the location of the operator. That should be operational by now. Sooo…If we can get our hands on that system." She pumped her fist excitedly. "We should be able to pinpoint where the pilots are!"

Cole stood, pulled Diana out of her chair and gave her a bear hug. "Beautiful and smart." He chuckled then asked, "What have I got myself into?"

❖ ❖ ❖

9:00 a.m.

Goodman escorted Cole and Diana into his office and they took seats at the conference table where two other agents were already seated. Their nametags read Scott Hundley and Mike Baktiari.

Goodman slid two brown file folders across the table, one for Cole and one for Diana. "Standard contract for each of you.

Fixed price, twenty-five thousand each and the government is waived of any liability in case either of you is killed or injured."

Cole smiled. "And this folder will self-destruct in thirty seconds."

"Tough business you're in, Cole," replied Goodman. He stood and walked over to a side table where a pot of coffee and clean white cups were set out. "Either of you like any coffee?"

"No, thanks, I've had enough already today," replied Cole.

Diana's head was down as she read the contract. She shook her head side to side without looking up.

Cole pulled a pen out of his pocket and signed two contracts, one original and one copy. He slid the original back to Goodman and flipped the folder closed on his copy. He slid the folder aside then placed his folded hands on the table in front of him.

Diana turned toward him, her nose and forehead scrunched up and one eyebrow raised. "You're not going to read it?"

"Standard stuff."

"For you, maybe. Not me. This is my first one."

"Take your time," replied Cole.

Six minutes passed in silence as Diana read the contract. Then she reached into her brown leather pouch and pulled out a pen and signed it. Goodman sat with his hands clasped behind his head. Cole's left elbow was on the table and his head rested in the palm of his hand. Diana looked at Goodman first then her gaze shifted to Cole. He made eye contact with her and they smiled.

"What?" she blurted, her eyes wide and mouth open. "It's my first one."

The three of them laughed then Goodman declared, "Good to have you guys on the team." He slid a temporary FBI identification card across the table to each of them.

Cole began, "I think we have a way to nail them."

"Already?" replied Goodman. "Let's hear it!"

"I'll let Di explain. She did all the homework." Cole slid

his chair back away from the table and turned to face her.

Diana's extemporaneous brief lasted forty minutes. She described the drone's capabilities; ten to fifteen minutes of flight time; twenty-knot maximum speed; operators not more than two miles way; drones controlled by radio waves. Finally, she disclosed her knowledge of the system that can track radio waves in a five-square-mile area and triangulate the location of the drone operator. "That should be operational by now," she concluded.

Goodman's attention was anchored on Diana. "This is fantastic." He gripped the edge of the table with both hands. "This is really good!"

Cole picked up the conversation. "The way I see it, we'll need two teams. One team with vehicles, a second team that can go airborne and rapidly take down a vessel at sea." He looked at Goodman, who was listening intently with his elbows on the table and his fingers pressed together to form a steeple. Cole continued, "We know that one drone came from the bay. I think we should assume the operator was on a boat. So, we'll need a helo assault team for that. However, we also need to assume it's possible that this operator is on land somewhere and flew the drone over water to position it there and then flew it in from the bay."

"With such short air time, I doubt that," replied Goodman.

"Agree, but we have to account for that possibility."

Goodman nodded. "Concur."

"I think the ground team needs four vehicles. If it turns out both operators are on land, we'll need to break that team up."

"Concur," Goodman said as he nodded again.

"The rest is easy," Cole said. "When we know the location of the operators, we take 'em down. Standard tac-op."

Goodman turned toward Hundley and Baktiari. "You guys have any thoughts?"

Hundley and Baktiari exchanged glances and then shook their heads.

"Okay then." Goodman slapped his hands on the table. "I'll make arrangements for the teams."

"Unless you have an objection, I'd like to be with the air assault team and have Di with the ground team," Cole suggested.

"I don't think that'll be a problem," replied Goodman. "In fact, you have more experience than my agents, so if you agree, I'd like you to take charge of the teams."

Cole nodded his acknowledgement.

"Again, I'll make the arrangements," said Goodman.

"Great. Then the only thing we need is the FAA system." Cole turned toward Diana.

"I can make some informal calls and see what we need to do to get it but," she faced Goodman, "I think the request will need to come from you formally."

"No problem. Find out what's required and I'll make it happen."

❖❖❖

Monday, June 13th, 1:00 p.m.

Cole received a call from Goodman on Monday morning asking to meet with Cole and Diana somewhere in East Beach so he could put eyes on the op-area for situational awareness. Cole suggested they meet for lunch at the East Beach Delicatessen and after that, he could show Goodman around the neighborhood.

Goodman, a consummate professional, arrived precisely at the agreed upon time. Cole and Diana were seated at one of the round, white-painted tables to the left of the entrance. It had been the only table available when they'd arrived a few minutes earlier. There were a few East Beach locals there but most of the patrons were the lunch crowd from the nearby Little Creek Naval Base. They decided they needed more privacy so they ordered sandwiches and soft drinks to go.

White sandwich bags in hand, they loaded into Cole's olive green Club Cart. As Cole slid into the driver's side, Diana hopped onto the jump seat in the back and assured Goodman she was perfectly fine there, so Goodman sat in the passenger seat.

"I thought we could head down to the clubhouse and eat our sandwiches on the deck there," suggested Cole as he pressed the accelerator pedal. The electric Club Cart jumped forward then rode smoothly up 26th Bay Street toward the Bay Front Club.

"We can talk while we ride," continued Cole, "and I doubt that there will be many people sitting on the deck so we should be able to talk freely there."

"Perfect," replied Goodman. "I need to see the clubhouse anyway. I'd like to place a twenty-four hour watch on the place in case they do any exchanges at other times."

Cole turned toward Goodman. "Yeah, I suppose it wouldn't hurt to do that, but…" His gaze returned to the road ahead. "…the way I see it, they can only do their exchange first thing in the morning. Right after sunrise."

"What makes you say that?"

"Well, think about it, Blaine. They can't do it at night because the pilots need to be able to see when they drop and retrieve. I'm sure the drones have video cameras, but it's doubtful the drones would also have a light. That would be too much weight." Cole braked to a stop and checked traffic before he crossed Pleasant Avenue. "So that rules out nighttime."

He continued to drive toward the Bay Front Club. "I also doubt that they would attempt to make an exchange during the late morning or afternoon. You'll see when we get there, the club is right next to the beach and the neighborhood pool. If the weather is nice, and it has been lately, there will be a pretty good crowd of people on the beach during the day. So if they tried it during the daytime, there would be people there, watching and asking questions. So it really narrows the window of opportunity to right after sunrise."

"You make a good point. Maybe I'll just set up a morning watch."

Cole parked in front of the Bay Front Club. It was a warm day and the sounds of the pool crowded with neighborhood kids buzzed as they stepped out of the cart.

Goodman continued, "But I could probably augment the

watch by hiding some cameras in the area."

Cole nodded.

They found three wooden rocking chairs on the deck facing the beach, sat, and opened their lunch bags.

Cole ate half of his club sandwich before he turned toward Goodman and asked, "Have you heard anything from the FAA about the drone tracker?"

"Yeah, I did," Goodman replied. "We're good to go on that but the earliest they will be able to get it here and set up is Wednesday or Thursday."

"Okay. I'll be here at sunrise for the next few days just to watch." Cole leaned his rocking chair forward, closer to Goodman. "I'm assuming you don't want me to try to snatch the packages, realizing that if this is what we think it is, there will be classified information in one of those satchels."

"Yeah. We're on the same page, Cole. The goal remains to catch these suckers. If you snatched a package, they would just relocate their drop site." Goodman took a bite of his sandwich and gazed toward the horizon. He swallowed, turned back toward Cole then continued, "We need to stick with the plan. Get the tracking system in place and then nail 'em."

"Have you got the team assignments?" asked Cole.

"Yeah. The ground team will have four agents, each with a vehicle." He turned toward Diana. "You can ride with Baktiari, the team lead." Goodman's gaze shifted back toward Cole. "If you want to go along on the air assault, I'll have a helo turning at sunrise over at Little Creek. There will be three agents geared up every morning until this ends. I figure you will want to be the fourth."

"You figured right."

"I'd like the four vehicles strategically placed within the two mile area so the one closest to the location of the operator can pounce quickly. The others should be able to join rapidly."

"I can help you pick the locations," offered Cole. "I know the area pretty well."

"Figured you did." Goodman smiled then asked, "By the way, when was the last time you fast-roped out of a helo?"

"It's been awhile," answered Cole. "I hear it's like riding a bike, though."

Goodman chuckled, still slowly shaking his head from side to side. "You're one of a kind, Cole. One of a kind."

"Thank goodness for that!" interjected Diana.

❖❖❖

Thursday, June 16th, 1:00 p.m.

After Cole met with Goodman, technicians from the FBI installed hidden cameras to provide twenty-four hour monitoring of the Bay Front Club tower and a two-man surveillance team was posted between four and eight o'clock each morning. On Wednesday afternoon, a team of technicians from the FAA arrived and began installation of the drone tracker.

The team lead contacted Cole at eleven and informed him there would be an operational test of the system at one o'clock.

Cole and Diana walked the two blocks from his house to the Club to meet with the team lead and observe the test. As they approached East Beach Drive, a young woman wearing jeans, a red Nike golf shirt, a shoulder-length ponytail, and tortoise shell eyeglasses emerged from a white, nondescript van parked across the street from the Club. She asked, "Are you Draper?"

Cole walked in her direction and answered, "That's me. And you are?"

"Joanne Posner." She pulled her Agency badge out of her back pocket and held it for Cole to see.

"Call me Cole. And this is my partner, Diana." He extended a hand to shake and motioned with his head toward Diana. "I appreciate the call this morning. We would love to see the test run of this system."

"Be happy to show it to you, but first can I see some identification?"

Cole looked at Diana with a wry smile. She gazed toward the ground and bit her lower lip. "Sure, no problem," he replied.

Cole removed his temporary identification from his wallet and Diana removed hers from her pouch and handed them to Posner.

"This is a high-priority job," Posner said as she perused their identification. "You guys obviously have heavy pull with the FBI."

"Yeah, well I think the priority on getting this system operational is based more on the reason we're here than on our pull with anyone at the Bureau."

"Yep, s'pose. Well come on in the van and we'll run the test and show you how it works." Posner slid open a side panel door on the van.

Inside, the back of the van was surprisingly empty. There was one computer monitor, keyboard and a small Dell CPU tower fastened to a metal desk. One seat bolted to the floor in front of the monitor and two seats bolted to the floor against the opposite wall. There was one other technician seated in the driver's seat.

"So this is how it works," Posner said. "The system uses the drone's own radio links to identify and locate the drone when it's flying where it's not supposed to be. And it triangulates the origination of the radio beams to locate the operator."

"That seems too easy," said Diana. "There has to be more to this system than what's in this van."

"Oh, and there is," replied Posner. She stood facing Cole and Diana with her arms down and hands interlocked in front of her. "We've set up six antennas around the perimeter of the two-mile grid that agent Goodman provided. And this was a particularly challenging setup, since part of the grid is over water. We had to set up two antennas on barges in the bay. These antenna receivers passively detect the direction of controller's radio guidance signal to the drone. That guidance signal direction is then transmitted to a receiver in this van that is connected to this CPU." Posner pointed at the computer tower next to the monitor. "The software then triangulates the directional signals and pinpoints the location of the operator. If there are three or more intersecting lines, the software will rate the probability of that position as high."

"That's pretty cool," declared Cole.

Posner leaned forward with her hands on the table. Her gaze turned toward Cole and she was beaming. "Let's run the op-test."

Cole put his hand on Diana's back and gently pushed her forward as they moved closer to get a good view of the computer monitor. The monitor had a map overlay of the grid area that allowed the system technician to pinpoint locations.

Posner picked up a small two-way radio and spoke into it. "This is Joanne, are you ready to run the drone?"

"All set," came the reply.

"Let's do it."

Posner faced the monitor and spoke over her shoulder toward Cole. "I don't know the location of our drone operator. I just told him to go pick a spot." There was a silent pause. "In a moment, you'll see a drone icon on the screen." Another pause was interrupted by an alert tone from the computer that sounded like a sonar ping. "There. The blue circle." She pointed at the icon on the monitor located in an area on the map overlay labeled Pavilion Park.

"Impressive. Is that where the operator is?" asked Cole.

"Not necessarily."

Posner's fingers quickly tapped instructions on the keyboard and several lines appeared on the monitor. They intersected at a point south on the grid and one-and-a-half miles from the van location. A red circle marked the spot of the intersection on the beach near the entrance to Little Creek inlet.

"There's the operator." Posner stood straight and turned toward Cole and Diana. Her finger remained pointed at the monitor. "He must have placed the drone in the first location then drove to the second location to operate it and try to trick the system."

Cole smiled. "This is great!" He rubbed the back of his neck and thought for a moment. "Only one thing concerns me. If the drone pilots see the van parked here, it may spook them and they might bolt before we can take them down."

"Yeah, we've already talked about that," Posner answered. "We're going to move to the other side of this bow-tie-shaped park. That's where we'll be tomorrow morning."

"All right, we're good to go for tomorrow," declared Cole.

"Call signs?" asked Diana.

"Oh, yeah. Glad you reminded me. Posner, you'll be Buckeye. Diana, your team will be Wolverine. My team will be Badger." Cole smiled toward Diana then said, "Good thing I brought you!"

Diana half smiled and gently punched him in the shoulder.

❖❖❖

Friday, June 17th, 5:15 a.m.

Cole stopped for a coffee at the Starbucks at the Little Creek Navy Exchange on his way to a helicopter launch and recovery zone across the street from the base golf course. The grey, SH-60 Seahawk helicopter was on the ground and three agents wearing black tactical gear with the letters FBI stenciled in white were loading more gear on the Seahawk. He parked in the field about a hundred yards away from the helo to ensure the car did not kick up any objects that could damage the helo's turbines during takeoff. He finished his coffee, strapped his Glock 9mm handgun around his waist, placed his two-way radio in a shoulder harness and strapped that on, then walked over to join the agents near the helicopter.

One of the agents stopped loading gear and came over to meet Cole. As he approached, Cole recognized him from their earlier meeting. "Hundley, good to see you." They shook hands and Cole placed his hand on Hundley's shoulder as they walked toward the Seahawk. "Do you have all the gear?"

"Roger, sir," replied Hundley. "Your tac-gear is in the back of the helo and the pilots have done their pre-checks and Foreign Object Damage walk-down. We're ready to go."

"Good. Sunrise is at five forty-five. Let's get the bird turning at five-thirty and launch right at sunrise. I want to stay airborne for about an hour. If nothing happens, we'll end it today and come back again tomorrow, and every day after that until we catch these guys."

"Roger."

❖❖❖

Diana drove Cole's golf cart to the East Beach Marina parking lot and saw Baktiari standing with three other men next to four black Chevrolet Impalas parked along a row adjacent to Pretty Lake Drive. They were each wearing black tactical gear. She parked the cart and, as she got out, Baktiari approached her.

"Good morning, Ms. Shelby," he greeted her. "We've got some coffee over here if you're interested."

"That would be great."

She walked with Baktiari to the car farthest from her where an agent was already pouring coffee from a thermos into a white Styrofoam cup.

"All we have is powdered cream and some sugar packets. Hope that's okay," said Baktiari.

"That's fine," replied Diana. "I need a kick-start at this time of day. Anything will do."

The agent handed Diana the coffee and she took a sip with both hands on the cup. She remained silent, sipping her coffee as the agents waited. After a few moments she apologized. "I'm sorry. You guys are waiting for me and I'm just in my own world here." She then continued, "We need to go to four separate locations that should surround the two-mile grid that we think the operator will be in." She pulled four area maps, with grid marks, out of her pouch and handed copies to the agents. She pointed at four red marks on the map. Each location was chosen to ensure that each vehicle could converge on a spot within the grid in less than two minutes.

"Agent Baktiari, if it's all right, I'd like to ride with you and be in position number one." She pointed to that position on the map.

"I was going to suggest that," replied Baktiari. He then directed the other three agents to take the remaining three positions.

"Gentlemen," Diana continued, "Cole has assigned us call signs Wolverine One, Wolverine Two, and so on."

They conducted radio checks using both their hand-held radios as well as their vehicle-mounted radios.

Diana looked toward the east. "Sunrise is at five-forty-five. We should be ready to go by then."

Baktiari nodded and said, "All right, man up. Let's take our positions and stay alert. Assuming this goes down this morning, when we're given a location, Diana will radio that grid spot to you and we all need to converge on that spot immediately. Weapons should be drawn but only return fire if fired upon. If at all possible, we want an arrest, not a stiff." He perused the faces of the agents. "Any questions?"

The four agents shook their heads. "Okay. Let's go."

❖❖❖

5:58 a.m.

Joanne Posner was seated at the desk with the computer monitor in the drone tracker van and she held a grande mocha latte from Starbucks in her hand. She faced sideways, engaged in a conversation with another system technician when she was interrupted by the alert tone that sounded like a sonar ping. She quickly placed her mocha latte on the desk and swirled in her chair to face the screen. The other technician stood over her left shoulder and he also focused on it. A blue circle appeared in the top right and the map overlay showed the location of the point on Pretty Lake Drive between 27th and 29th Bay Streets. The circle remained stationary for a few moments then moved on a true north bearing in the direction of the Bay Front Club.

She picked up her two-way radio, keyed the mike and spoke. "This is Buckeye. It's show-time, folks."

A second sonar ping alert sounded and she switched the radio to hands-free operation and placed a headset and microphone on her head.

"This is Badger." The reply from Cole sounded distant with a lot of machinery noise in the background. "Standing by for grid coordinates."

Posner heard Diana's voice through the headset. "Wolverine, ready."

The second blue circle appeared over water near the starboard side of the Little Creek channel buoy and headed southwest in the direction of the Bay Front Club.

Posner pulled the microphone closer to her mouth. "We have two bogies and they are both moving toward the Bay Front Club." She tapped a few more keys. "Stand by, I'm going to triangulate the location of the operators." She then tapped the monitor to zoom in on each position. *Great. Got it!*

"This is Buckeye. Wolverine, your contact operator is at grid location D42. On the map, that is the Bay Point Marina parking lot."

"Acknowledged," replied Diana.

"Badger, your contact operator is at grid location E3. That looks like it is located near the Little Creek channel buoy where the drone flight originated."

"Roger," replied Cole.

❖❖❖

Diana and Baktiari were in their idling vehicle in the East Beach Shoppes parking lot across Shore Drive.

She keyed the mike on her radio and spoke. "Wolverines, this is Wolverine Prime. Close to positions closer to Bay Point but do not enter until told to do so. We can't take him down until he brings his drone back to him."

"This is Wolverine Three." The speaker crackled. "From where I'm parked, I have eyes on the target. He's about a hundred meters away from me. I'm parked behind a hedgerow and concealed well. He's in a silver Benz AMG."

"Sheeww." Wolverine Four whistled. "That's serious coin."

"Let's keep our eye on the ball," Diana said. "What is the target doing?"

"He's definitely operating the drone. He's in the passenger seat with a computer in his lap and a controller joystick in his right hand."

"Great," she replied.

"This is Wolverine Three. The good news is there is only one way to exit Bay Point. If we block that off, he'll be trapped."

"Good."

"There's one more thing."

"Go ahead."

"He's in uniform. A Navy Lieutenant."

❖❖❖

The Badger team Seahawk launched at sunrise and flew at two thousand feet in a two-mile square, returned to the landing area and hovered at thirty feet then lifted airborne again. The purpose of this pattern was to give the appearance the Seahawk was on a training exercise. Team Badger headed north on the first leg of the pattern. Cole was seated next to the open side door and he peered through binoculars toward the Little Creek Channel buoy. Cole spoke into his microphone inside his tactical gear helmet to the others in the helo. "There it is, gentlemen." He pointed to a yacht, about eighty feet in length, with a black-and-white hull. "Captain," he addressed the pilot, "just stay in this pattern until I'm told the drone is back onboard and then we'll go take it."

The pilot turned in his cockpit seat and gave Cole the thumbs up signal.

❖❖❖

Posner continued to monitor the location of the drones and the controller operators.

"This is Buckeye. The drones are maneuvering near the Bay Front Club tower." She tapped her fingers on the desk. "I think they're making the exchange."

"Badger here. Everybody get focused. This is going down soon."

One of the blue circles on Posner's monitor broke off and headed north-northeast toward the grid coordinates of the controller."

"Badger, this is Buckeye." Posner wiped some perspiration off her forehead with the back of her hand. "The drone is returning toward grid location E3."

"This is Badger, call out when the points converge."

Posner felt her hands begin to shake. *This is not like training. I'm either jacked, or scared to death!*

The second blue circle on Posner's monitor headed southeast toward the controller in the Bay Point parking lot. "Wolverine, the drone is moving toward the controller in Bay Point."

"Acknowledged," Diana replied.

Posner's hands were shaking and her mouth was dry. She looked over her shoulder and made eye contact with the second technician. His demeanor didn't waver, and he put his hand on Posner's shoulder. "You're doing great. Just stay focused," he said.

The first blue circle on Posner's monitor merged with the red circle located at grid location E3.

"Badger, this is Buckeye. The drone is united with the controller."

"Roger, Buckeye. Badger team is going hot," replied Cole. "Great work, Buckeye."

The second blue circle merged with the red circle located at grid location D42.

"Wolverine, this is Buckeye." The technician's grip on Posner's shoulder tightened and she reached up and gripped his hand. "Drone is with the controller."

"Understood. Wolverine out."

❖❖❖

Diana switched channels and spoke to team Wolverine only. "Team Wolverine, converge on the target."

As Baktiari floored the accelerator, the Impala lurched forward with a screech. The scenery on each side was a blur as they sped down Pretty Lake Drive. Ahead of them Wolverine Four slid through a left turn off of 29th Bay Street toward Bay

Point. Wolverine Two followed on Pretty Lake Drive.

"Wolverine Two, block the exit in case he runs!" she shouted into her microphone.

"Roger. Block the exit."

Baktiari flew through the entrance to Bay Point and executed a hard left turn. With the tires screaming, he entered the parking lot.

Wolverine Four approached the Benz from the rear, Wolverine Three approached from the right side and Wolverine One from the left side. The tires screamed as the three vehicles braked hard to stop and surrounded the Benz.

Diana was the first out of her vehicle. She crouched behind her open door and aimed her service revolver at the suspect. Baktiari was seconds behind and Wolverines Three and Four were almost simultaneous with their weapons drawn.

"FBI," shouted Diana. "Hands high above your head and face this way."

The Navy Lieutenant held a brown leather satchel in his hand. He closed the Benz trunk lid and looked around. First toward Diana, then his gaze moved to the other agents with their weapons drawn on him. His posture straightened, eyes wide and mouth open. He dropped the satchel at his side and several reams of cash fell out. Diana made eye contact with him then he raised his arms above his head and fell to his knees.

❖ ❖ ❖

The pilot of the Seahawk banked hard left and descended to fifty feet. In less than a minute the Seahawk was within twenty-five yards of the sleek yacht and slowing to a hover. Four men were in the yacht's open-air bridge. As the Seahawk approached two of them pulled handguns out of their jackets.

"Gunner," commanded Cole through his headset gear. "If they fire on us, you are weapons free, and Captain," he directed his order toward the pilot, "show them our starboard side so they can see they're up against a fifty-cal."

The pilot maneuvered the Seahawk as directed and began

a slow approach to hover over the bridge.

Cole leaned out of the helo and looked down on the yacht as Hundley prepared to throw out the fast rope. The yacht's propellers began to churn up white foam and one of the four men ran off the bridge, down a ladder and inside.

"They're running," shouted Cole.

The yacht accelerated and pulled away from the Seahawk.

"Gentlemen," the pilot announced, "when the vessel reaches its maximum speed, I can match it but, the drop will be dicey."

"Do it," Cole replied.

The yacht accelerated to twenty-four knots and held steady at that speed. The pilot caught up to the yacht and matched speed. He yawed in and maintained his starboard aspect in case the gunner needed to take any action, then maintained position above the yacht's bridge.

"Go!" commanded Cole.

Hundley dropped a thick rope that hung from the hooks inside the door. Before the end of the rope had reached the deck of the yacht, he began to slide down the rope like a fire pole. The other two agents, then Cole, followed at ten-foot intervals. In less than a minute, all four were on the deck of the yacht with their assault weapons drawn.

The Seahawk pulled away and maintained a station off the stern of the yacht.

Cole immediately slid down a ladder. As he advanced forward toward the cabin area, he felt the deceleration of the yacht, fell forward, and caught a beam with his free hand to maintain balance. He heard the ripping sound of a paper shredder from a cabin on his left.

Cole kicked open the door and was rushed by an assailant wielding a raised hatchet. As the hatchet came down, Cole dropped his assault pistol and grabbed the assailant's arm with both hands to stop the blow. They struggled for a moment then Cole wedged his shoulder under the armpit of the attacker and body slammed him into the bulkhead. The attacker screamed in pain and his dislocated arm went limp. Cole had his back against him and kept him pinned against the bulkhead. He swung his left arm backward and forcefully connected his elbow with the attacker's jaw. His entire body went limp. Cole stepped away and allowed the unconscious man to fall to the deck.

Cole stepped over him and stood next to the shredder. He picked up the satchel and peered inside.

He heard Hundley enter the cabin area. "Cole, we've secured the vessel." A few more footsteps then Hundley stepped through the broken cabin door. "The crew is topside, restrained with zip-ties, and the Norfolk Police and Coast Guard have been notified. Their boats are on the way to clean this up." Hundley looked at the man on the deck. "You need any help?"

"Nah. I think I have this under control." Cole half smiled then handed Hundley the satchel. "Looks like he shredded a few pages, but not much. And there's a thumb drive in there as well. I don't think he had time to wipe it clean."

Hundley looked at some of the papers in the satchel. "These documents are labeled top secret!"

❖❖❖

Friday, July 1st, 9:00 a.m.

Cole met Goodman at the Sandfiddler Café for breakfast. Over an omelet, toast and coffee, they discussed the status of the investigation and charges.

"I'll start with the bad news," said Goodman. "The yacht is owned by the Chinese embassy in Washington and everyone taken into custody was a diplomat who worked at the embassy."

"I can see where this is going," replied Cole.

"Yeah, they threw the diplomatic immunity card on the table."

"Figures," grumbled Cole. He tossed his knife on the plate with a clang.

"State has revoked their credentials and they have all been sent home and are prohibited from ever returning to the

States."

"Yeah, well that's international diplomacy for ya. Nothing we can do about that," conceded Cole. He chewed and swallowed a bite of his omelet. "What about the Lieutenant? What's his story?"

"Lieutenant Anthony Cleveland. He was greedy. Lived a lifestyle that far exceeded the salary of a lieutenant. He worked at the Naval Shipyard on a Naval Sea Systems Command team that was developing plans for the next generation destroyer. He was slowly feeding the technical plans to the Chinese."

"Is that what was in the pouch?" asked Cole.

Goodman leaned forward, closer to Cole. "Yes. He was feeding them information in increments. The Chinese paid him twenty-five thousand for each drop."

"Well, I hope he spends the rest of his life in a federal prison."

"He will," replied Goodman. "His attorneys wanted to plea bargain but this has federal-level attention. The Attorney General said, 'Not only no, hell no.' We've got enough evidence on him to make this a slam-dunk case."

Cole couldn't help but smile when he heard that.

"Of course, he's very remorseful now," Goodman added.

Cole sat back in the booth bench, placed his arm on the bench top and shook his head.

Goodman continued, "I assume you and Diana know that you'll be needed to testify."

"With pleasure." Cole finished the rest of his omelet and then placed his napkin on the table.

As they stood to leave Goodman asked, "You have anything big on your plate in the near future?"

"Yeah," replied Cole. "Diana and I need to run some errands."

FIRST LANDING
BY WILL HOPKINS

This Fourteenth day of June, in the Year of Our Lord 1607
    It is now gone a fortnight since we were marooned upon this desert strand of the great Chesepiook Sea. Our meager supplies exhausted, pitiable shelter ravaged by Tempest, and Prayers of rescue gone unanswered these many days, Mr. Trumble and I prepare to strike from this strange and forsaken place for unknown Western territories, Devout in hope of meeting our lost contingents. I leave this account as a true Record of our trials and discoveries, so that it may aid and guide those who come after.
    May God be merciful to who next reads these words.
    s, George Hapencourt, Virginia

April 26
    For these hundred and forty-four days we have danger'd the winter Atlantic, risking gales, calamity of the Bermudas, and deprivations of the every sort, all for the hope of faire landing on the Virginia coast. Finally we have it. This morning near sunrise the boy Joseph Dobb, a'perch the main rigging, crowed landfall off the bow horizon. While this news caused great stir and jubilation amongst our crew, the Rev. Hunt has called for three days' prayers of Thanksgiving before we venture ashore. More than one murmur arose for stringing the

poxy Right Reverend from a windward yard, as fitting his so lofty station. Captain Newport, master of our ship Susan Constant, and perhaps more devout than his rummy language and hard rule do betray (though I suspect his piety waxes with prospect of increase share in the London Company) silenced our little mutiny. So the cook's man doles our morning ration of infest'd meal and foul water. I now look out to those distant woods rosed in dawn's light and cannot help but feel like Tantalus.

April 29
 Our Deliverance this brave morning. Aboard the S. Constant's main launch, I am at station on the prow, watching for lurking shoals before our course. Mr. Jonas Trumble, a dour though dependable man of Sussex, mans the near oar. Captain Newport himself leads our landing party. Fourteen other men aboard, four with muskets and steel armor should we encounter savages or Spaniards. Rev. Hunt rides atow in the skiff, along with Mr. McIntyre and an oaken Cross to be stood at the place where we land. Our Corps slaves the oars, racing the green Sea to our new shore. I will resume this passage once we reach land. Now to my watch.

❖❖❖

 It is perhaps middle day as I write this from the comfortable hollow of a leeward dune. We roved the empty beach and sand hills through morning, after Rev. Hunt led our moppy congregation in Hymn and Prayer, claiming all these lands for King James, with this empty Cape to be called Henry for His eldest son. Concluding this ceremonious occasion we began to explore the ground inland of our landing site. It is, as may be fairly described, a desert. Not a sight of walking animal, berry or nourishing fruit, nor watery spring. A sand mountain rises to the southwest just inside the seaward dunes, though its steep slopes collapse under the feet of those seeking to climb for vantage over the inland forests. After several unprofitable hours we repaired to the beach, where some of our party then combed for oysters, only to find the succulent innards robbed, no doubt by the kites and jackwings that circle endlessly above the shore. Word now passes that the Captain prepares to muster a small regiment of musketeers and able men, apparently to include myself and Mr. Trumble (per his small competence in the Spaniard language, learnt to him during claimed trading voyages along the Africa coast), to trek inland for evidence of superior shelter and replenishment. I must suspend this Account as our line now forms for the advance.

❖❖❖

Havoc! Commander Hazelton of the Fleet Guard and two of his armed troop (the third musketeer remained with our main party) organized the orderly march into the forest alee the dunes. Our foray stalled in the tangled vines and swamp, no better than a quarter-league from our Ocean camp. Hazelton ordered Geyson, a boatswain of knavish character but useful wiry frame, to worm through the devilish thicket consuming our progress, with the objective of finding a path inland. Now, by this hour the sun had low'd into the far trees, and the all fresh airs had deaden'd in those black woods, rousing clouds of ravenous flies to swarm and torment us unendingly. I was elected among the party to urge Hazelton for retreat, on the grounds that we may refit and determine a more suitable route in the new light of morning. As I offered this case, an unholy whoop sounded from inside the forest, raising general alarm among us, followed by the form of Geyson brashing the thorny vines and mudded ground, an arrow shaft affix'd into his shoulder! Despite our protests he raced for the beach, blood trailing his steps across the peat. On his heels came more sounds from the leafy interior and as Hazelton hotly ordered his guns to bear on the source, I glimpsed a pair of wild, yellowed eyes inside a ruddy head, peering from a knot of Cypress. Our Commander shifted to direct fire, only to have an arrow keen his hand. This triggered a fury of smoke and sound from the guns, the reports echoing in the primitive wood and the savages feeling the hot sting of our shot. They fled into the darkness, animal-skinned and barefoot, each grasping a bow, blood a-trickling their peppered backs.

❖❖❖

Dusk. Our wounded party rests about the shore and recounts our tale of encounter. McIntyre and the Reverend attend to Geyson, who lies on a pallet set near the Cross. Hazelton, with bandaged hand, has deployed the gunners to defend from further attack, also setting a watch seaward to warn of approach by Spanish ships of war, as the black-souled Iberians may be in trick and league with these savages. Trumble and I go to collect wood and limbs drifted by the waves and set a fire. One of the oarmen has killed several fat gulls, which, with a ration of sorry ship's meal, will furnish our buffet for the evening.

April 30
After a watchful and tentative night, glad news this morning. Captain Newport has decided leave this cursed place for more protected and promising landfall westward, where his charts showed several spacious rivers which may offer acceptable site for a permanent Fort. On a rising tide (both of Sea and our good humor) the crew began to strike the unhappy camp for return to safety of the Susan Constant. After bestowing aboard our wounded and equipment, we pushed off the launch into the surf, leaving the Cross and our Prayers of Thanks and Claim on the blowing dune. Once beyond the breaking seas, the Captain ordered Mr. Trumble and myself to board and untether the little skiff, and tend it toward the barque Godspeed, for reasons unsure (we complied with hope that G.Speed be better provisioned than our flagship).

❖❖❖

Oh, woes! I record this an hour hence, upon a rough brace inside our little boat, fearing ebbing fortunes. Our skiff, not much bigger than a good-sized coffin though not stoutly built to abide 'til doomsday as is that graveman's box, has but a single mast and sail (which Trumble hoisted only to discover dry-rotted canvas torn in several places). We have made hurried repairs using a length of twine unravel'd from the bowline, but this paltry jib offers little truck against the faire east wind now raking the main of our Fleet. Godspeed is rigged and underway, her master perhaps unaware of our newly ordered rendezvous. Our hails to her helm go unanswered. We steer as best we can for her retreating sails; the faster S. Constant and Discovery are already half-down the watery horizon. With fortune we shall gain and take them.

May 1
    Lost. Two nights' reach on a sou'easterly wind, we have surely entered the Chesepiook, a Sea of unknown extent lying inland of the Great Ocean. Our Fleet has vanished as the evening sun into the western horizon. Alone, we make way within portward sight of unbroken and dismal-looking beaches and wooded hinters, the surf making landfall too perilous even if we desired to venture onto those landings. The wind carries scents of pine and honeysuckle. Yesterday eve Trumble spied a large fish in our wake. Fearing a shark or sea monster, I fashioned a harpoon by rough-hewing the handle of our single oar with a knife (found in the modest keep at our boat's bow, along with a satchel holding a small copper'd ship's chest of wax'd candles and Eucharist wine used at our new Pointe Henry). The creature soon flashed beneath the skiff and I rose to strike, only to see that he was a grey dolphin. So free was the fish to swim between the Atlantic and this inland Sea, Trumble observed, that these waters must indeed be deep and vast like the Ocean itself. Comfort us this did not. Our self-consolation was paired drams of the Holy drink, though it now be more vinegar than claret (I vouch the latter coursed o'er our R. Hunt's plump lips a-many lines of longitude east). At the least I may use the chest, etch'd with the good name Susan Constant, for storage of my nibs and precious papers.
    At dawn we drew nearer to what appeared as a gap in the

otherwise unbroken beach. The growing light confirmed such, giving sight of a capacious lagoon and reedy marshes behind the inlet. Anticipating salvation, we made to steer for this haven, only to be fought back by a conspiracy of tide and wind. A best we are able to tiller within a half-mile of the shore or else be borne into the empty recess of northern waters. The little Bay recedes as Eden as beat westward with the lifting sun. We have left perhaps one ration of stale water and hard cracker.

May 2
Afternoon. We have spent our supplies. Trumble leans across the gunwale, scooping water to wash across his gums. I must warn him that to drink this brine will be his death. Still, I cannot blame him; the Spring sun in these tropics burns like high summer to an Englishman. I rest in the shadowed stern, washing my kerchief in the slowing passing current, and setting it dripping upon my scalp as a means to cool. It is of little utility, as salty rivulets run into my eyes and burn. The stubborn wind prevents our landing; at best we can trim the shore not a half-mile off. Our hope saps with each hour.

May 3 or unknown
How strange a place. Perhaps this is heaven as we have died? I write as best my memory permits, fevered as it was from lack of drink. It is early morning on what I believe is the third day of May, though I might have slept through't and it now be the fourth morning. I honestly know not which, such was my exhausted state. This then is my approximate account of our deliverance from the prison Sea.

❖ ❖ ❖

Around evening last as we sailed, the shore wind subsided and calmed, perhaps with the cooling air or from our entreaties to the Almighty. Soon came fresh breezes, stirring then coming faire from the nor'east. I advantaged our newfound fortune and steered on an opposite bearing toward shore. The boat heeled on the run, making smart speed as I could determine by the fast lap of water against the hull. In the gloaming, as the moon rose to greet her husband night, appeared a hint of a cut into the silver'd beach. I played out the sheet lines and headed us for it, making steady way until perhaps a hundred yards out when came the sweep of an outflowing current. In this excitement, Trumble exclaimed that we have discovered a little Creek, no doubt graced with saving fresh water and wild things on which to feast! Carried by contending wind and this outgoing tide we finally secured landfall on the eastern bank of the creek maw, bow dragging and bumping along the sandy bottom. There we quickly disembarqued into a low surf rolling about our feet. Two good heaves and we drove the skiff up onto the dry beach, which hemmed a line of low dunes. To the west, across the flowing channel, an opposite beach with deep woods behind disappeared into a westward mist. In the darkness we set out over the dune and down along the bank of our little Creek, which shone softly under the orb'd moon. I recall following the shining water for some distance. Then nothing.

❖❖❖

So much for our late landfall. I record this from the mossy bank of a small pond set in the midst of a pine forest. It appears to be late morning. How we arrived here I remember not. By some blessed quirk of nature's heavenly design, this water is fresh and clear, though not a quarter-mile from the salted and undrinkable Sea. Trumble snores away (more noise from this taciturn fellow than during all our hours asea!) on a mattress of boughs stripped from the small trees lining the near bank. We've sated our thirst in the life-returning waters, and dined on the sweet flesh of an unknown reed that flourishes here.

May 4
Stranger things still. Trumble and I left our camp this morning, drawing a careful map on which to make our return. We walked back north to the Sea to inspect our skiff (which, with proper repair and supply, may now deliver us westward

and to our Company) and survey for sign of rescue. Tracing our steps in the sandy ground, we climbed the gapped dune and down onto the beach, dead empty save for the in-rolling waves! After some search, Trumble discovered a furrowed line, which we judged to be from the dragging keel of the skiff, leading into the water. While he conjectured that the incoming tide must have borne the little boat out to Sea, the remnant beach flotsam left by the high water did not reach the spot where we beached the skiff that night. We now sit atop the seaward dune, waiting on the in-running tide in hope that it may return our only boat. This is doubtful, as all we see is the unbroken blue horizon against a clear sky. Trumble intends to gather wood for a signal fire. I now set down this journal to aid him in this project (no matter how futile). He remains thick-minded as the timber he carries.

❖❖❖

I resume this Account from the confines of our inland camp. No luck with our signal fire, as I wagered. We burned piles of drifted wood throughout the afternoon, laying atop wet sea grasses to raise thick smoke so that a high-mast watchman may better spy us. With no response to our beacon and desiring to escape the Sea winds before night, we retreated to our camp in the lake pines. We have managed a small fire to roast some of the reeds, and Trumble has discovered that one may burn the hollow shafts and draw soothing smoke from them as a clay pipe! Tomorrow we will begin on a more substantial camp. For tonight, I too have built a leafy bed and wish for sleep.

A Week Past
    I have expended my inks, but luckily have found a means to fashion a writing nib from the charred tips of willow. It is a good thing that I resume this journal, as further mysteries have risen. And we are not alone here.
    The luxury of our inland camp wanes. The loss of our boat has deprived us of working materials with which to construct shelter. We have used limbs and leafy boughs to make a

canopy against the elements, though this proved woefully insufficient during a sharp rain. More, our constant reedy diet strains our stomachs and strength, owing, I expect, to its lack of fat and salt (at least the poor ship's gruel offered the meat of mealy bugs). Our pond, while providing ample drink, contains no fish that we can determine. Trumble did succeed in capturing a small turtle, which we cooked and ate several days ago. It sustained us for a day, but we have since been forced to hunt for vegt'bles and game in the nearby areas (Trumble is fashioning spears for this purpose). Our larder remains empty.

Now to the matter. Yesterday, Trumble and I ventured into the woods along a broken stream that feeds the several ponds about our camp. After perhaps an hour's ramble we came upon a clear pool fed by springs, headwaters to these lakes, we presume. Down in the water we peered stones bright like yellowed jewels. Trumble extracted one of the number, only to find it a flinty rock a'sparkled in some mineral peculiar to the waters. We marked this place Diamond Springs on our expanding map.

Still unfed by afternoon and feeling the weight of a heavy sun, we decided to retreat for yet another repast of roasted reeds back at our camp. Trumble decided to try one last probe into the near wood, making joke (how misery thus improves his odd temper!) that perhaps he'd spear a bear or other beastie that could keep us fat and fed us through the season. He made three more steps, then without a word dropped to a knee, turning and gesturing for me to hurry upon. As reached him, he pulled me down and tapped a finger to his lips, all the while pointing into a brambled tuft maybe ten yards off and intently watching its shadowed branches. I followed but saw nothing for several moments, and then there, in the high grass before the leaves, I saw the fixed eyes of a man. At that instant our spy must have realized his position was betrayed, as he leapt from his cover and turned running for the far woods. Though the form was swaddled in deerskins, we estimated it to be not of a grown man but of a boy of perhaps ten or so years. Trumble called to the native; on that the boy turned for one last look then disappeared into the trees.

Fearing this encounter a prelude to general massacre, Trumble and I sped forthwith back to our camp to fashion a hasty defense. What we discovered on returning, however, abated our concern, at least for the immediate time. There, next to the banked coals of our fire, were five fish, skinned and salted, rowed atop a plank of a fragrant wood. Perplexed, I suggested this was the work of an industrious hawk or gull, until Trumble noted the fishes were each carefully knotted and bound with grass twines. We conducted a tentative search of the adjacent hedge and trees, finding nothing but a single set of footprints in the soft earth. They bent 'round to the direction of the woods where disappeared the boy-savage. 'Tis strange, but perhaps these people possess more Christian charity than do most of the men in all of old England?

Now to the fishes. After some debate as to whether these gifts might be tainted by our hosts with potions or foul venom, our hunger o'ercame us and we baked the fish on a fire kindled with the resinous plank, which burned with considerable heat and imparted a fine taste into the assembly. (I will happily report that it was an excellent supper, the best we have tasted in nearly a half-year.) Under moonlight we enjoyed more of Trumble's smoking reeds, later banking the fires and repairing to our beds. He resolved to keep first watch in case the native men come upon us during the night. With a full belly and cooling night air I am to sleep.

May 12, as I will best estimate it for purposes of this Journal
More astonishments. Trumble arose early, taking morning sanitary relief and scrounging the woods for firewood. He has returned directly with something else in hand, and has awakened me rudely to show it.

Before us is a basket of most intricate weavings, using grasses of select sizes and color. It brims with an odd fruit, candle-shaped and rowed with small yellow berries. Trumble found this and another batch of salted fish near the trail of footprints that we discovered yesterday evening. It seems the natives seek to fatten us more—I hope not for the slaughter! We plan to cook part of this feast and strike out for more exploration. Perhaps we will meet our young benefactor.

May 14
At last, after these trying months. Oh simple days of contentment and leisure! Our search as planned in my last entry went empty, with no further encounter with these benevolent natives. Sustained by our kitchen and fairing weather, we decided this morning, after breakfast on the roasted yellow'd fruits, to explore westward to the shore opposite the little Creek. Returning to the beach where the distance across was most narrow, we waded then swam across the flowing waters (a blessing, in that we had not bathed in many weeks) to make land on the opposite beach. Mr. Trumble found a breach in the dune, which led us into a long, grassy interior copsed in black oaky trees gnarled and bent to the sea winds, and vale'd by dunes on either side. Further westward passage through this land revealed it a peninsula, north'd by Sea and a broad lagoon along the south.

We traveled for perhaps three or four miles, the ground intermittent with fine sand and loamy earth. At this point the dunes gave way to clear flats overlooking the coast. There (I estimate not five leagues distant) across a narrow in the Sea, stretched a western shoreline! Trumble and I searched its forested limb, hoping for sign of our lost Fleet, even though we lacked means to reach across the long fetch. Our plan was then to build a signal fire, but as we saw no sails or signs of Englishmen, we decided to return to our camp for the night. Before leaving, Trumble noted inviting woods to the south that might offer promise of exploration on another day. I thusly marked these on the map and we departed.

On the return journey, while swimming across our little Creek, Trumble spied a greeny spiked lobster clinging a log. He speared the creature and carried it to shore, going back to capture four more in similar manner. These were rounder and more fierce than lobsters which we are familiar, but placed upon hot coals yield a flesh as delicious.

We then set about for rest at our pleasant evening camp, bellies full of meat and roasted fruits. Mr. Trumble even became talkative during our relaxation, expanding on the events of the day and their portent. Our discourse leaned toward scheme for deeper exploration into the western peninsula, with hope of finding a route to the destination Rivers marked upon Capt. Newport's map and thus remarriage with our vanished fleet. (I warrant that the far shore spied on today's foray may play in this discovery.) Suddenly, in the early twilight a flight of ev'birds scattered from a tree near by the lake edge. Hard upon came a rush and blur, which Trumble exclaimed to be a hunting hawk, then the fell of a small bird into the near grass. Our search of the ground there uncovered not the bird but a trail of ruby blood and the imprint of light feet across the field and into a wood. After these we followed until there in the dimming light stood our native, revealed not as a boy but rather young maiden by her bare breast and composure of face. She held an arrow, upon which pinned the small prey'd bird. When Trumble called out she turned and flew swift as a swallow into the forest. To what end she came near our camp we could not determine. Still, our good fortune rises, and we make plans to return to our discovered peninsula and its far coasts and woods tomorrow.

May 17

Oh harrowing days! This tale of which I now write still colds my blood, yet I will try to render it truthfully.

On the night of which I last recorded, Mr. Trumble and I retired to our pallets and honest sleep, as we were much worn by the busy day. At a dark hour yet nearing dawn (this based on the position of the sinking moon and the stars of the summer triangle), I was awoken by crashes in the hedging grass and then rough hands upon my arms and neck. Terrified, I looked into the wolf'd eyes of three native men, faces painted with black'd and reddish marks as revealed by the shining moon and the embers of our cooking fire. One held a spike against my chest, jabbing it closely as I struggled to escape my arrest. The two others held cudgels poised ready for strikes on my legs. A matched party was upon Mr. Trumble.

These men—I hesitate to name them savages as their work was carefully executed and most skillful—then bound our hands with strips of hide and fashioned a length of coarse rope around our waists, joining us together like a loose team of oxen. In this manner we could stand upright and walk, though running flight was an impossibility. After short discourse among the raiders (in a tongue unrecognizable) we were shoved and marched south into the forest.

By sunrise we entered into a grassy lea bounded by pinewoods and twisting creeks. Skirting these, we marched onward, no pointing path evident through the fields, occasionally prodded by one of our jailer's spear. Perhaps an hour more we passed through a thin wood edging the bank of a wide river. There we were sat down into the hull of a dug'd out tree and paddled across to the nearest spit of land. Closer I noted the finger of grey smoke rising into the clear morning sky. A party of men, all clad in deerskin like our jailers, waited there on the close bank. As our boats drove up into the watered ground, several of these men pulled us roughly onto dry shore. Followed close by, we were paraded hence to a clearing where spread a native village. Five oblong lodges made from hewn limbs and woven marsh grass rounded a central fire. The ground was bare and worn, evidence unsettling that a large body of people lived here. Near the nestling woods, several naked children stood quietly and watched us as one might consider creatures within a traveling menagerie. Elsewhere in camp women worked wooden bowls of meal into round forms and hanging these to bake on sticks set by the fire. (Our presence must have enkindled modesty as they would not look to us.) Here we were detained for onward of a quarter hour, all the while the aroma of the breads tempting our empty stomachs. Once a young man of our party addressed me in words unknown yet oddly familiar. His eyes held both mock and menace.

Anon a man of ceremonious clothing and manner appeared from the drap'd door of the center-most lodge and beckoned our keepers to come forth. Rough shoves followed as Trumble and I were manned through the parted curtains and into the main hall of the lodge. Even now I shiver at thought of the sight. There at the facing end of the long room sat a man of flinty visage, bedeck'd in elaborate skins and bright feathers of blues and green, perched atop a seat raised chest-high from the packed loam floor—no doubt the Chieftain of this strange community. To the flanks stood men in lesser feather'd clothing and young soldiers weapon'd with spears or artfully carved clubs. A fire burned eagerly in the center of the otherwise dark room, its smoke disappearing through a vent arranged in the o'erhanging roof. Mr. Trumble and I were bundled forward and forced to kneel on a reeded mat.

Their King sat silent, keeping our gazes (which we steadied to conceal our growing unease) while veiled talk commenced among the elders. Soon these turned heated, with one elder of most warlike appearance proclaiming loudly and gesturing in our general direction, while another seemed to counter him (I know not why). Their words unknown to me, all I could surmise was that our poor necks were at the wager. Then, in the midst of these advocacies, the King raised a hand, beaded and rattling with beach shells, bringing abrupt silence in the assembly. With sweeping motion he commanded a fierce-appearing man, who stepped at us carrying a scabbard of leg's length. Nearer to us, he pulled from it a silver'd sword of fine work and honed edge, then raised it above the head of poor Trumble. Certainly, this instrument was not the product of these impoverished and backwards heathen! The swordsman held as if for signal and at this horrible moment the elders began their final appeals at the King (he remaining unmoved) as the most belligerent spat and holler'd "Espan!" while pointing at Trumble's poor head! This caused Mr. Trumble to cry "No!" and gibber in his coarse Spanish tongue. I was amazed as the fiery old man gibbered back in some reply, leading Trumble to shake his head violently and shout English!

English! To this our accuser appeared sharply surprised, and began hushed conference with the King for several minutes. All the time the sword hung above Trumble's poor head.

The exact events that followed remain unclear to me, as we were swiftly hustl'd from the Lodge after a new judgment by the King caused shouts and general confusion. I do remember the bright sun scalding our eyes as several men ushered us from the village and down to a waiting boat, on which we were sail'd back across the river and left alone at the far bank. Leaving, I spied the young maid who aided us over the several days watching our progress from a spot hidden in a small wood. She betrayed no sign as to her involvement in this adventure.

On the far bank we bade quick farewell to our captains, unmoved as Charons plying this mysterious river, and made forthwith to the near woods. There we found cover'd refuge and recounted our experience. Even now, I may only wonder that these natives, having met the cruel Spaniards (hence their recognition of the Iber's tongue and their possession of a Toledon blade, no doubt swag and boot won in battle), believed Trumble and me to be of that vile race and so sought to kill us. Thanks be to God that Englishmen landing here earlier showed Christian benevolence! After a brief (still fearing for our bowed heads) Thanksgiving, Trumble and I raced northward to the thin safety of our camp. By Providence and the guiding Grace of the ev'steady Pole star, we found the sweetwater lakes and our modest home by early darkness.

It is gone four days now since our capture and release. After a wakeful night, Mr. Trumble and I determined the second morning to abandon our exposed position for a more secluded and remote place. Our reasoning thus, that the hotter of these natives may prevail to seek us out, Englishmen or no, and exact some punishment upon us. Gathering our rudiments (the box and meager satchel from the vanish'd skiff, and a few pikes untouched during the heathen raid) we struck north along the Creek to the Sea, wading into the tongue-ing waves that erased our footprints, then swimming to the Eastern Beach of yon narrow peninsula. There we encamped in the sea dunes, digging a hutch into the lee-sand amongst thick grass and vines. Later, we raised a weather awning of thatched leaves (styled on the natives' cabins, I readily concede), which now hides us from the winds and preying natives. This perch affords us view of the Sea from which to monitor any sign of our ships. Alas, those waters remain empty, save for the wheeling gulls and far-endless waves.

I end this passage for the afternoon. Rising clouds threaten from the west and I doubt the coming night.

❖❖❖

Present Day

"You better come on up, Lonnie Ray. Your burrito's gettin' cold."

"Give me a second."

"These damn things are good." Junior Pratt wiped a smear of cheese off his chin and watched a seagull wheel above East Beach Drive. The white and gray bird soared out over the dunes and the deep blue water of Chesapeake Bay. Junior knuckled the last wad of tortilla into his mouth, then tossed the 7-11 wrapper into the ditch where Lonnie worked.

"Jackass."

Junior lit his after-lunch Winston. "What you doin' down there?"

Lonnie set down the shovel and flicked open his pocketknife. "Looks like somebody buried something in the sand."

Junior took a good pull and listened to Lonnie's blade scrape across something. He couldn't tell what it might be, seeing how the little excavation was blocked by Lonnie's sizable tail.

"Here we go," Lonnie declared, hefting himself to the lip of the ditch. He plopped a small, blackened chest on the sandy dirt.

"What is it, a cigar box?"

"Must be some good smokes if it is. Damn thing's made

out of copper."

"Huh." Junior leaned down for a closer look. "What's that writing on it?"

Lonnie Ray wet his thumb and ran it cover the dented lid. "Who the hell is Susan Constant?"

"Got me. Anything inside?"

Lonnie Ray fingered around the corroded lid, but couldn't find a way to open the thing. "Almost like somebody had waxed the seal." He gave it a shake. Something rattled around inside. "Sounds like papers maybe."

Junior snorted. "Probably receipts from one of the flop houses that use to be back in here." He tossed the stub of Winston. "Come on, pitch that damn thing and help me with that next run of pipe."

Lonnie crawled out of the ditch with the box under an arm and scrapped his boots on a piece of two-by-four. "Nah. My daughter can take it to show-and-tell at school tomorrow. You know how kids love mysteries."

FORAYS INTO SAILING
By Mary Jac O'Daniel

    The sea and its turning tides have always beckoned me. I'd always been fascinated by the ocean and often dreamed about living on the beach, looking out my window, and seeing the waves crash against the sand. I loved the romantic notion of the sea caring so much about the land that it formed dunes as it swept up the sand.
    As a teenager, I'd happened upon a poem called "On the Dunes," which encapsulated everything I loved about the ocean. Written by Sara Teasdale, it found a way to express the mystery, longing, and beauty of the ocean in a few stanzas. It surmised that if there were any life when death was over, the beaches would know her. It implied that she would come back, and went on to say that if her life seemed small, or that she was scornful, she would improve after death. The poem ended by saying that if anyone wanted her, all they had to do was stand on the seaward dunes and call her name.
    Something in the words touched my tender sixteen-year-old heart. I could picture someone, an older person—perhaps me—standing on the dunes and calling a loved one's name. The desperation of someone hoping to hear an answer from the sea as they softly spoke their loved one's name was easy for me to envision.
    A framed copy of the poem had been given to me years

ago from a friend who knew how special it was to me. The simple words have followed me through many career and Navy moves. Today, it sits on our shelf in our East Beach home, a memory of a beautiful day, and a reminder of my love for the ocean.

❖❖❖

When we'd first moved to the seaside community of East Beach, I'd watched from our balcony the Wednesday night sailboat races. I longed to be on one of the boats, jumping the sail. Or standing at the bow as the boat motored out to the bay and yelling, "Clear," signaling that it was okay to make the turn out of the marina. One Wednesday, I walked down to the marina. I knew no one who sailed, and knew very little about sailing. I had a feeling I would be back up on the balcony drinking a glass of wine and watching the race very soon, but I gathered my courage and went up to the first sailboat I saw. All they could say was no. And I still had wine waiting for me.

❖❖❖

The first boat I came to was one that normally had ten to fifteen people on board. They always looked like they were having fun and enjoying themselves. I walked up to a stocky redhead I presumed was the owner.

I brushed at the strands of hair that had fallen from my ponytail and took a deep breath. "Do you need any crew tonight?" I politely asked.

The man put his beer down and then looked up at me. "We're full tonight. It's Brian's birthday, and we're expecting over fifteen people on board. I'm sorry."

I tried not to look dejected. I looked at the copious bottles of alcohol lying around. I liked to win. This might not be the boat for me. "Thanks, maybe next week," I said as I backed away from the pier.

He took another sip of his beer. "We normally have room. Maybe next week," he said as he set his beer down.

I walked down to the next dock. I didn't see anyone who

looked like they would be racing, but there was an older man and woman sitting outside their boat. I caught their eye as I walked up the pier. The woman smiled at me. They looked friendly enough.

I stopped in front of their boat, a fiberglass beauty that looked new. "Hi there. I'm Emily. I'm trying to find a boat to crew on tonight. Do you happen to know anyone that needs crew?"

The man looked up from his newspaper. "I'm Tom and this is my wife, Evelyn." He looked down the dock and quietly counted. "Well, you're on the right dock," he said, pointing in front of him and to the right. "There's four boats on this dock that I normally see go out. I bet one of them would let you go along."

Evelyn looked up from her book and nodded her head. She pushed her glasses up and peered up at me. "They're all good people. I bet you won't have any problem getting on a boat."

I started to get excited. Maybe I would actually get to sail tonight. "Thanks so much." I was about to ask specifically which boats went out when I heard someone behind me.

"Ma'am, do you want to sail with us tonight?" The voice sounded older, kind and grandfatherly.

I turned around and saw a man with white hair and the bluest, kindest eyes I had ever seen. He wiped a trickle of sweat from his forehead and looked up at me.

I walked toward the boat and looked to see who else was on board. My husband had asked that I find a boat that was coed. "Yes," I said. I turned slightly to get the sun out of my eyes. "I have very limited experience," I explained. "But I'm willing to learn," I added.

A younger man popped up from below deck. "You going to come with us?" He asked hopefully. He was tall and lanky, with jet-black hair. He appeared to be about twenty years old. I shifted from side to side. *I prefer you to go on a coed boat.* Does an elderly man and a college kid count as coed? I looked back at the older couple I had just been talking to.

Tom smiled and nodded. "They're harmless. They'll bring

you back the way they found you."

That sounded encouraging. And it's not as if we were going far. The races were about four miles, tops. "I think it would be a riot to go with y'all," I said. "How many people do you normally have for crew?"

"Let's see." The young man looked up at the sky in thought. "We normally have Ryan, Jim, Stephen, Dan and sometimes Ronna."

A girl! They have a girl that crews. This might work!

As I was sizing up the situation, the older man held his hand out. "I'm Jim," he said.

"I'm Emily," I said as I shook his hand.

The younger guy came forward and put his hand out. "I'm Pat."

"Well, come aboard. The others should be here any minute." He disappeared below deck and popped up with a beer. "Want one?" he asked.

I was still standing on the dock. I did a quick look at the people I was about to entrust myself with over the next two hours. They seemed legit and harmless. I went aboard and had a seat in the cockpit.

"We had another partner that sailed with us, but he died a couple weeks ago," Jim told me. He held his beer up to the sky. "We haven't been able to sail as much without him. The others are sporadic and sometimes we don't have enough crew." He flipped a switch beside him and took the cover off the helm.

"Oh, I'm sorry. What was his name?"

He gave me a lopsided smile. "Thanks. We all miss him. His name was Marco." He shielded his eyes from the sun and looked out past the marina into the inlet that led to the bay. "Marco started some of the big races around here. He did so much for the sailing community." Jim rubbed lightly at his eyes.

I remembered seeing fliers at a local restaurant for a fundraiser for Marco's widow. He'd had salt-and-pepper hair and intense brown eyes. At one point, I had asked my server about him. She'd told me he was one of the old-timers and a fixture in the sailing community. Now I was sailing on his boat.

"Are we racing?" a new voice asked from the dock.

I turned to look in the direction the voice had come from and saw three more people hurrying down the dock. A couple of middle-aged men, and a younger person that appeared to be mid-twenties.

"Aw, looks like we have new rail meat," the younger guy announced. He smiled and nodded his head at me.

I gave him a timid smile. *What the heck is rail meat?*

He jumped onto the boat. "I'm Ryan."

"I'm Emily," I said.

"So, do you have any experience on boats?" Ryan asked. He pulled a line onto the boat and looked back to me.

"Does jumping in the water while fishing count?" I asked.

Ryan leaned his head back and laughed. "Absolutely. No worries, we can teach you. The biggest thing is to watch out for that thing. It's the boom." He pointed to his ear. I could see a vague scar and some disfiguration. "You don't want that thing to hit you."

"Okay, so watch my head. Any other tips?" I asked.

"Yea, stay aboard." He pointed to the water. "Don't fall in the drink."

As we motored out, I wondered how many people had fallen in the drink. There was little time to ponder falling in the water as people started moving around me.

"Let's take the condom off of her," I heard Pat say.

Condom? No wonder my husband asked me to be on the coed boat. I quickly ascertained that they were removing the covering from the mainsail and I jumped up to assist.

As we motored out of the marina and into the inlet that led to the bay, I followed the lead of the crew and helped place all the covering below.

When I came back up, one of the guys asked if I wanted to jump the sail. I had no idea what jumping the sail was, but why not? I was here to learn.

At five feet two inches tall, I quickly learned what they

meant by jumping the sail. I was literally jumping, pulling, and using whatever leverage I could on the lines to get the sail up. At last I looked up and saw the sail was up. I heard someone yell, "Made."

The water appeared calm and still. I felt relief that my first competitive sailing experience would be a calm one. I was wrong. As soon as we rounded the corner to head into the bay, I saw whitecaps on the water and felt gusts of wind in my face.

"Looks like you picked quite a day to join us. You ready for this?" asked Dan, the captain.

I gave him my best grin and said, "Bring it." I felt like I was going to throw up. "Where should I sit?" I asked.

Pat walked over to me and pointed to the deck. "You'll sit here and shift from side to side as we tell you. Your first few times out you're rail meat."

I looked at the uninviting whitecaps and cold water, and hoped I would not fall in and become bait.

Pat must have seen the fear in my eyes. "Don't worry. We have to come back with the same amount of people we left with. We won't lose you."

How comforting. I took my seat next to him on the deck, my hands holding on to a small rail by my thighs.

I turned to face the captain and saw his eyes widen.

With no time to react or ask what was going on, I turned my head as a very cold wave rushed over the bow of the boat. It hit me full force and left me drenched and cold.

I wiped the wet strands of hair away from my face. With my hands not holding anything, I felt myself slip off the deck toward the rail. I put my foot in front of me. It caught on the wooden rail lining the deck.

I quickly made my way back to midships and held on as another wave came over the bow. I could hear words but couldn't understand them over the roar of the wind. I ducked my head, trying to get some warmth.

Turns out, the word I hadn't heard was "tacking."

When the boat tacks, you typically want to move to the high side of the boat. But I hadn't moved so was now on the low side, with water sloshing over the side. I was practically vertical, holding on for dear life and looking anxiously at the captain.

"Get to the high side," someone yelled.

I now understood why they called people "rail meat." I grabbed whatever I could to pull myself up and crawled my way over to the other side of the boat. *Pay more attention, or you're going to wind up in the drink.*

"Marco would love this," Pat said.

"Really?" I asked.

"Oh yeah. He would be cussing up a storm and loving every minute of it. I guess you're taking his place."

I couldn't help but laugh at the absurd notion. Me, a person who knew nothing about sailing, taking the place of such a highly regarded man. What a joke.

He scrunched up his eyes. "Only he didn't care much for women sailing on the boat."

Yep, what a joke.

Another wave came over the side of the boat. Now every article of my clothing was wet. I had stubbed my toe scurrying to the other side of the boat, I was freezing, and it turned out that the shoes I was wearing had no traction, so I was slipping every time I had to change sides when the boat tacked.

"Tacking," Jim yelled. I heard him this time and hurried to the other side of the boat.

"Watch the boom," someone yelled.

I ducked, and felt my feet slip out from under me. I slid into the rail and saw the boom was exactly where I had just been sitting. This was not what I had expected on my maiden sailing voyage. And whoever this Marco person was, he was clearly angry. I was not sure what he was madder about: the fact I was a woman; or the fact that I, this little gal from Texas who knew so little about sailing, was supposedly taking his place.

"Is it always this way?" I asked Pat, who was sitting next to me.

He looked at the waves crashing around us. "Nope, this is

a pretty rare night. Congratulations."

Yep, Marco was angry all right.

It was cold, I was wet, and the gusts of wind were intense. My body was covered in bruises. It was glorious.

Trying to stay on the boat and not get hit by the boom, I had forgotten one important fact. We were racing. I looked in front of us and saw several boats. There were more behind us.

"So, what place are we in?" I asked Pat.

Pat looked intensely in front of us. "All of the boats in front of us are in a different class, or they owe us time."

"Owe us time?" I asked.

"It's based on their rating. Some boats owe us as much as five minutes," Pat said.

"What about the boats behind us?" I asked.

Pat looked behind him. "You see the red boat about two hundred feet back?" he asked.

I looked where he was pointing. There was a red boat, very similar in structure to the one I was on. "Yeah." I nodded.

"They're our competition."

My competitive nature took over. I wanted to win! I narrowed my eyes and looked up at the sails. The tails were flying, which meant we were in the right path of the wind. We had one more turn to make and then we would be at the finish line.

I looked at the captain to make sure I heard the cue for when he was tacking. The whitecaps were all around us. I was still cold, but now I was focused on winning.

"Tacking," he yelled out clearly.

I hurried to the other side of the boat and looked behind me. I watched as our competition prepared to tack.

"Was that a good tack?" I asked afterward.

Pat was also watching. "It was, but I don't know if they'll catch us. It's going to be close." He looked up at the sails and then eyed the boat. "Yes, it's going to be close."

I gripped the rails and looked over the side. We had two hundred feet before the finish. I didn't know one could feel such adrenaline going only five knots. It was exhilarating.

"Put all the weight on the low side," Dan yelled.

I sat down on the rail, my feet dangling over like the rest of the crew. I felt the water skimming over the top of my feet. I heard the horn blow as we crossed over the line. We won! My first race ever, and we won. I forgot how cold I was, how I almost fell in the water. All I knew was I wanted more.

"Looks like someone got the bug," I heard behind me.

I turned around to see Dan smiling at me. "Yes, I think I do. That was amazing."

He handed me a beer. "We didn't get to have one during the race." He clinked his beer against mine and smiled.

"Thanks," I said. I opened the beer and was about to put it to my lips.

Dan put his arm out. "No, you have to give some to King Neptune first."

Puzzled, I watched as he poured a small amount of beer into the water.

Monkey see, monkey do. I poured a tiny amount in the water. "To Neptune," I said. And silently, I gave a toast to Marco as I took my first sip. *I'm a terrible replacement for you, but I'll try to learn and I'll try to give back the way you did.*

❖ ❖ ❖

Later, back at the bar, I asked other people about Marco. The stories flew as quickly as the drinks. He was a curmudgeon. He barked orders. But always, after the race, he was jovial and kind. One thing I learned about Marco was that I had big shoes to fill. This man was loved by many. He was a pillar in the sailing community of crusty old men.

People came up and introduced themselves. "What boat are you on?" they asked. When I replied I was on the Black Spider, the next question was always the same. "How?" Little did I know I had just walked on to one of the best and most notorious boats in the area. It had been pure luck. I was in the right place at the right time. Any other week, it might have been different. I might have started on a different, less competitive boat. However, that's how life is; you have a completely ordinary day that somehow changes your life.

❖❖❖

I've been sailing now for two years. So many experiences have been added to that day.

I went to a boat renaming ceremony and learned that you should never mention the former name of the boat again. I have gone on overnight races and slept on the boat. I have jumped in the water at the end of a late fall race, even though it was cold outside. These are all experiences I never dreamed of as a carefree girl back in Texas.

So, here's to Marco. I wish I could have known you and learned from you. I hope that you are smiling on us all and that you know no one could ever take your place. I can't even attempt to try. I think of you often when I'm hanging off the side of the sailboat, the water skimming over my feet, and the adrenaline rushing through my veins as we pick up speed. I look up at the sail blowing in the wind and give small thanks.

I think of you when I'm walking on the beach, gazing at the sand dunes. I wonder if you were like the person in the poem. I wonder if the tawny beaches know much of you. And sometimes, when I'm standing on the dunes, I quietly say your name. I thank you for the love you poured into the sailing community. A community I now love.

A small tribute, but from what I've heard of Marco, he would have appreciated it.

THE GATLINS COME TO EAST BEACH

By Elizabeth Kimball

Raindrops meandered down the foggy train window and obscured my view of the bumper-to-bumper traffic outside. My raincoat and purse lay in a damp heap beside me, and my leather flats were soaked through. Friday evening traffic in D.C. was a snarl of busses, trucks, and commuting vehicles, all jockeying for position in the fastest-moving lanes out of town. Headlights blazed and windshield wipers whipped back and forth—a reflection of the commuters' agitation at the delayed start to the weekend.

I, too, was anxious to get out of town. The workday had been a blur of meetings and my hastily consumed lunch was a distant memory. I brushed raindrops off my purse and rummaged inside for a granola bar and my phone. I needed to tell Eric the train had been delayed, and wouldn't arrive in Norfolk until after 8:30 p.m. My stomach rumbled as I unwrapped my snack. During my last visit home, my mother asked how I stayed so skinny. "It's simple," I remembered answering. "Lots of stress, meetings scheduled all over Capitol Hill, and no time for proper meals." It was not a model to follow.

I glanced around the sparsely occupied train car. It felt

decadent to have a window seat with a view, an extra seat for my bag and coat, and no one to bump into me. I never got a seat on the D.C. Metro during my claustrophobic morning commute. I boarded at the fifth stop on the Orange Line and was lucky to squeeze through the door when the train pulled to a stop. Snagging one of the orange-upholstered seats was unthinkable. I often watched trains go by before spotting just enough space in the doorway for my bag and me. Usually three more people than could comfortably fit would push onto the car, and we'd all stand in awkward silence, swaying and jostling one another, until we neared the city center and the ratio of boarding to de-boarding passengers tilted toward the latter.

In stark contrast, this Amtrak car was quiet and practically empty. It shared a similar musty odor with the metro cars—a fragrance that was especially perceptible when it was wet outside—but at least there was plenty of space for the air to circulate. I dusted the granola bar crumbs off my navy blue suit skirt and rummaged in my bag once more for my trusty blue notebook. I was relieved to find it hadn't been soaked during my mad dash to the train station. I flipped to the page of "Norfolk notes" I'd taken during my conversation with Meg. My husband, Eric, and Meg were both naval officers, and Meg and James Stein were the reason Eric and I had started dating. Meg and her family had recently been stationed in Norfolk, and when I told her we, too, were being stationed in Norfolk, she teasingly asked if we were following her. She was going to be out of town when we arrived, but she gave me restaurant tips and offered to let us stay at her home while we house-hunted.

Eric's assignment to Norfolk had come as a surprise. We had been given orders to Charlottesville, Virginia, four months earlier. I had started my job search and we had signed a contract on a sunny little apartment. But, one month before we were set to move, new orders came through. When I asked Eric how much time we would have to cancel our plans in Charlottesville and make new arrangements in Norfolk, he responded, "Since they needed me there yesterday, we have one month."

Eric and I hadn't yet celebrated our first anniversary and I was still naive about "Navy life." We talked a lot about the different assignments Eric might receive and where we might move. But, I had been filtering this information through my own experiences. I had moved several times, but I had always been able plan a move well in advance with few surprise changes. Nevertheless, I was determined to be positive and flexible. This might actually work in my favor, I thought. I hadn't had much luck with my long-distance job-search in Charlottesville, and I might find better options in Norfolk. Job searches were tough in the best of circumstances, and I could see how a Florida-licensed attorney with no ties to the local community might make an unlikely candidate for most positions. As these thoughts swirled in my mind, I remembered something my grandmother used to say: "Each day has enough trouble of its own." She was paraphrasing Matthew 6:34, and it always encouraged me. The job search could wait. First, we needed a place to live.

As soon as we got the orders to Norfolk, Eric had reached out to one of his former commanding officers who had retired in Norfolk. Captain Stanton told Eric that he and his wife, Ellie, had built a home in a beautiful new neighborhood in the East Ocean View area called East Beach. This did not align with Eric's memories of the neighborhood ten years before. "It's different now," Captain Stanton told Eric. "You'll see. Stop by and we'll show you around. Ellie would be happy to help you look for a place." Ellie was a real estate agent, and Eric told me she was very warm and kind.

Eric had exchanged a few emails with Ellie and told her we were looking to rent a three-bedroom, two-bath home. Our "nice-to-have" list included covered parking, a gas range, and outdoor space for plants. Ellie had warned Eric that there weren't many options on the market at the moment, but she assured him she would set up some viewings. Eric had driven down earlier in the week to visit his new command, and once I finished my workweek in D.C., I was taking the train down to join him for our one-day house-hunt.

Meg and James were renting in Ghent—the "hip" Norfolk neighborhood near downtown. Meg, who was also lactose intolerant, recommended the vegan cheese at Y-Not Pizza and the vegan frozen yogurt at Skinny Dip. I knew very little else about the area, and even went around saying "Nor-folk" rather than "NAW-fahk," as is the local custom. Eric had been stationed in Norfolk long before we were married—back in his "early SWO days" as he referred to his time as a surface warfare officer. Eric told me he spent so much time on the ship he rarely had time to explore the area.

I, never having experienced the rigors of military service, couldn't imagine living somewhere without having the opportunity to exhaust its cultural offerings. Give me three days in a city and I'd map out an itinerary so chock-full of destinations your legs would ache just to look at it. Just ask my friend Sarah, whom I'd exhausted with museum trips when we studied together in Toronto, Ontario. When I first moved to Washington, D.C., I explored the city at every opportunity. I visited museums, gardens, outdoor markets, and shops. D.C. had so much to offer and I loved every minute of it. I wanted to apply the same concept to Norfolk, and search out its hidden treasures.

❖❖❖

The hours passed quickly, and soon my train was pulling into the Norfolk station. Harbor Park, home of the Norfolk Tides, loomed large and bright in the darkness just past the train platform. I gathered my things and smiled at the sight. Eric and I had attended many Washington Nationals games during our dating relationship, and it seemed fitting that this new chapter was beginning near a baseball stadium.

It didn't take long to spot his searching face, shielded from the glaring platform lights by his well-worn Red Sox baseball cap. At six feet, two inches, Eric usually stood "head" if not "head and shoulders" above a crowd. He flashed me a smile as he spotted me and swiftly closed the distance between us.

"Hullo, Love!" he said, and bent down for a quick peck. "How was the trip?"

"Productive," I said, and changed the subject. "I have a crazy idea!"

He laughed. "Of course you do."

"It includes pizza," I said.

He briefly stopped scanning the platform for my bag to suspiciously scan my face for clues. "How are you going to eat pizza if you can't have the cheese?"

"Meg and James live two blocks from a pizza place that serves vegan cheese," I announced triumphantly, "and they're open until ten!" My dairy restrictions were cutting into some of his favorite "cheat" meals—pizza being chief among them.

As we made a dash for the car, I rattled off other restaurant ideas I had gathered while perusing my Yelp app on the train. "I found a few local coffee shops, too. Cure—also in Ghent—is said to make delicious macaroons and a decadent lavender mocha." Eric held the passenger door for me before dashing around to the driver's side. The car's interior was quiet and dark, and I sank back into the leather seat as Eric pulled off his baseball cap and swept a hand through his close-cropped auburn hair. His eyes twinkled in the glow of the dashboard console.

"You know, I've also been doing some research," he countered.

"What have you learned?"

"Before your train arrived, I drove around and found some neighborhoods we might want to drive through."

"Excellent," I said. "I'll map us to Y-Not Pizza, and we can stuff our faces while you tell me what you found."

Before long, we were passing the retro neon-lit facade of the Naro Cinema and searching for parking. We found a space halfway down a side street and Eric neatly maneuvered us into it. I was grateful he was an expert at urban parallel parking. Growing up in central Florida, where sprawling concrete parking lots are as plentiful as alligator- and snake-infested lakes, I didn't have nearly as much experience.

Back out in the downpour, Eric held an umbrella for us and pulled me close. Our waterlogged shoes squeaked and slurped as we made our way down the dimly lit sidewalk to Y-Not Pizza.

"This is really good," I said through a mouthful of pepperoni. The garlic knots had long since disappeared and the large pepperoni pizza with half-regular, half-vegan cheese was nearly gone as well. The butter literally dripped from the steaming garlic knots, and savory chunks of fresh garlic covered the top. It seemed my public duty to write a good Yelp review, as I so depended on the good reviews of others, and I wanted to start while the experience was fresh in my mind.

"So," Eric said, licking a bit of marinara out of the corner of his mouth, "Ellie has several houses to show us tomorrow. Two are in their neighborhood, and two are not. She suggested we meet at their house around 9:30 a.m. tomorrow."

"Sounds perfect," I said. "I can't wait to meet them."

Eric nodded to the waitress that we were ready for the check. I wiped my greasy fingers and drained the last drops of ice water from my glass.

"How many stars should I give them?" I asked.

"For the review?" Eric clarified.

I was forever starting a sentence mid-thought, but Eric almost always knew what I was talking about. "Yes, I'm thinking four-and-a-half. I've been told that five simply leaves no room for improvement."

Eric signed the bill with a flourish, slapped the leatherette book closed, and maneuvered his large frame out of the booth. "That works for me."

❖ ❖ ❖

The next morning, we chose a route from Meg and James' house that took us past a Starbucks drive-through. (Most of our routes were anchored by coffee shops.) Between reading directions off my phone, I surveyed our surroundings. There was no dearth of payday lenders and used-car lots, nor grocery stores of all types. I grew up with Publix, Goodings, and

Albertsons, but since leaving the south, I had never found a bakery quite like Publix.

After moving away from home, the idea that no one made bread as good as Publix prompted me to start a self-proclaimed "food quest" in each new town where I lived. I knew there were other establishments that made some food or dish better than anywhere else, and if I focused on finding that new gem, I wouldn't waste time missing what I couldn't have. During law school, I went on a macaroni-and-cheese quest. In my defense, I moved to Michigan during an especially cold January, and because I was freezing and far from home, macaroni and cheese was the perfect comfort food. In Washington, D.C., it was hamburgers. I had a busy schedule and bills to pay and burgers were plentiful, quick, and usually inexpensive. Good Stuff Eatery won that quest, hands down. *Hmm, I should come up with a new food quest here.*

"We turn left at the next light," I said, glancing up from the map and ending my carbohydrate-filled daydream.

"Well, that makes sense," Eric said wryly. "Otherwise, we'd end up on the Little Creek Amphibious base."

I had been so wrapped up in my thoughts, I hadn't realized that East Little Creek Road was about to end at an entrance to one of the area's naval bases. Eric had explained to Ellie that he wanted a short commute to compensate for the pain of his current commute: Springfield to Annapolis. The Stantons' neighborhood fit the bill perfectly; it was five minutes from the Little Creek base and only 15-20 minutes from Naval Station Norfolk. The light turned green, and we turned onto left onto Shore Drive, crested the bridge over Little Creek, and there it was—East Beach—with the thin blue line of the Chesapeake Bay glistening over the rooftops.

It is said that individuals who are left-brain dominant process information using quantifiable data, and are more logical and analytical. Right-brained individuals, by contrast, tend to be creative and process information in colors, feelings, and emotions. I tend to be right-brained, and when I first spotted the bright pastel hues of the beach-style houses, I was immediately reminded of home.

In the early 1990s, Celebration, Florida—not far from my hometown—was built in the New Urbanism planning style to be a utopian, walkable community. Homes, businesses, restaurants, and schools sprang up out of Kissimmee pasturelands in a colorful fusion of Colonial, Classical, and Victorian architectural styles. At Christmas, soap-bubble "snow" would rain down on tourists and residents strolling the downtown Main Street. I had often thought it would be fun to live in such a beautiful place.

Yet, here I was, in Norfolk, Virginia, turning onto the aptly named Pleasant Avenue, experiencing a moment of déjà vu. We were passing shops and homes painted in bright pastel colors, modeled after various architectural styles. I realized I was clutching Eric's hand—which normally rested on the gearshift knob—as I leaned forward drinking in the sights. I didn't know such a place existed outside of Florida, let alone in the little-known-to-me area of Hampton Roads. This was even better than Celebration. It was Celebration-on-the-Beach, and I loved the beach.

We pulled up to a periwinkle blue home with a wide porch and white shutters. An American flag fluttered in the breeze, and an arrow-shaped sign next to the door read "Beach This Way!" We knocked on the door and Captain Jack Stanton promptly appeared.

"Come in, come in!" he said, graciously gesturing for us to come and sit down. "Don't mind Bermuda," he said, over the long, deep barks of their German shepherd who was ensconced in a large, plush bed in the corner of the living room. I sank into their deep, leather sofa. "She'll settle down in a minute," Captain Stanton explained. Bermuda eyed us warily from her corner kingdom, and soon lay down her head as if it would be too exhausting to properly protest our presence.

A moment later, Ellie came into the living room and immediately folded me into a warm hug. "You must be Cate! Eric Gatlin, how long has it been? Ten years?" She hugged Eric and begged us to sit back down.

"This is quite a place you've got," Eric said appreciatively.

Ellie beamed. "We love it here. We can just see the bay from our second-floor window and we have the most wonderful neighbors. There's always something to do! We have Bunco groups, a book club, a neighborhood Bible study, a writers' guild, and there's a concert in the park next Friday." Ellie passed us two folders filled with the listings she'd selected. "I have two homes to show you here in East Beach and two in a neighboring community, just to give you a feel for the area."

"Don't let me keep you," Captain Stanton said, standing. "We can catch up later." We said goodbye and piled into Ellie's SUV.

On our way to the first rental home, Ellie explained that East Beach was modeled after the towns of Seaside and Celebration—having been built by the same architects and urban planners—and it was intended to form not just a neighborhood, but also a community. The first rental we visited was a two-bedroom apartment that fit comfortably within our price range. It didn't have a gas range, a porch, or large windows. The modest ceiling height and lack of built-in light fixtures made the space feel close and dark. I frowned at Eric, and he nodded as if he agreed that we could mentally cross this option off our list.

The second listing was a three-bedroom condo in a four-unit building modeled after a large plantation-style home. The home was white with towering, black-shuttered windows, and a large, columned front porch that wrapped halfway around the building. Inside, the twelve-foot ceilings, bright wood floors, white walls, and surrounding windows made the modest living space feel bright and expansive. Moving from the dark two-bedroom apartment to this open space, I felt as if I could stand up straight and breathe more freely. (I knew I could be a bit overly dramatic about these things, but it definitely felt different.)

"Look, Cate," Eric said, pointing to the kitchen. "It has a

gas range!"

Ellie laughed as I lovingly swept my hand across the granite countertop and took in the stainless steel appliances. "They finished out this unit with top-of-the-line appliances," she told us as she read from the listing. "It's larger than the last unit we saw, and has one dedicated parking spot behind the building." I wandered around the large island in the center of the kitchen and surveyed the layout. The open floor plan placed the kitchen and living area at the center of the unit. This space was surrounded by doors leading to all the other rooms in the house: a bedroom off the living area, the master bedroom with an en-suite bath at the back of the house next to the second guest room, a full bathroom just on the other side of the kitchen island, the stacked washer and dryer and one closet. Sunlight streamed through the large front windows, filtered by the plantation blinds. The front porch wrapped around the exterior and looked like the perfect place for some potted plants. I started to mentally place our furniture in the empty space: the red sofa there with a bookcase on each side, and the glass-door hutch between the two bays of windows.

Ellie glanced at her watch. "Shall we keep going? The next two homes are in another new neighborhood called Ridgley Manor."

The next two options were both two-story condos with nearly identical layouts. The living room, kitchen, and master suite were all on the first floor. The second floor housed two bedrooms, a hallway bathroom, and one of the homes had a windowless bonus room over the garage. Each had a single-car garage, a small, fenced back area, and more overall square footage than either of the East Beach listings. These condos were center units with shared walls on both sides and fewer windows. Perhaps it was because I was a Floridian, or because I'd spent three cold winters in Michigan, but whenever we went house-hunting, I immediately noticed a lack of interior light—artificial or otherwise.

After seeing the last condo in East Beach with its towering ceilings and open layout, these townhomes couldn't help but feel darker and more segmented. They also didn't have gas ranges. Even the tiny fenced yards felt less welcoming than the open front porch we'd just come from.

I had already pictured myself leaning out over the porch railing of the East Beach condo, talking to neighbors as I watered my plants and they walked their dogs. I saw myself reading a book next to Eric on that same porch on a lazy Saturday afternoon. And, of course, Ridgley Manor couldn't boast about "a two-block stroll to the Chesapeake Bay" like East Beach.

I hated to admit that my mind was made up, but I soon realized that it was. I was anxious to find out what Eric was thinking. Did he want the garage and the extra living space afforded by the Ridgley Manor homes? He didn't crave the closeness of the beach as I did, and of course the gas range was a special perk for me. It's a good thing I never developed the habit of biting my fingernails, I thought, or else I'd be doing that now.

"Who's hungry?" Ellie asked cheerfully, as we got back into the car. "There's a cute little place I want to show you called The East Beach Sandwich Company. It's right at the edge of my neighborhood. You'll love it."

Soon, we were munching our way through sandwiches and salads, discussing the relative merits and drawbacks of both neighborhoods. "You're closer to the highway in Ridgley Manor," Ellie noted, "and they have similar neighborhood amenities to East Beach. But, of course, East Beach has the Chesapeake Bay." Eric asked about property values, crime rates, and taxes. His decisions were based on facts first and feelings second. I had more trouble subordinating my feelings to the facts.

I speared a Kalamata olive and a heart of palm with the tines of my fork. This was what my work lunches were missing: delicious toppings. I often took homemade salads to work, but they were just something I halfheartedly tossed together at the end of the weekend or the night before. They were healthy, but hardly appetizing. I made a mental note to add olives and heart of palm to next week's grocery list.

"The commissary is only ten minutes away," Ellie was saying. That would be a new experience, I thought. I almost felt like a faux military spouse living in Northern Virginia. I had learned the area as a single, federal government employee, and after becoming Mrs. Gatlin and a Navy wife, I continued shopping at the same places and hardly ever visited the area bases. Now, I could develop a new "normal routine" to include shopping on base.

"That was a really good sandwich, Ellie," Eric said as he pushed back his chair. "Thanks for introducing us to this place!" He offered me the last of his BBQ potato chips. I shook my head. I'd already eaten my own bag of chips and also a huge pickle. The pickles had been swimming tantalizingly in a giant glass jar beside the cash register and I couldn't resist a good dill pickle.

I also thanked Ellie. "We will definitely visit this place again!"

"The neighborhood often gathers here," Ellie added. "Did you notice they even deliver to the beach?" she asked, winking at me.

I laughed. "That would be fun." Ellie waved goodbye as she walked back to her car. Eric and I set off, hand-in-hand, to walk around the neighborhood and talk about what we'd seen before returning to our car.

Pine needles littered the shady sidewalk. Ahead, we could see two young boys throwing a Frisbee with their dad. We walked in silence, each lost in our own thoughts.

"So, what do you think?" Eric asked.

I smiled and hesitated. "No. You first. Which neighborhood did you like best?"

"Well," he said. "Each has its merits, but I think you'd be happier here by the beach."

I looked up quickly. Excitedly. "Really?"

"Yes," he said. "I know you like the feel of this neighborhood, and we don't know when you'll find a new job. I know it's going to be a big change for you, and I think it would be nice for you to be able to walk to the beach and relax while you look for a job."

I absentmindedly studied the pine needles on the sidewalk. "You certainly know me well," I said. "I would love to live by the beach, but I thought you'd prefer a garage and more square footage."

"Well," he said. "A garage would be nice, but I liked the openness of the second place in East Beach, and I think we'll enjoy the neighborhood activities."

I smiled. "I wouldn't mind a few distractions while I continue the job hunt."

He put an arm around me as we walked. "We'll just take it one step at a time."

❖ ❖ ❖

We returned to Northern Virginia, but not before telling Ellie we wanted to move forward on the sunny condo in East Beach. She told us she couldn't wait to be neighbors.

The intervening month passed quickly. Before I knew it, I was hugging my coworkers goodbye and commuting home to Northern Virginia for the last time.

I had known this day would come and that Eric's job in the Navy would lead us to new places every two years. The idea of new towns and things to explore was exciting, but now that "moving day" was here, it felt a little daunting. I had used the month to lay as much groundwork for my job search as possible. I plied my friends and colleagues for information on the area and connections in Hampton Roads. I set up informational meetings through friends of friends and applied to as many jobs as possible. After hearing nothing back, I told myself things would improve once I had a local address and extra time to hunt and interview.

Our possessions were safely loaded into the moving van on a Friday afternoon, and Eric and I and caravanned down to Norfolk that evening to beat the movers to the new condo. It was wonderful that this move was only four hours door-to-door, and we could drive down in a single evening, me with my backseat full of potted plants, and Eric with the valuables, air mattress, and overnight necessities. I had packed a box filled with paper towels, the coffee maker, garbage bags, toilet paper, towels, sheets, a shower curtain, antibacterial wipes, paper plates, and plastic silverware, to hold us over until we unpacked. We camped out on an air mattress that first night and got up early the next morning to help unload the truck.

The move went smoothly and only a few items were damaged. Eric immediately started his new job and I started unpacking. Ellie had stopped by during our move-in and brought us a "welcome" beach bag filled with beach towels, magazines, and a BBQ lunch. She had given me an encouraging hug, a knowing look, and then had to hurry off to show another house.

Ellie had moved nineteen times over the course of Captain Stanton's military career, and she was a fantastic source of knowledge, both for moving and military life. It wasn't until I started talking to Ellie that I began to realize how little I understood about military life. Eric had bought me a book called *The Navy Spouse* and Ellie loaned me an old book called *Welcome Aboard: A Service Manual for the Naval Officer's Wife*. I planned to study both after I'd opened a few more boxes and located the silverware. It turned out to be a good thing I'd packed plastic silverware and Styrofoam plates in the box of necessities. The boxes labeled "Kitchen" had sofa cushions and sheets in them, and the "Living Room" boxes had pillows from the bedroom and books from the guest room. It seemed the labels only reflected the last item packed in the box, and I had no idea which box might hold the silverware.

I turned on the stove a few days after we moved in and discovered—too late—that the previous tenants had used foaming oven cleaner and it hadn't burned off during the cleaning cycle. It dripped down into my chicken casserole, which had to be thrown out. Next, the combination washer/dryer had to be replaced. During one of my trips to the Laundromat, I realized how grateful I was to not be starting a new job at the same time. *Things certainly happen for a reason.*

One Friday evening, we decided to attend a neighborhood social event to take our minds off the moving-in hiccups. The oven was now clean and functional, so I brought a heaping plate of brownies to share. As we mingled, we quickly learned that our neighbors identified each other by their dogs and houses. "Where do you live? Oh, the house across from the Montessori school? Yes, I know it. I'm in the yellow house with the large front porch on 28th Bay. Yes, right next to Janice and Mike in the blue house with white shutters. Have you met Toby, their cocker spaniel?" Everyone was very welcoming and encouraged us to keep coming to all the events we could. They were planning a Rat-Pack inspired evening the following month, and another outdoor concert.

❖❖❖

A few weeks later, I got a call from Ellie.
"What are you doing later this week?" she asked.
"Unpacking."
"Still not done?" she asked, laughing.
"Not hardly!" I said, chagrinned.
"Well, you need to get out of the house. Come to lunch with Kimberly and me. She lives just up the street from you in the big blue house, and she's a fellow Navy wife and artist. You'll like her a lot."

I didn't argue. I knew Ellie was right. I really did need to get out of the house. My lunches had devolved to PB&J or sad salads without any of the fun toppings I'd planned to start using. It was all too easy to either sit amongst the half-unpacked boxes and search all the job sites, or pad around in an old T-shirt and shorts and rearrange the books. I wasn't feeling very well, and I wasn't sure if I'd eaten something funny or if I was catching a cold. I definitely needed a distraction from the unpacking and the unemployment.

Ellie connected us all by email, and suggested we meet at Taste Unlimited on Shore Drive. Kimberly offered to pick me up since we were just a block apart.

Through the shutters, I saw Kimberly pull up and walked out to meet her. We talked about painting and drawing, two hobbies I always enjoyed but hadn't spent much time perfecting. She told me about her favorite art supply store in Virginia Beach called Jerry's Artarama and I made a mental note to visit it later.

Ellie was waiting for us when we arrived, and I ordered chicken soup and a BBQ side salad. We ate on the second floor, which had a nice view of the market below. Ellie had been volunteering that morning with East Beach Buddies, an elementary school reading program. She explained that a group of neighbors volunteered at a local elementary school and read with first- and second-graders for one hour each week.

"You should join us sometime!" Ellie encouraged.

I told her I'd like that.

Kimberly told us she was planning to go to The Tidewater Collection—a charity boutique on the Naval Station Norfolk—later that afternoon. "We could go after lunch," she suggested, "if you want to see where it is." I told her I would love to come. I certainly wasn't busy.

"It's not far from The Treasure Shop," Kimberly added. "That's the base thrift shop."

I had no idea there were thrift stores on military bases. When I'd lived in Florida, I'd often gone "thrifting" with my mother, and as I moved around, I'd always hunted out the local thrift stores to browse through the books and dusty vinyl records.

Ellie hugged us and dashed off to a meeting, and Kimberly and I set off for The Tidewater Collection. It was a long, narrow-ish shop inside the lobby of a Navy Gateway Lodge at Ely Hall. I browsed the tasteful assortment of nautical home décor and jewelry, and chose a red and gold enamel bracelet with tiny gold anchors for me, and nautical note cards for Eric. As we checked out, Kimberly and the volunteer behind the desk explained that volunteer spouses ran the store and all the shop's profits went to support various military charities.

"You should volunteer," Kimberly encouraged me. She

pointed to the purple sheet next to the cash register, which explained how to join the local officer spouse association and volunteer at the shop. I tucked one inside my purse.

I had, admittedly, fallen into a rut. I went grocery shopping, watered my plants, unpacked, cleaned around the still-packed boxes, went to informational interviews when I could get them, looked for new restaurants online to try with Eric on the weekend, and visited the library. On the weekend, we attended church and explored or just rested. Volunteering would definitely get me out of the house and allow me to meet more people.

Later that night, I emailed Ellie to tell her I wanted to be involved in East Beach Buddies, and signed up to volunteer at the Tidewater Collection.

❖❖❖

Two more months passed, and as the calendar pages turned to October, I began to feel like a new person. There was a hint of fall in the air. A cold snap the previous weekend had turned the green leaves on the neighbors' crepe myrtles bright red and orange. I'd started volunteering at both The Tidewater Collection and with a non-profit public policy organization. I was involved with East Beach Buddies and volunteered at our church.

All my new activities paled in comparison to the miracle growing inside me. A small, black-and-white sonogram photo now hung on our refrigerator. My new doctor told me we could expect our little addition to arrive late the following spring. I had made it to the second trimester, and I was no longer feeling nauseous and exhausted all the time. I had also begun to find purpose in this period of professional limbo.

My excitement for the adventure had returned. Eric had started his own food quest to find the best shrimp and grits, and he was already a huge fan of the dish at Tupelo Honey Cafe. Shrimp made me queasy—pregnant or not—so I decided to continue my burger quest to see if anyone could unseat Good Stuff Eatery as the reigning champion.

As I stepped out onto my front porch, I knew it was exactly 8:00 a.m. because I heard the sound of "colors" being played over loudspeakers on the Little Creek base. Depending on the direction of the wind, some mornings I could even hear colors from inside the condo. This morning, it drifted sweetly through the trees and even the birds seemed to sing along. I paused and turned to face the direction of the loudspeakers. Listening to colors always made my heart swell with pride for my country and for my husband's work.

When the last note played, I started down the stairs to the beach with Ellie's beach bag and towel under my arm. It was a warm day, and I wanted to soak up the last bit of sun before fall set in. Down the street, I could just make out our neighbor, Mike, walking Toby, the cocker spaniel. I patted my slowly growing stomach and smiled. "I think we're going to like it here, Baby. I really do."

THE MERMAID
By Jamie McAllister

Tad Phillips lifted the last box from the trunk and trudged up the walk to the house. His brother Jason stood on the wide front porch, a bottle of beer in his hand.

"Hey man, you want a drink?" Jason asked.

Tad dropped the box and accepted the bottle his brother had fished from the cooler at his feet. He twisted off the cap and closed his fist around the small metal disk, distracting himself for a moment with the pain from the crimped edges gouging into his palm.

"Want to talk about it?"

Tad shook his head.

"C'mon, bro."

"I'm fine."

Jason took a pull from his bottle and set it on a small table next to him. Crossing his arms, he leaned against the porch railing. "Twins tell each other everything."

Tad clutched his bottle and looked his brother square in the face. For the past thirty years of his life it had been like looking at his own reflection, but that was changing. Both still shared the same light-brown hair that fell over their foreheads, as well as the same blue eyes and dimples. But where Jason had six-pack abs, Tad now had a layer of flab. Jason's jaw was as chiseled as when the two had graduated from high school, but Tad had looked in the mirror the week before and noticed jowls lurking around his face. He hadn't had the guts to look in the mirror a second time to either confirm or deny their existence.

"It's not good to hold it in," Jason continued.

Tad gulped his beer. He opened his mouth and Jason lifted one eyebrow. When Tad belched, Jason frowned.

"I'm going inside," Tad said, placing his empty beer bottle on the railing next to his brother. He pushed open the front door and entered the large foyer. Jason and his wife, Chrissy, had said he could crash at their home in East Beach until he found another job and a new place to live. They had only been in the house for a few weeks, so Tad wasn't certain where everything was yet. He did know his room was upstairs, third door on the left.

Chrissy met him at the top of the stairs. "Tad! We're so happy you're here." She wrapped her arms around him, laughing as her large belly came between them. She stepped back, rubbing her stomach. Long dark hair cascaded down her shoulders and framed flushed cheeks.

"How're you feeling?" Tad asked. Chrissy had always been sweet to him. His problems weren't her fault.

"Huge," Chrissy admitted. "I think I might be having a whale."

Tad smiled. The front door slammed open and he jumped.

"Where is he?" demanded a woman's voice. "Tad?"

Tad peered down the stairs as his girlfriend, Katrina, stomped toward him.

"My boyfriend loses his job and his apartment in the same day, and I have to find out about it on Facebook?" She crossed her arms over her chest, long red nails catching and reflecting the light.

Tad groaned. "Who posted it on Facebook?"

"Your mother."

Tad couldn't stand the thought of his mother telling the entire world he was a loser. He wanted the ground to open up and swallow him whole. Did Virginia have sinkholes?

Katrina's arm snaked across Tad's shoulders, the clump of metal bracelets on her wrist jangling in his ear. "Aren't we going out?" she asked. "Isn't that new art exhibit opening in downtown Norfolk tonight? You said you would take me."

Tad felt his heart sink even lower, something he hadn't thought possible. All of his coworkers from his old job would be there. How could he show his face?

"It's been a long day, Trina," he said, shrinking away from her tight embrace. "I'm going to stay here and take it easy."

Katrina yanked her arm from around Tad's shoulders, grazing his earlobe with her bracelets. Her green eyes turned to fire.

"I'm sick of missing out on things because of you." She clutched her purse in her fist and wheeled around, thundering down the stairs. The front door opened and slammed closed.

Tad stared at the floor. He didn't dare meet Chrissy's eyes. He wanted to avoid the pity he knew he would see there. He mumbled something unintelligible, stepped into his bedroom, and quietly shut the door.

Fighting the urge to hide under the bed, Tad dumped the box on top of the others next to the closet and flicked on the lamp. He stared out the bedroom window, which overlooked the Bay Front Club next door. The club was the heart of the East Beach community, and it looked like the heart was beating tonight. People milled about by the pool and played games on the sand. Just a few steps away the Chesapeake Bay sparkled in the last rays of the fading sunlight.

Sitting alone in this unfamiliar room would only force him to dwell on his new job title—unemployed—so Tad grabbed his jacket from the bed and headed out to the beach. The sun had set and the sound of the waves mingled with the voices and laughter coming from the party next door. Darkness had fallen and the temperature had dropped. Goosebumps broke out along Tad's arms and he shivered as he looked out over the water.

A streak of moonlight drew his gaze to the surf. He strained to see through the gloom and made out a long tail wiggling on the sand. Had a dolphin ended up stranded on the beach? If that were the case, he knew he had to call someone but he wasn't sure who. His eyes moved up, above the tail. Long silver hair, dripping with water, covered milky white shoulders and hung down to a trim waist. A slim hand lifted in greeting, and the tail slapped against the water, the sound echoing in Tad's ears.

He shook his head and peered again at the surf. Waves slid onto the sand and slithered back to sea. The party next door had broken up and the beach was empty. Tad headed back into the house, convinced he needed a drink.

❖❖❖

The next morning, Tad awoke to shafts of light burning through his eyelids. Terrified he had overslept and would be late for work again, he jerked straight up in bed. His head swirled and he gripped the mattress with his left hand. Slowly he eased back down.

What had happened? Where was he? The events from the day before leaked back into his mind. His job and his downtown apartment were both gone. He was staying at his twin's house in East Beach.

Tad cracked open one eye as his last memory from the night before came back to him in full force. Had he really seen a mermaid?

The bedroom door opened and Jason entered carrying a basketball in one hand. "Want to be part of the Saturday morning pick-up game?" he asked, balancing the ball on the tip of his index finger and grinning as it twirled. "It's gonna be a blast."

Tad shook his head.

"C'mon, you need to do something to forget about your troubles for a while," Jason said. He tossed a pair of shorts and a white T-shirt on the bed. "I don't want you wasting time looking through boxes for your clothes, so wear mine. Be ready to go in twenty."

Tad remained rooted in the bed. All he wanted was sleep, not an early-morning basketball game. He thought about his brother, who was letting him stay in his house and eat his food for free. He sighed and put on the clothes before heading downstairs.

Chrissy greeted him with a smile and a plate of scrambled eggs and bacon. "Breakfast of champions," she announced, setting the plate on the kitchen table.

Tad sat down and took a bite. His favorite foods did make him feel a little better. He took another bite and Chrissy beamed as she buttered a piece of toast.

After breakfast, Tad and Jason walked to the house next door, where a neighbor had a basketball hoop set up in the driveway. Tad recognized a few of his brother's friends, but he could only recall seeing them a few times before. Since it was Saturday morning, no one wanted to talk about work, and Tad was grateful. He laughed and joked, the stress he had felt ebbing away like the tide. When the ball rolled down the alley and under a truck parked in the street, he offered to go chase it down.

Tad squatted and peered under the truck, and that's when he saw her. Her long green tail filled the space under the vehicle, and the salty tang of the ocean slipped into his nostrils. Her thick silver hair trailed down her back. She lay stretched out on the asphalt, muscular arms reaching for him and a smile on her face.

Tad froze. Was this the mermaid he thought he had seen last night? He stared, unable to believe she was real. He reached out a hand to touch her tail, and was shocked to discover how wet and cold it felt. The mermaid's violet eyes were beautiful, and he wanted to crawl under the truck and rescue her.

Jason's voice interrupted his reverie. Tad narrowly avoided thumping his head against the truck as he backed out from underneath it. His brother stood behind him, a concerned look on his face.

"You okay?" Jason asked.

Tad nodded. "Yep. Just had to find the basketball."

Jason looked down at the ball in Tad's hands. "Looks like

you succeeded. Can we get back to the game now?
Tad glanced once more at the asphalt under the truck, but there was nothing there. He followed Jason back to the group of guys and once again got caught up in the game. But he couldn't shake the feel of the mermaid's tail beneath his hand, or her violet eyes. How could something he imagined seem so real?

Tad and Jason called it quits about half an hour later. As soon as they got back to the house, Tad headed straight for the shower. Afterwards he stretched out on the couch in the living room. His plan was to watch a movie, but he fell asleep before his hand even touched the remote.

❖❖❖

The sound of a wailing siren jolted Tad awake. He glanced at his cell phone and saw his mother's picture pop onto the screen. He let the call go to voicemail and hoped she would leave a message he could return later. The phone went silent for a moment and Tad let out a sigh of relief. He leaned back against the pillows and closed his eyes. The phone wailed again, emitting the frenetic tone his mother had insisted he use to signal her calls.

Tad debated whether or not he should turn off the phone, but he knew there was nothing stopping his mother from getting in her car and driving down from her house in Newport News, except maybe tunnel traffic. But even the usual backup at the Hampton Roads Bridge-Tunnel was no match for his mother's concern. Avoiding her calls would only make her worry more.

Tad snatched the phone from the edge of the coffee table, took a deep breath, and answered. "Hello?"

"Why didn't you pick up?"

Hi to you, too, Mom.

"I was sleeping," Tad said, rubbing his eyes.

"I hope you're not getting sick, on top of everything else," Mrs. Phillips said.

"I played basketball with Jason this morning and it wore

me out."

"Oh." Mrs. Phillips paused. "So, do you have any leads for a new job? What about a place to live? You know you can't stay with Jason forever."

"I'm sure something will open up soon."

"It's too bad you can't have better luck, like your twin. Jason's business is doing so well, and he just bought that beautiful new home. I can't wait to hold that new grandbaby, either. You should think about starting a family, Tad."

"I'll think about it, Mom," Tad said. "I gotta go. I'm getting another call."

Tad said goodbye and slid the phone onto the coffee table. He considered trying to go back to sleep, but too many thoughts were racing through his mind. A walk along the beach sounded like a much better idea. He would never admit it out loud, but he hoped to catch another glimpse of the mermaid.

The shifting sand made walking difficult, but once at the water's edge the wet sand felt firmer under his feet. Tad inhaled deeply, letting the salty air clear his lungs. A breeze blew through his hair and he brushed the stray strands from his forehead as he began to walk.

A large wave rushed toward him and he dodged left to avoid it, but he was too late. The wave crashed over his feet, soaking his sneakers. Biting back a curse, Tad lifted his foot to shake his sopping shoe. Before he could do so, he heard a voice.

"Tad!" The voice sounded strange, like the speaker had a foreign accent

Tad whipped around, searching for the source. He saw her at his feet, long silver hair churning in the waves. The water swirled around his ankles, but he no longer cared.

The mermaid smiled at him, one hand gripping his ankle. Her violet eyes were framed with thick dark lashes. Tad stepped back, too stunned to speak.

"You're not real," he whispered, glancing around him. Other walkers and joggers passed by without even a backward glance. "If you were real, people would stop to look at you."

The mermaid continued to smile. She grabbed his other ankle and pulled him toward her. He sank to his knees in the sand, waves crashing against his chest. The mermaid let go of Tad's ankles and wrapped her arms around his neck, pulling him closer. He wanted to forget all his troubles and lose himself in those violet eyes.

"Hey buddy, you okay?"

Tad looked up and saw an older man wearing a pair of swim trunks peering down at him. An ear bud dangled free so the man could hear Tad's reply.

Tad looked around, searching for the mermaid. His hands swished through the foamy surf, touching only grains of sand and broken bits of seashells. He stared up at the man, who had pulled out his cell phone.

"Do you need me to dial nine-one-one?"

Tad scrambled to his feet. "No! No, I just dropped my iPod. I'll have to buy a new one."

The older man's expression changed from compassion to suspicion. Tad closed his eyes. *He probably thinks I'm on drugs.*

Tad kept his gaze on his feet as he jogged toward the house, refusing to look at anyone. *I'm cracking up. I'm being chased by an imaginary mermaid.*

When he twisted the doorknob on the back door of his brother's house, Tad's hand was shaking. He could still feel the mermaid's arms around his neck and his legs felt like they were made of taffy. He staggered into the kitchen and steadied himself against the granite countertop. Glancing over at the refrigerator, he caught sight of a magnet in the shape of a mermaid. The long green tail and silver hair looked familiar. The tiny mermaid winked and extended her arms, beckoning him toward her.

Tad extended a finger toward the fridge and touched the mermaid magnet. It felt hard and lifeless, not at all like the mermaid he had just seen on the beach.

The back door opened and Jason and Chrissy walked in carrying several large shopping bags. Both stopped in their tracks when they saw Tad poking the magnet.

"Hey Tad," Jason said cautiously, approaching Tad as if he were a wild animal. "What's up?"

Tad didn't know how to answer. He slowly pulled his finger back and let his hand rest at his side. Rather than try to make up a good excuse, he decided to pretend as if nothing had happened.

"Just grabbing some orange juice," Tad said, opening the fridge and pulling out the jug. "I'm thirsty after my walk."

Jason and Chrissy didn't look like they believed his story, but they were too eager to show Tad what they had bought for the new baby to dwell on his weird behavior. While Chrissy and Jason pulled toys and games from the shopping bags, Tad reached behind him, lifted the mermaid magnet off the fridge, and slipped it into his pocket.

Tad spent the rest of the afternoon and evening filling out job applications online. Around midnight he decided to call it a night. He closed the laptop and tucked it under his arm before heading upstairs. He dropped his shorts on the floor and heard a faint thump. Curious, he picked up the shorts and reached in the pocket. The mermaid magnet! He had forgotten all about it.

He jiggled the magnet in his palm and tossed it in the air a few times. What had compelled him to pull it from the fridge? He had had mermaids on the brain, that was all. The stress he had been under lately had made his imagination kick into high gear. Once he landed a new job and could afford to rent another apartment, he could put all this nonsense behind him.

Tad put the magnet on the night table next to the lamp. He would return it to the fridge first thing in the morning, before anyone could even notice it was gone. Stretching his arms over his head and yawning, Tad climbed into bed and pulled the covers up to his chin.

❖❖❖

The next morning, Tad woke up feeling better than he had in weeks. He hopped in the shower and sang his favorite song while he lathered himself in soapsuds. He heard his phone ding in the bedroom while he was toweling off, and when he checked his messages he saw he had an e-mail from one of the companies he had applied to the night before, asking if he was available to come in for an interview the next day.

By the time he had gotten dressed and walked downstairs, he was whistling. He ended the tune when he saw Chrissy standing in the kitchen, frowning at the refrigerator.

"Are you okay?"

"I don't see my lucky mermaid magnet," Chrissy said. She shifted to look between the counter and the refrigerator. "Where could it be?"

Tad's optimism surged yet again. Not only had his own luck turned, he could also play the role of hero and surprise Chrissy by finding her favorite magnet. "Oh, I'm sure it will turn up," he said, smiling. He poured himself a cup of coffee and sat down at the table, jumping up immediately.

"I just realized I forgot my phone," he lied. Chrissy, still searching for the magnet, nodded but didn't turn around. Tad bolted from the room, ran up the stairs, and stopped short next to the night table.

The mermaid magnet was gone. Tad distinctly recalled placing the magnet on the night table right before he went to bed. He wracked his brain, trying to remember if he had seen the magnet that morning when he had gotten up. Had it been there after he had taken a shower? Maybe it had fallen under the bed. He dropped to his hands and knees and searched every square inch of the carpet around the bed. He rooted through his pockets, although he was sure he had left it on the table. He even searched the bathroom, but the magnet was gone.

Tad returned to the kitchen. Chrissy had also given up her search and was eating a bowl of oatmeal with strawberries on top. She looked sad, and Tad wanted to cheer her up.

"I'm sorry about the magnet," he said, sitting down across from her. "How about I pick you up a new one after my interview tomorrow?"

Chrissy's face lit up. "That's great!" She reached across the table and patted his hand. "I'm so proud of you. Looks like your luck is turning around."

Tad took a sip of his coffee and nodded. "I think so. The company I'm interviewing with is one I wanted to work for right out of college, but I took a position with my old employer instead. I can't believe they called me back so soon."

"You're going to do great at the interview," Chrissy said, stirring her oatmeal. "And don't worry about buying me a new magnet. It was silly of me to think that an object could make good things happen."

"It's not silly," Tad said, smiling as he looked out the window at the Chesapeake Bay. A silver head bobbed in the waves, and then a shimmering green tail flicked out of the water. Who knew mermaids could be such good luck?

MULE'S BIG DAY
BY WILL HOPKINS

"Mule?"

"Sure, baby. Anything you want. Just lay off that drum, huh?"

Bang. "Hey, you here? It's gettin' late." Bang, bang.

Mule Dantone cocked an eye toward the nightstand. The alarm clock numbers swam like fish in an aquarium. He blinked and elbowed up on the ten-dollar mattress. A bottle of Gordon's gin stood in front of the clock.

"Whew. Thought I'd hurt myself this time," he said, flopping back down and rolling an arm to the other side of the bed. "For a second I…" He expected warm, soft shoulder but got empty pillow.

"Huh? Hey, now where'd you go?" Mule forgot his hangover and sat up, scanning the bedroom for a yellow dress, but the only trace of last night's blonde was the scent of Rexall perfume and menthol cigarettes.

Plates rattled down in the kitchen.

Mule managed a little grin, remembering she (was it Linda?) promised to make him pancakes. He slipped out of bed and pulled on the pair of slacks hanging from the doorknob, patting the hip pocket to confirm that his wallet was still there.

The refrigerator door clanked open. Something thudded on the floor. A guy said, "Dammit."

Mule froze.

More shuffling and scraping from the kitchen.

Mule inched over and hefted the Louisville Slugger he kept by the dresser. He choked up on the grip and crept downstairs.

"Don't even have a towel in this dump." A man bent over the linoleum, trying to mop up milk with the TV section of the *Virginian-Pilot*.

Mule hauled back on the bat, banging it into a cabinet.

"I thought I was gonna have to come up and get you," Tasco Plate said, turning his head up. "What's with the bat?"

Mule slumped against the wall, dropping the bat on the dinette table. "Damn, Tas. I thought somebody had broken in." His head throbbed.

"Shit, they'd have to be hard-up or drunk to rob this place." Tasco balled the sopping paper and tossed it over into the sink. He cast an appraising look at Mule. "You look like hell."

"People over in Forest Lawn Cemetery feel better than I do this morning." Mule uncorked the aspirin bottle he kept on the windowsill, downing two tabs with half a warm beer left on the counter. He noticed the red lipstick around the pop-top.

"Your date split?"

"Huh?"

"The blonde from over at Cozy Inn." Tasco laughed. "Said she looked like Veronica Lake. You was calling her Pretty Lake."

"Yeah." Mule rubbed his gut and tried not to look like he was trying to picture her in his head. "I need a cigarette." He reached for the pack he kept handy on top of a portable television. For the second time this morning, Mule got thin air.

"Hey, where the hell is my TV?"

"Don't look at me."

"That little hellcat stole my damn TV set," Mule stammered. "Brand-new Japanese job. Just made the last payment." He stared at the clean rectangle on the kitchen counter, right beneath an empty power outlet.

"I warned you about bringing these gals home."

"Well, at least she didn't get my wallet," Mule said, patting his back pocket.

Tasco took a bite of pickle and wiped the brine off his chin. "You check inside?"

Mule hmmphf'd and opened the leather. Just his lucky penny fell out. "Well, I'll be damned."

"Tried to tell you, son. Want a pickle?"

"I swear I'm gonna…" Mule pulled on the stale beer. "I'm gonna call the cops."

Tasco laughed.

"Well, then I'm going back to the Cozy tonight and find Little Miss Blondie."

"She's probably a long-gone redhead by now, pally. Gals like that work a bar then get the hell out of town." Tasco fingered another pickle from the jar. "How much she get?"

"Thirty-four bucks. And I got rent due."

"Ouch." Tasco put the empty jar back in the icebox. "Don't worry it. We'll figure something out. Meantime, it's a nice morning. What do you feel like doing?"

"Same as we always do, I guess."

"Let's go down to the beach, get some air, maybe do a little fishing like we talked about last night."

Mule shrugged a little. He didn't remember that discussion, but he was always up for a little fishing. "Let's go out back. Don't want the landlady to see me."

The boys took the kitchen door out to the cinderblock patio. Mule grabbed a clean shirt from the clothesline and his flip-flops from the cement birdbath. They followed the sand path around to 24th Bay Street and padded toward the beach.

"Sure is pretty out this morning," Mule said, squinting up at the big cumulus clouds out over the Bay. "Hold on a minute." He swooped up the paper from a neighbor's driveway and unrolled the front page.

Tasco leaned over for a peek. "Anything good?"

"Nixon won't turn over some damn tapes to them Watergate fellas."

"Shee-it."

"Yeah." Mule snorted. "Let's see, weather's sunny, mid-eighties."

"See, I told you it was gonna be a good day."

❖❖❖

"What the hell you two doing up so early?" Bit Waters wiped down the intake of the outboard hitched to his plywood skiff. He'd beached the boat at the edge of the tide line.

"Hey, Bit." Tasco lit a Lucky and tossed the match out on the warming sand. "Catching anything?"

Bit lifted the lid of a foam cooler, revealing six fat croakers on ice. "They're biting just off Little Creek. Hooked these in ten minutes." He plopped down the lid. "Man, Mule, you look like hell."

"So I hear," Mule said, shaking his head.

"Little boat time and a cold beer will fix you up. Y'all want to go out? I got extra poles."

"We might just do that," Tasco said. "Whatcha say, Mule?"

"Let me get something to eat first."

"Well, I'm shoving off in an hour. Come on down if you want." Bit went back to fiddling with the Evinrude.

Tasco and Mule climbed to the top of the dune and looked around. The little seaside village of East Beach was shaking off Friday night and coming to life. A few cars rumbled down the numbered Bay streets, kids zipped by on bikes, lawn sprinklers swirled on a couple of the fancier cottages with Bermuda lawns.

"Hey, what's that smell?" Mule asked, sniffing the air like a retriever.

"Bacon, I think. Somebody's got a grill going." Tasco lifted his nose in the direction of 25th Bay. "Let's have a look."

They tumbled down the sea-grass path and crossed over to the alley behind 25th Bay, where blue smoke plumed from the back of one of the shotgun bungalows tucked into a stand of live oak.

"It's coming from Jeep's place," Tasco said. "C'mon." He cut a path through the maze of junked cars and jalopies rusting out in the backyard. Benny Sherman was in a bathrobe, frying a pound of bacon on a hibachi sitting on the hood of his peacock Oldsmobile with "Jeepers the Clown" painted across the driver's door. Under the red and blue script, Benny's artist cousin had ventured a portrait of Jeepers in full makeup. It looked like a raccoon.

"Why you cookin' outside, Jeep?" Tasco asked, stepping over an old muffler.

"Hey, boys," Benny said. "Stove's busted and I had some charcoal. I figured, what the hell? It's a nice morning out and this way I don't smoke-up the house. Grab some if you want it." He pointed the spatula at a line of burnt-brown strips cooling on a paper towel by the hood ornament.

Mule grabbed several.

Benny chuckled. "Damn, Mule. You look…"

"I know, like hell," Mule said between chews. "I'm just hungover."

"He got rolled last night," Tasco said, nibbling a piece of bacon. "Gal took his money and his TV."

"Man, your TV? That's—"

A pinecone ricocheted off the fender of the Olds. "Heehaw! Jeepers! Jeepers!" Two boys danced the Jeepers Jig out in the alley.

"Get out of here, you little bastards!" Benny yelled. The boys took off running, laughing and hollering heehaws.

Mule went for another strip. "Yeah. So now I'm busted and I gotta make rent Monday."

"Huh," Benny said, fingering the two-day stubble on his chin. "How'd each of you like to earn an easy twenty this afternoon?"

"I ain't fencing hubcaps again," Tasco said.

"Nah, nah. This is all legit." Benny ducked into the car and came out waving a flyer. "Got me a gig over at the amusement park. I could use some help setting up and fending off the drunks."

Mule took the flyer in his greasy fingers.

> *Miss Ocean View Park Pageant*
> *Saturday, July 16th at 4:00-6:00 p.m. in the Park dance pavilion.*
> *24 Beautiful Girls! Fireworks! Door Prizes!*
> *Music by Zig Gordon and His Polka Kings*
> *Norfolk's own Jeepers the Clown, your master of ceremonies*
> *BEER ON TAP*

"Twenty bucks for a couple of hours?" Mule asked.

"Cash money. After the show, of course."

"Who's paying?" Tasco asked, arching an eyebrow at Benny.

"Don't worry," Benny said. "The Park's covering expenses. They'll pay us right out of the front till."

"Damn, Mule," Tasco said. "This sounds pretty good."

"We're in," Mule said, licking his fingers. "What do we need to do?"

"Swing by around two. That'll give us plenty of time to drive over and set up." Benny lifted the fry pan off the coals and dumped the hot grease on the sand. "And put on some clean clothes. One of the TV channels is gonna be there."

❖❖❖

"We need to get spiffed up."

Mule sniffed his shirt. "Smells okay to me."

"I mean get us some haircuts," Tasco said, tossing his 7-Up bottle in the trashcan at the Dockside Marina.

"Why the hell do we need to waste a good morning doing that?" Mule asked, patting his stubbled flattop. "Plus, it'll cost three bucks."

"You heard Benny. We're gonna be on TV with all them beauty gals. I'll front the dough."

"We'll miss out on the fishing trip with Bit."

"Which would you rather do, handle some flopping

croaker or a good-looking brunette?"

Mule smiled. "Yeah, twenty-three of them gals are gonna need some consoling."

"Now you're thinking. Come on."

❖❖❖

Mule shouldered the door into Jonesy Barnett's joint over in the shopping plaza by the Little Creek Bridge. Jonesy was working the stub of a White Owl and running a razor down the jowl of a customer springing for a hot shave.

"Morning, boys. I'll be with you in a minute."

"Don't shortchange me none, Jonesy. I'm paying you six bits for this shave."

"Damn, Pete. Didn't recognize you under that soap," Tasco said.

Mule plopped down with last month's *Playboy*. "What, you going to a funeral or something, Pete?"

"Wedding this afternoon. Old lady wants me cleaned up."

"Anybody we know?" Tasco asked.

"Fish Nelson's daughter."

"Lord," Mule said. Jonesy winked and made like he was racking the slide of a 12-gauge. Everybody chuckled.

Jonesy cranked the chair upright and wiped the missed patches of foam off Pete's face. He dusted on some talc and held up the mirror. "Now you're ready for Hollywood."

Tasco gave a two-note cat whistle.

Pete ran his fingers across a baby-soft cheek and checked for blood. "Hey, now that looks okay." He climbed out of the chair and forked over the money. "See you boys around."

"Say congratulations to Fish," Mule said, his head cocked sideways behind the May centerfold.

The doorbell tinkled closed after Pete stepped outside, still stroking his clean mug.

Jonesy snapped a fresh towel. "Who's next?"

"Worst first," Tasco said, slapping Mule on the shoulder.

"Shh…" Mule shuffled over to the chair.

"How you want it, Mule?"

"The regular. High in the front, flat on top and nice and tight around the ears."

Jonesy flicked on the clipper and started buzzing. Ten minutes later he was butch-waxing the front ridge of Mule's hair. "There you go." He spun the chair so Mule could admire himself in the wall mirror.

"Now that's one handsome SOB right there," Mule said, touching the razor-edge of a sideburn.

"How about a little Clubman?"

"Sure," Mule said with a sly smile. "Ladies love the Clubman."

Jonesy splashed the tonic on Mule's neck, and then dosed himself a little.

"Tasco's paying. I'm busted."

"You musta had a big night," Jonesy said, wiping down the chair.

Mule mumbled something.

Tasco stepped over for his turn. "He sure did. Get a load of this..."

❖❖❖

Mule and Tasco stepped out onto the sunny sidewalk like they owned East Beach. The feeling lasted a minute.

"Let's get some lunch."

"Oh shit," Mule said, nodding at the smoking Plymouth angling their way. Its curb feeler sparked along the curb until the driver's door glided to a stop right in front of Mule's unzipped fly. A shock of raven-black dye job poked out of the open window.

"Where's my money, Mule?"

"Hey, Blanche. We're on the way to the bank right now. Then I gotta run some Saturday errands. How 'bout I drop it by tomorrow?"

"Errands," Blanche snorted. "Where, down to the Thirsty Camel?"

"Nah, nothing like that. See, I got me a job this afternoon that..." Mule tried to think of something plausible.

"Listen. Get me them lousy forty dollars in an hour or I'm calling Dwayne and gettin' you evicted."

Dwayne was Blanche's brother-in-law and a Norfolk deputy sheriff. He and Mule went way back.

"Now don't go and do that. Look, how about I get you half now and the rest first thing tomorrow morning?"

Blanched crushed her Pall Mall in the dash ashtray and sighed. "I should get my head examined. Remember, an hour." She turned up Charlie Rich on the radio and drove off in a cloud of blue exhaust.

"I only got six bucks," Tasco said.

"Don't worry, I got an idea." Mule looked out across the cars to the neon and stucco glory called the Jolly Roger.

The boys dodged traffic on Shore Drive, jogging into the dirt and oyster shell lot of the most venerated beer joint in East Ocean View. A couple of cars slouched by the building.

"You ain't thinking of robbing the place are you?"

Mule laughed as he hopped over a broken Schlitz bottle. "Nah. Just follow my lead."

It took a few seconds for their eyes to adjust to the dim light. Somebody had painted over the windows so the only illumination came from the pinball machines and a string line of fiesta lights above the bar. A couple of kids in Oxfords and Birdwell trunks leaned on cues by the pool table. College boys from over on the West Side, Tasco figured. A new guy manned the taps, reading the morning paper. Mule walked over.

"Where's Zeke?"

The bartender dipped the top of the sports section. "Zeke who?"

"Zeke Mulholland. He manages this dump."

"Never heard of him." The guy went back to reading the paper.

Mule walked over and kicked in the side of the juke. "Black Dog" barked and whimpered quiet in mid-guitar riff.

"Hey, that was my quarter, asshole," called one of the kids at the table.

Tasco sat on the edge of the pool table and spun the nine

ball into a side pocket. "Not your dog show, junior."

"Hey, we ain't having no trouble in here," the bartender said.

Mule hitched back over to the bar and clapped a meat hook hand on the 'tender's wrist. "You're right about that, pal. So don't even think about that sawed-off Mitch keeps by the sink. Now, give the magic signal and get Zeke's ass out here, pronto. Tell him it's Mule Dantone."

The 'tender looked back and forth between Mule and Tasco, who was tap dancing a pool cue along the lip of the bar. *Could be the cops for all I know*, the 'tender thought. He shrugged and fingered a button by the register. A faint buzz sounded behind the wall, then a door marked "Staff Only" swung open.

"I told you not..." The angry little guy in a Pink Floyd tee shirt sweetened up real fast when he saw Mule's flattop glistening under a fiesta light. "Mule! How you doing? Man, I swear I was coming to see you tonight."

"Uh-huh. Been two weeks."

Zeke gave an anemic grin and a head-tilt back to the smoky room behind the door, where four dopes hunched over a blanket spread next to boxes and beer kegs. One rattled a pair of dice. Zeke went confidential. "Listen, I'm teeing up a couple of suckers in there. I'll have your dough and then some by nine o'clock. Promise."

Mule peered around to see the craps game. He shook his head and draped a ham-sized arm on Zeke's shoulder. "Here's what I'll do. You give me thirty in cash right now and I'll forget the other twenty."

Zeke wasn't an accountant, but those numbers added up A-okay for him. "Deal." His hand shot into his jeans and came up with a wad of bills. He snapped off three tens. "Here you go." He turned to the barman. "George, give these guys a beer on the house, willya?"

Tasco tossed the cue and scooted over to claim his prize. Zeke gave Mule a smile. "Say, how 'bout comin' in for a few rolls?"

Mule took his free beer from Tasco. "See you 'round, Zeke."

The door banged open behind a shaft of sunlight and a guy wheeling a handcart.

"Coca-Cola man, coming through," announced Lenny Wilkes. He steered his clinking load up to the bar. "Hey, Mule, Tasco. Y'all are in early today." He passed a ballpoint and clipboard to Zeke. "Eight cases. Sign here."

Zeke clicked the pen and initialed the invoice. "Set 'em over there." He handed the clipboard back and went to pocket the pen.

Mule caught his hand. "Let me see that damn ballpoint."

Zeke shrugged and forked it over.

Mule played with the pen, tilting it just enough so the hula girl swayed in the little plastic window. "I'll be damned."

"Cool," Zeke said, watching the show.

"This is my damn pen," Mule said. "Keep it on my dresser. Where'd you get it, Lenny?"

"I bummed it from a gal over at the Tradewinds. She was hustling some guy to drive her to Virginia Beach. Told me to keep it."

"What she look like?"

"High miles and a few dents but still running. Big damn beak on her. Looked like a buzzard or something. Fire engine hair."

Mule shot Tasco a knowing look. "She's still in town, all right. Let's roll, Tas."

"Come on back tonight, boys," Zeke called. "We got some dancers on at ten." The juke started back up.

Mule checked the bills once he and Tasco got outside.

"Damn, Mule. You just left twenty bucks on the table in there."

Mule snorted. "Lucky I got thirty out of the little weasel." He folded the money into his shirt pocket. "Let's go pay Blanche then get sandwiches over at the Cutty. I'm buying."

"Good. All this high finance has got me hungry."

Mule and Tasco chucked their empties in a cement planter

by the door and headed back to 24th Bay.

❖❖❖

Around two o'clock, Tasco's Impala rolled to a stop in the drifted sand along Benny's front yard. Tasco didn't need to blow the horn, since Benny was sitting on his gear case out by the curb, smoking a Viceroy and brushing the lapel of his purple zoot suit. Two empty beer cans sat by his two-tone wingtip.

"Hey, boys." Benny hefted the case festooned with Jeepers the Clown and a disconnected phone number, and ambled over to the car. "Don't mind driving do you, Tas? My heap won't start." He popped a back door and followed the suitcase onto the bench seat.

Tasco eased out of the loose sand and steered for Ocean View Avenue. "You all set?"

"Yeah. This'll be a cakewalk." Benny used a hand mirror to swab on some greasepaint. "Stop at the Tinee Giant, will ya? I need a pack of cigarettes."

Saturday afternoon traffic gummed up the main intersections as drivers looked for a place to park near the beach. Tasco finally bounced the car into the lot and nosed into a space. Benny passed a five over the front seat. "Pack of Vics and a carton of Schlitz for the car."

Tasco took the money. "Want anything, Mule?"

"Get me a Dreamsicle if they got it."

"On me. Take it out of the five, Tas," Benny said, painting on his trademark big eyebrows.

Tasco hopped up on the sidewalk as a convertible slipped into the spot next to the Impala.

"Hey, ladies," Mule purred to the two women climbing out of the olive green Cougar. "How y'all doing?"

One bent down to look at Benny in the back of the Impala. "You lose a bet or something, Bozo?"

Benny kept on brushing. "Get bent, honey. It's a living."

Tasco held the door for the two laughing women as he stepped out of the store. He dumped the sack in the back window and slid into the driver's seat. Keys jangled and a minute later they were back on Shore.

Benny cracked three cans and passed two up front, along with Mule's Dreamsicle.

"How do I look?"

Mule turned around. "Like a damn zebra. Maybe you oughta add a red nose or something. One of them rubber ball-lookin' jobs." He licked his ice cream.

"Nah. Everybody does that jive. Plus they get hot and don't look right on camera."

Tasco slowed behind a line of cars snaking in to the amusement park lot. "Damn place is jumping." The Space-a-Whirl tower loomed just ahead, twirling a fleet of sheet-metal rockets. "Where do I go, Ben?"

"Park over there in the VIP section. I got us a dash pass."

The trio finished off the beers, locked the car, and headed for the midway.

❖❖❖

"Where are the dames?" Mule looked around the open-air dance floor, a concrete slab set next to the Ferris wheel.

"They usually show just before the contest," Benny said, adjusting the plastic flower on his lapel. "They're probably slipping on their suits."

"Huh." Mule gave an appreciative gaze over to the bathhouse.

Tasco Zippoed a cigarette. "So what do we need to do?"

Benny pointed to the crew hammering the last nails into the plywood stage. "Tas, go over and see if the sound guy is all set up. Mule, you slip over to that rack of stage lights and make sure a couple of spots are pointed to where I'll be standing. I want to look good for the cameras. After that, y'all can look around and get rid of anything somebody could throw. I gotta unpack my props." Benny tapped his suitcase.

"I did it myyyy wayyyyy—" Tasco worked the mic with his best Sinatra until the speakers went *bzzt*!

The electrician killed the juice to the amp. "Hey, you're

gonna scare off customers with that crap."

"What, you tone deaf?" Tasco stuck the mic back in its holder. "I thought that was pretty smooth."

Mule clapped and waved from up on the light truss.

Benny had disappeared in the direction of the beer tent.

Twenty minutes later, Tasco dumped the last soda bottle/potential missile in the barrel trashcan. "That oughta do it."

Mule wiped the sweat off his brow. "Somebody could still throw a shoe at Benny, I guess, but this is good enough. What time is it?"

"We still got twenty minutes," Tasco said. "Let's go get some beers and look around."

They scooted around the gathering crowd and headed for the midway.

"Hey, there's the Lucky Ducky," Mule said, pointing to a plywood booth where a fleet of little yellow ducks bobbed and raced around a zinc sluice. A sailor held one of the dripping ducklings.

"What the hell is this 'Try Again' jive?" the sailor said, looking at the message painted on the duck's bottom. "I thought you said everybody wins."

"I said almost everybody." The platinum blonde barker running the Lucky Ducky concession at the edge of the midway gave a practiced little pout. "How about another chance, handsome?"

"This damn thing's rigged," the sailor said, plopping the duck back in the stream. "Took my last quarter."

"Shove off, Popeye." The barker turned to the passing throng, waving her hand up and down the rainbow shelves of stuffed bears. "Step right over folks and try your luck for just two bits. Everyone's a winner!"

"Hey, Diane." Mule leaned on the counter, shirt unbuttoned to show a little chest hair.

"Well, Mule Dantone. Where the hell you been keepin' yourself?" She leaned down and gave him a healthy peck on the cheek. "Mmm, you smell good, honey."

"You working this game or not, lady?" A gambler banged his quarter on the counter. "We want to fish some damn ducks."

Diane turned to the guy, who sported an oil-stained Texaco shirt and a skinny girlfriend. "Beat it, Gomer. The ducks are on break."

"Well, I ain't ever…"

She went back to Mule, elbowing the counter so Mule could get a bird's-eye down the vee of her leopard-print blouse.

It worked. "Uh, I've been working night shifts down at the piers. Crimping my social life a little. Been thinkin' of you, though."

An accordion sounded a high C from over at the dance pavilion. Zig held the note and worked the mic. "A-one, a-two…" The Polka Kings busted into a murderous rendition of "Bad, Bad Leroy Brown." A few couples started dancing.

"You're sweet, Mule, honey. Say, now. I get off in a couple of hours. How 'bout we get a few drinks somewhere?"

"Heehaw!" Honk! "Hey everybody! Welcome to the Miss uh," (hand over muffled mic) "oh yeah, the Miss Ocean View Park Pageant. I'm Jeepers the Clown," (a few claps) "and we got a bevy of gorgeous beauties from all over town competing for the crown tonight. Just get a load of this pulchritude, I'm tellin' ya!" Honk! Honk!

Benny tooted his brass horn and jabbed a gloved hand at the line of young gals at the corner of the stage. The WVEC camera lights panned in their direction, showcasing a sea of emerald bathing suits, pearl-white teeth and waves of hair. Benny eased over to get in the camera shot. "Now before I introduce our first contestant, let me tell you a good one I heard just the other night—"

"Shut up and introduce the girls, dumbass!" Others in the crowd echoed this general theme.

Honk! "Hey, folks, just to remind everybody, we're on live TV tonight, so let's make sure we show the viewers out there some good-ol' fashioned Ocean View hospitality!"

"Go to hell, you goofy son of a bitch! Bring out the

broads!"

The camera kept rolling.

"Okay, okay, keep your damn shirts on," Benny muttered, half-off mic. "Zig, can I get a little musical accompaniment, please." The Kings launched an up-tempo "Some Enchanted Evening." "Our first contestant, hailing from the beautiful Camellia Acres section of Norfolk…"

Mule turned back to Diane. "Well, now. We might just be able to arrange something. What say I—"

A woman screamed from up on the Rocket.

"Mule! Mule!" Tasco was over by the stage, yelling and pointing his Pabst longneck up at the roller coaster.

Mule spun around and caught a glimpse of the Rocket just as it catapulted down the first dip. A shock of fire-red hair trailed from the seat of the last car.

"Well, I'll…" Mule tossed his cigarette and pushed through the crowd for a better look.

"Mule, baby, what's…"

Tasco met him at the edge of the dance floor. "You see that gal? Red hair, big schnoz, just like Lenny said."

"That was her, all right. Ridin' there between a couple of guys. Come on." Mule pushed open a path to the coaster entrance.

"…Miss Carla Ginowski from, uh, here it is, East Belvedere. Now ain't she an image of elegance, folks?" Honk!

Mule and Tasco shoved to the front of the line just as the Rocket zoomed overhead on the rickety tracks, showering everyone with rust and paint chips.

"Hey watch it, Mack! No cuttin'!"

Mule heaved his girth over the waist-high fence and dashed up the ramp, Tasco on his heels. Too late. The coaster rumbled to a stop and the carnies were already raising the safety bars.

Mule locked eyes on Dolores. For some reason he now remembered her name. He dug into the planked walkway like a bulldog going after the milkman.

Dolores saw him coming.

She said something to one of the guys, who got a load of Mule barreling their way. He quickly unhitched the bar and jumped out with the girl on the far side of the tracks, the third guy in tow. Dolores shot Mule one last look, then melted into the crowd of riders staggering off the coaster.

Tasco caught Mule by the belt just as another train of cars roared past the platform.

"Dammit. Almost had her."

Tasco searched through the old wooden track supports. "There! They're heading for the parking lot."

"Come on. We'll cut through the midway."

The boys ran down the covered walk, bay on one side and a menagerie of cheap hustle games, funhouses and tunnels-of-love on the other, the whole way zagging around kissing couples and kids eating cotton candy. They burst out of the midway and into the dance pavilion, smack in the middle of the TV picture. The camera guy hollered as Mule bowled head-on into a couple of sailors, sending the swabs and their beers flying. Then somebody threw a punch.

Honk! "Now come on, folks! Let's all just have a little—"

A shoe sailed across the picture and hit Benny on the head. That's all it took. Shoving and fights broke out. People rushed the concession stand and grabbed free beers. The cops blew whistles and waded into the riot. Miss Glenwood Park pushed Miss Norview and took her crown. Benny tossed his horn and dove into the melee. The TV director yelled for somebody to cut the feed.

❖❖❖

"There they go!" Mule pointed at the end of lot, where Dolores and her confederates were piling into a blue Torino.

He fell into the Impala as Tasco fired the V-8. They fishtailed out of the parking space, slinging gravel, honking at people to clear a path. The Torino got lucky with the traffic light and hauled west onto Ocean View Avenue.

"They're heading up Willoughby Spit," Mule said, one hand on the dash. "We're gonna lose 'em!"

"Hold on." Tasco gunned the engine and spun the wheel, bouncing the Impala across the curb and onto the avenue in a shower of sparks. He stomped on the gas to swerve past a city garbage truck and ran a yellow, two hundred yards behind the Torino.

Blue lights and sirens popped on back at Granby Street.

"Damn cops," Mule said, glancing out the fastback window.

Tasco worked the gas and brakes, swinging the dice hanging from the rearview as the Chevy swerved through tunnel-bound traffic.

They were gaining on the Ford.

Brake lights flickered a half-mile up as cars jockeyed onto the I-64 ramp. "We got 'em, Tas!"

An electrical cord snaked like a black mamba from the Torino's passenger window, whipping and snapping in the slipstream. Then out flew Mule's Japanese TV, bouncing along the pavement, dead in the path of the Impala. Tasco tried to veer but he was hemmed by a station wagon. The TV crashed into the Impala's grille, busting out a headlight before tumbling past the right fender. Mule watched the remains of his sixty-nine-bucks-plus-interest cartwheel by and scatter across Ocean View Avenue.

"Son of…"

"Hey, they're dumping something else!"

A hand with red fingernails shot out of the Torino's window and loosed a stream of what looked like confetti into the wind. A dollar bill stuck on Tasco's windshield.

"That's my damn money," Mule yelled, half-mesmerized at the sight of cold cash floating across the road. "Stop the car!"

The hand gave a little wave then pulled back in the Ford, which accelerated westward.

Mule jumped from the still-rolling Impala, dodging traffic and scooping up bills. Other drivers were pulling over and trying to do the same, as horns blared and tires squealed. A sedan rear-ended a flatbed carrying a load of port-a-johns over in the eastbound lane. The two Norfolk black-and-whites whistled by, sirens on and lights flashing, trying to nab the Torino before it made the Hampton tunnel.

Tasco sat on the lip of the Impala's hood as Mule walked back with a fistful of ones.

"How much you get?" Tasco shook out a Lucky and passed the pack to Mule.

"Fourteen lousy bucks," Mule said, pulling out a cigarette and getting a light from Tasco.

"Well, you can make rent."

"Yeah."

They watched the stragglers scurry around, hunting for free money. A couple of kids passed by, carrying a float down to the beach.

"Hey, what do you want to do tomorrow?"

"Same as we always do, I guess."

My 2nd one for your fun! Love! Gina

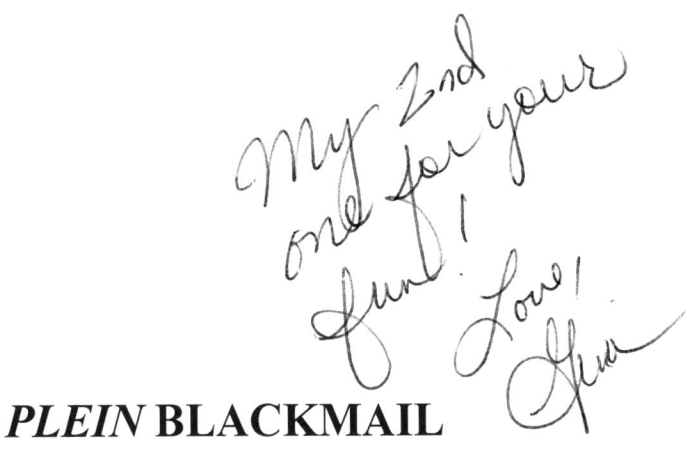

PLEIN BLACKMAIL

By Gina Warren Buzby

"Miss Warren?"

"Who's calling, please?" I asked cautiously.

It was almost midnight and I didn't recognize the number, yet the voice sounded very familiar.

"This is Bob Skaddon, with WAKY-TV Twelve."

Oh, that's how I knew his voice. He does the nightly local news.

"I'm sorry to call so late, but we want to interview you tomorrow about the body you found in the creek today. Would you mind?"

I didn't want to relive the ordeal so soon, much less on TV. I hesitated. All I could think about was the pale blue grimace of the dead man I had discovered floating in Little Creek just twelve hours earlier. The only thing good that had come out of the day was my meeting the oh-so-cute Detective Will Addison of the Norfolk Police Department. He had called earlier in the evening to check on me and to ask me out to dinner! Still, the horrific discovery of that man's body was going to haunt my dreams for a long time to come. *If* I could ever get back to sleep.

"I understand your concern. I'm sure it has been a harrowing experience, but we really hope you'll agree. And, at the risk of sounding trite, this is a double bonus for me, as I've been wanting to meet you. I live in the neighborhood and have seen you out painting. I bought one of your landscapes from the Bay Beach Gallery a few months back. I love having it in my home."

Even in my sleep-aided stupor, I still managed to gush. "Okay, sure."

I wrote down the details and then immediately fell back into a deep sleep, thanks to the numbing force of a wonderful pill.

❖❖❖

The next morning I awoke with a jolt. *I'm going to be on TV? Interviewed?* Suddenly feeling very unsettled, I looked for the business card for Will, the cute detective. I had never met this Bob Skaddon, I had never been interviewed on TV and I had never discussed finding a dead body before. "Unsettled" was putting it lightly. Will had been very sympathetic during the filing of the police report and maybe he'd have some good advice. His contact information was somewhere around my nightstand. After finding the card on the floor, I phoned him immediately.

He answered on the first ring. "Detective Addison."

"Hi, Detective. This is Lizzy Warren. From yesterday?"

"Hi, Lizzy. Please call me Will."

Oh, that velvety voice…mmmm, love it.

"Yes, Will. I'm looking forward to it. In the meantime, WAKY-TV 12 has called and wants an interview later this morning. Is it okay if I do this?"

"Well, that's your right. But, of course, we prefer you stick to the facts and only those that you shared with me yesterday."

"I was just thinking. What if Bob Skaddon asks me questions that you haven't?"

"Bob Skaddon is going to interview you?" Will asked.

"Yes, he called last night. I'm to meet him today at the Bay Front Club, here on the beach," I said.

"Perhaps I should come over and be there when you are

interviewed, just to help if I can?" he quickly offered.

Yessssss! I'd feel so much better, in more ways than one.

"I would appreciate that Detec…I mean, Will. Thank you. I'll see you later."

❖❖❖

We all met at the Bay Front Club in my East Beach neighborhood. The mid-morning sun highlighted the dunes beautifully as we stood outside on the porch next to the slightly weathered rocking chairs. The cameraman was ready and Bob, dressed in a gray suit with a yellow tie, stood nearby. I had chosen my "uniform" of a black short-sleeved, cotton sweater and cropped khaki pants. Focusing on what to wear, how to stand and my diction were all pieces of loving advice from my mother when I'd called to warn her I would be on TV.

"Present yourself as the poised, confident young woman I raised you to be. You never know, there might be a future beau or collector out there watching!" she had said.

Eye rolls soon followed.

As I was assessing the results in the clubhouse hall mirror, Will walked in through the side door looking simply handsome in a gray shirt with the sleeves rolled up, no tie, black pants and a badge on his belt.

Will addressed Bob Skaddon first. "Well, hello Bob," he said snidely as he put out his hand for Bob to shake.

Bob had a microphone in one hand and notes in the other and didn't make an effort to shift his items. He just lifted his chin in a dismissive acknowledgment.

As the producer directed us outside on to the clubhouse deck, Bob frowned and asked, "Will, isn't the Norfolk Police Department too busy to be hanging out during TV interviews?"

"Miss Warren asked me to be present, for moral support," he said, smiling at me. *Swoon.*

"Okay, let's get this going then," Bob said, rolling his eyes.

I took in a deep breath of fresh ocean air and reveled, briefly, in the relaxing scents of sand and surf. I dreaded being on TV…once again.

❖❖❖

Two days later, I met Will at the Ocean View Pier café overlooking the Chesapeake Bay. He'd come straight from detective work and I'd caught an Uber ride over from the Bay Beach Art Gallery where I was the manager and artist-in-residence. There was a pleasant, early evening breeze on the terrace overlooking the surf, but this had to win the prize for "Weirdest First Date Ever." Will dominated the conversation with stories of dead bodies, bullet holes, guns, ammo, drowning, signature strangulations, meth-amphetamines, and, oh yes, *rigor mortis*. And that rib-eye steak had looked so delicious and juicy when it had arrived on my plate. So much for that. As cute as he was, I was not sure if I could continue to date a police detective. Will was very enthusiastic about his work. The problem was, his work was gross!

I'd been on enough first dates to know this was an odd one. Don't get me wrong, I am not a one-night-stand kind of girl, I'm just very picky. My mom actually threw me a small surprise party, cake and all, when I was sixteen to celebrate that I had dated a boy for over three months. She thought so many of my dates were adorable. Later, she'd only be disappointed and mad with me for breaking up with them so soon. "He had such hairy hands, Mom!" was one of my declarations. Or, "But he went bankrupt playing Monopoly after only fifteen minutes!" I had standards. Fast forward twenty years and here I am, still single. Every available guy now looks like a possible soulmate. What can I say? I am on "the hunt." I have wanted to be married—to the right guy, of course—for a long time. My sister was married; all thirteen female cousins were married; and all of my classmates from the woman's college I'd attended were married. Everyone I knew was married. Not to mention well into starting their families. I have been in fourteen weddings!

Always the bridesmaid, never the bride.

I don't understand. Why was I the one stuck dating guys

who only wanted to talk about dead bodies with purple faces? "My Detective" was awfully cute, though. Even the waiter gave him a big smile and flirted a little. I guessed I should give Will a break because the bizarre crime scene was our only common ground thus far. He was just a little too enthusiastic about the gory details that would only add to my nightmares and troubled sleep.

The flirting waiter brought Will a refill of water and forgot mine. I gazed into Will's eyes and tried to seem very interested as he explained to me how the eyes of a dead man begin to bulge out of the skull with time, especially after being strangled, shot and sent surfing down the Chesapeake Bay, as had happened with my "Mr. Dead." *Ewwww.*

And I'd been about to try one of those white, buttery, round baby potatoes. I stuck to the asparagus. Will must have noticed my face and the change in my fork's direction, because he politely switched the subject.

❖❖❖

It was a new day and a painting day. I focused on that and not on the dichotomy of the prior night's date. It had ended pleasantly with Will sincerely asking me about my art and ambitions. He was a good listener after all. He gave me a ride home and walked me from the car to my carriage house gate. There he'd given me a kiss on the cheek before saying goodbye and that he would like to call again.

Had that meant he would "like" to, but wouldn't? Or that he would actually call again? *You're overthinking, Lizzy. Stop it.*

Aside from his intense, modern-day crime-fighting career, I thought Will was refreshingly old-fashioned. He was romantic, especially after the Virginia Beach surfer I'd dated the previous month who'd wanted to move in with me after just one date! Probably only to save on his rent.

On my calendar, I tried to carve out at least two days from my weekly gallery work schedule to focus on *plein air* painting. *En plein air* is a French term used for painting outdoors, and I especially enjoy the opportunities to do so in my new neighborhood of East Beach. We have the golden sand dunes, beach, Chesapeake Bay, breakwater, parks, fountains, marinas, and beautiful homes on tree-lined streets all in one easily accessible area. The two days I chose each week depended heavily on the weather. Thankfully Ingrid, the gallery owner, gave me the flexibility of painting on the prettiest of days. Also, the *plein air* paintings have proven to be big sellers in her gallery, and that is a win-win for us both.

As I set up my easel, I was reminded of the last time I'd done this, down on the east end of the bay beach, just a few days ago. Thoughts of my gruesome discovery came flooding back. That pink scarf floating in the creek, the blue body and the all too familiar face with a black hole in the forehead. Damn! Some of my favorite colors were going to have to find new associations very soon.

I focused intently on the darks and lights contrasting in the dune fencing and the shadows that fell below them this beautiful, summer morning. In the background, I heard the sound of a car with a loud muffler pull up close to the end of the beach access and turn off. I was too busy squeezing cerulean blue on to my palette when I heard footsteps behind me on the sidewalk before they were muffled by the soft sand.

Anytime an artist paints outdoors, they must get used to the many distractions that can interrupt their work. They can be tourists, locals, art lovers, beach goers, etc. who want to stop and watch what you're doing, only to comment on their Aunt Louise who also paints pretty pictures in her spare time. Or, they will critique your work after you've only placed three strokes of the pencil on the canvas. I try to be very patient with everyone and explain that I have to work quickly and I'm not ignoring them. My mom's voice is often in my head saying, "Always have a business card ready. Every person is a potential collector." I looked down to make sure I had brought business cards with me, in case the person I'd heard driving up was a potential collector.

I was just about to turn around to see if the person arriving for a morning beach walk might indeed be a collector when I felt something press into the middle of my back. It felt as if someone had taken one of my large markers and stuck the capped end, and pushed it, none too gently, against my lowest rib.

A low, male voice quickly said, "Don't move, don't scream, don't speak. Just pretend to keep on painting and you won't get hurt." Then I heard a *click, click* sound that matched a bad guy scene in any western movie—the good old pistol hammer being pulled back. I realized then that it wasn't a marker but a cold steel gun held at my spine.

I sat up straight as a debutante at her coming out. Once again, my focus on a painting had definitely been interrupted.

"Mr. Gun" continued to speak. "I want to know what you know about the man you found in the creek a few days ago. He had something in his possession that belonged to me and I need it."

My body shook as I continued staring straight ahead. Sweat was suddenly pouring from every inch of my body. It was hot and I was sweating, but at the same time shivering with fear. When I spoke, I stammered. "I never even touched him. The police have everything."

"That's just it, missy. You were out with the police last night. I followed you. I think you know more than you're letting on. Your cute TV interview didn't let on and I need to know. You were told something so spill it or I will spill you all over this pretty little sand dune you're painting."

"Lizzy! Lizzy!" a friendly voice called from the dunes. It was Elektra Davis, my landlady, walking Fred, her springer spaniel. She waved and stopped to pick up a "present" Fred had left on the grassy knoll they had just crossed.

The pressure on my back disappeared.

Mr. Gun said, "Damn. Okay, you're safe for now. Don't you dare call your boyfriend the cop, though. Trust me, I will be watching you. I need what's mine. Get it for me or you're dead."

I saw the sand fly off his black dress shoes as he quickly

walked to his car and drove away.
And then I proceeded to faint.
"Lizzy. Lizzy!"
I opened my eyes to see Elektra standing over me. My face was wet, covered with cold water, which Fred was happily licking off.
"Should I call nine-one-one?" Elektra asked.
"No, I'm okay. I'm just...too hot out here...already...I guess."
"Well, let's get you up and inside as soon as possible. Who was that man?" Elektra asked.
"Oh. Um, just a tourist admiring my work."
"Well, he has a very noisy car and was in a very big hurry. Are you sure you're okay? You need to head back home and cool off."
I brushed the sand off of my face and clothes.
"Yes, Elektra, thank you. By the way, what did that guy look like? I only saw a glimpse of his back as he left."
"He looked a lot like one of my favorite actors, Ray Liotta, just not as tall. Do you think he's going to become a collector?" she asked.
"No, I don't think so." Oh, he wants to collect, that's for sure.

❖ ❖ ❖

After three days, I considered myself finally married...to the recliner. Frozen in place. I was too frightened and bewildered to go anywhere. The phone rang, but I never answered it. Mom left messages, Will left messages, and someone left threatening silence and then hung up. I'd phoned and told Ingrid I was too sick to come in to work. She was not happy but I knew she didn't like germs any more than I did. If Mr. Gun was watching me, where would I go? As I nervously sat waiting for the inevitable arrival of Mr. Gun and his pistol, I heard the unmistakable sound of creaking wood as someone slowly climbed the steps to my carriage house apartment. Every muscle in my body tensed and I stopped breathing. This was not how I ever expected to spend my final moments on Earth, alone in my recliner.

There came a light tapping on my door. I jumped at the sound, as faint as it was. My skin crawled with fear, my eyes wide open.

"Lizzy? It's Elektra. Are you okay?"

"Oh yes, Elektra," I said, releasing the breath I'd been holding. "I just have a bad cold," I lied.

"Your mother called and asked me to check on you. I told her you'd fainted a few days ago so we're both worried. Plus, I wanted to ask you a favor, but only if you're feeling better soon. I could sure use a house and pet-sitter this weekend."

"Okay, thanks. I'll call you tonight. I'm just going to rest now, all right?"

"Sure thing. Let me know if you need anything."

Maybe that was the answer? I could hide out in Elektra's security-system-protected house with Fred for the weekend until I figured out what to do next.

I called an hour later and let her know I was feeling better and would happily house- and pet-sit for the weekend. I left the recliner and pressed the answering machine button. I listened to the two most recent phone messages. One from Will said, "The ball's in your court now."

He sounds so disappointed. Damn!

Another message—no number available—gave me the silent treatment. I figured that one was from Mr. Gun. Chills raced down my spine, as I knew he was watching me.

❖❖❖

Electra was a friendly landlady. She enjoyed a successful career as a commercial real estate agent, which kept her very busy. Occasionally she broke away from her clients to meet up with her husband who traveled a lot with his work. I'd house/puppy sat for them three times, and always enjoyed my mini vacation in their beautiful East Beach home. Their custom three-story house reflected her Greek heritage, defined by columns, molding, marble, and the occasional garden statuette.

It was so grand, I'd nicknamed it Castle Elektra.

When I went over Friday afternoon as arranged, Elektra handed me the key to the house and told me the new security code. "Oh, and Nadine is finishing up the cleaning today. She's upstairs now."

Nadine's Cleaning Services had an excellent reputation and was used by many of the residents in this area. Nadine and I had met during a previous housesitting assignment, and we'd figured out she'd been a high school classmate of my mother's.

I said goodbye to Elektra, hello to Fred, accompanied with an ear scratch, and walked upstairs to let Nadine know I was in the house.

I found her cleaning the sunken Jacuzzi bathtub in the guest bedroom I usually settled into when I housesat for Elektra. "Ah, my favorite place," I said as I entered.

Nadine winked at me. "I don't blame you a bit there, girlfriend. That tub has called out to me many times. It would be the perfect place to soak your cares away."

That's exactly what I'd hoped to do.

I went into the bedroom and began unpacking my things. Nadine walked in just as I placed a pepper spray canister on the bedside table.

"Well, now that's a new accessory. Why do you think you need that?" she asked.

"I, um…to ward off any loose dogs that might be too aggressive with Fred and me."

"Oh, okay." Her brow furrowed as she studied me. I picked up the canister and slipped it inside my pants pocket.

"Speaking of which, I think I'll take Fred on a quick walk. Look for us to be back before you leave."

❖❖❖

After being self-sequestered in my recliner, I needed the walk as much as Fred. But I steered him around every corner cautiously. I walked down just a few streets where I saw people mingling, and when there were none I pretended to talk on my cell phone. I watched for movement out of every corner of each eye. A girl can't be too careful, even in a neighborhood as safe as East Beach.

What am I thinking? I'm being threatened and blackmailed to find information on a dead man!

During a pretend conversation with my sister, the phone actually rang and I jumped. I looked down to see the caller ID. "Unidentified cell phone." I ignored the bone-chilling ring and walked a little faster, pulling a reluctant Fred behind me.

With a delayed tring-a-ling bell tone, the cell phone let me know someone had left a message. Fred had halted and was doing his business—on corner number five hundred, it seemed—so I played back the recorded voice mail message.

Silence. Mr. Gun leaving me a message again? I hurried Fred along and kept a cautious lookout as we almost sprinted back. But I didn't see anyone unfamiliar, let alone anyone in a loud car or a Ray Liotta look-alike.

I breathed a sigh of relief as I stepped on the front porch, unlocked the door, and then stepped inside Castle Elektra. Thankfully, there was a fenced-in backyard so if Fred needed to go again, he could go out the back door and take care of business on his own. No more walks for us. The few minutes we'd been out had been too edgy for my liking.

Nadine was just finishing up when I returned. As she mopped the last little area of the kitchen she told me, "Please keep that darn dog away from here so this house can be clean for at least five minutes!"

I held on to Fred's leash and collapsed into the living room easy chair.

"Girl, you look like you've seen a ghost!" Nadine said. "Are you sure you're over this cold Miss Elektra said you had earlier this week? Yeah that's right, I know everything. I got the four-one-one. She also told me you had a date with the handsome detective from the crime scene last week. Uh-huh, between me reconnecting with your mom and working for Elektra we have all compared notes on your little life and are living vicariously through you, the young, single, hot artist living in the carriage house. You might think you've got some privacy, but I hate to tell you, the Kardashian girls have got nothing on you. You have a fan club."

In one minute I was afraid for my life while walking a dog and the next minute I was giggling, thinking about these ladies being my fan club. I wished I could tell them everything. They would know what to do. But I couldn't put them in danger.

Nadine smiled as she wrapped up her work. "You rest up. I have to clean up at Mr. Swarthmore's across the street. His nephew just let him know he's flying in tomorrow for a visit and the place is a mess. Have a good weekend with Fred or whomever…and enjoy the tub!" She winked as she closed the door.

I locked it and set the alarm. Fan club indeed.

Okay, I needed a security checklist before camping out at Castle Elektra. I had my pepper spray, I had Fred, I had a security system and I had the weekend to figure out what I needed to do about this threatening Mr. Gun.

First things first. Dinner.

❖❖❖

As nervous as I was, I hadn't eaten in days. Being behind the new wall of security eased my tension a bit but released my appetite. What I needed right now was a bowl of Mom's pasta. She makes her own and always leaves me containers of spaghetti, ravioli, gnocchi, prosciutto, and the very best sauces. My tiny apartment freezer filled up quickly, so sometimes Elektra let me store extra goodies in her kitchen freezer. I headed there and picked out a generous portion of homemade spaghetti and sauce.

It would be colorful to say my mom is from genuine Italian stock and had learned these recipes from her great-grandmother in Orvieto. But she's just a South Carolina girl who happens to cook many things expertly and easily. The Italian cuisine is her favorite to make and mine to eat! The rolling of spaghetti noodles on the fork guided by the spoon is a trick I'd learned at an early age. It's a must for getting a robust bite of the perfect ratio of noodles to sauce. With the sauce defrosted then warmed in the microwave, the spaghetti boiled to ready and I sat down to enjoy my dinner. Just as I rolled the most exquisite twirl of pasta and sauce, Fred started to growl. Night had fallen and I'd closed the lower half of the plantation shutters for privacy. When I looked through the upper window, I saw it had started to rain heavily.

Damn, if Fred needs to go out, it's the fenced in backyard for him. No more walks.

Fred squatted down on his front two legs and growled again. At the front door. The trees rustled against the house and it all sounded too creepy. I shuddered a little but grabbed the remote so the TV could drown out the oncoming wind and rain.

"Calm down, Freddy boy, it's just the wind. I hope."

First level of security: I checked the metal lock on the door and reassured myself that it was secure.

Second level of security: I glanced over at the alarm system panel and saw the red light that confirmed it was prepared to warn me of a problem.

Third level: Fred, but he was now stretching out on his dog bed in the corner. Oh well, two out of three ain't bad. But, I did place the pepper spray on the kitchen counter as the final security measure.

❖❖❖

Keeping busy was important. Since I am not a reality TV fan, I focused my energy on one of my side projects. I lead a "Van Gogh and Vino" social painting event at the local sandwich shop once a month. The extra pay helped make ends meet, and it's also a lot of fun. It does require me to prepare a colorful, appealing, but most importantly, simple composition for each class. Once you incorporate alcohol (vino) into a classroom setting, you need to keep the project simple. With nothing better on the agenda this evening, and my spaghetti dinner finished, I decided to get a little work done for the next session.

I commandeered a corner of Elektra's kitchen and put down a small floor tarp and a plastic tablecloth to protect

Nadine's hard work. I set up the supplies I'd brought over from my carriage house and, after a quick inventory, realized I'd forgotten one important paint color. Gold. The painting for this month was going to be an anchor partially buried in a sand dune. A gold sand dune. Therefore, I needed the gold paint.

I looked out Elektra's back window toward my upstairs carriage house door. I had not turned the porch light on before I'd left. It had been a sunny afternoon and I was staying here overnight, so why bother?

Man, is it dark up there.

The courtyard, the stairs, and the door had all vanished in the wet blackness.

I put on my raincoat, grabbed a flashlight, and took a deep breath. Fred lifted his head slightly and looked at me as if to say, "You can go out in this mess, but I am staying right here."

I shot a smug look in his direction, turned off the alarm system, unlocked the door, flipped up the hood of my coat and headed out into the storm. As the flashlight angled a bit of glow across to the stairway, I pulled out my carriage house key, crossed the yard quickly and ran up the stairs. Once inside, I flipped the inside lights and set the flashlight on the table while I went in search of a bottle of gold acrylic paint. I found it right where I'd left it, in my paint box.

Wanting to be back in Castle Elektra as soon as possible and hearing new, loud barks from Fred, I quickly turned off the lights, locked the door and stepped out.

I was blinded by the sudden transition from bright light to stark darkness. Where was the flashlight? On the table inside, where it did me no good. And once again, I had forgotten to turn on the porch light.

A man in a dark coat bounded up the steps toward me. I couldn't see who it was. His hooded head was bent against the pounding rain, and he hadn't looked up to see me on the stoop.

It could only be one person. Mr. Gun! I reached into my pocket for my pepper spray. *Damn, it's on the kitchen counter!*

Thinking quickly, I popped the top of the paint bottle and threw the contents at my assailant's face, momentarily startling him. I slid around the dark figure who was grabbing at his face and yelling. I ran, screaming, back into Castle Elektra. Fred stood at the door, barking as loud as I had ever heard him. Locking the door behind me, I noticed pulsing red lights from across the street. Police cars! I opened the front door and ran outside yelling, "Help! Someone just tried to kill me!"

Nadine stood with one of the policemen and she ran to wrap me in her arms.

"Oh, darlin, I am so glad you're okay."

"How did you know?" I asked frantically.

"I saw some guy that looked like Ray Liotta peeping through the windows on one side of Elektra's porch and I called the police. I tried to call your cell phone but you didn't answer. Look, they have that fool 'peeping Tom' in the back seat of that police car. Didn't your detective man find you? I called him, too."

From around the back corner of the house, through the pouring rain, appeared a tall, dark figure. He walked over in his black, crumpled, soaked raincoat with his shoulders slumped and head hanging down. And, when he looked up, his face was so handsome, yet so angry and so very…

Gold!

❖❖❖

I held sweet Fred's face in my hands as I calmed him down and gave him a treat. Will stood at Elektra's kitchen sink wiping off the remaining gold acrylic paint. Thank goodness it was water soluble and the rainwater had helped to dilute the pigment. A faint yellow tint that included tiny bits of golden shimmer lingered on his skin. His fellow policemen had thoroughly enjoyed the sight. All of which had brought about angry lines and a tint of red fury to Will's face, creating an orange glow when mixed with the yellowish gold. These were memories and color references I was sure not to mention in his presence.

"Lizzy, we have to talk. When you didn't return my phone calls, I was worried, on a very personal level. Then when I got a call from your friend, Nadine, and simultaneously heard on the police radio that this guy was picked up in your neighborhood, I was extremely worried. He has a very bad rap sheet. We've been looking for him in connection to many other crimes, so we will make sure he is incarcerated and stays that way."

"Who is he?" I asked.

"He had ties to the dead body you found. As it turns out, he had some encrypted information on him that we had to decode and then utilize. I couldn't share any of this information with you, or anyone, and especially didn't want it to get out to people like Bob Skaddon and the press."

"That guy over there in the backseat of the car—I call him Mr. Gun—threatened my life over this information. And he's tied up with Mr. Dead? That's what I call the body I found. Now can you tell me what it was all about?"

"The information we found was on a thumb drive in a hidden pocket of Mr. Dead's suit jacket. It included your Mr. Gun's name and a list of other names of criminals who were building and managing meth labs all along the East Coast. It also had the addresses, their contact information and Mr. Dead had been using it to blackmail each name on the list. We think Mr. Gun was selected to retrieve the thumb drive and take care of the blackmailer. But Mr. Dead kept it hidden on him even after he ended up in the bay."

"The department thinks he murdered Mr. Dead? What's going to happen to him now?"

"Mr. Gun will go to prison for a very long time. And thanks to finding that list, so will a lot of his colleagues. This is going to be a big sting operation for our department and the state. But, after this craziness, I am just glad you are okay," he said.

"Oh Will, I had no idea what to do. I'm so sorry I didn't tell you. He threatened me with a gun to my back out in public, on the beach while I was painting! It was very frightening. My fear was he'd hurt my family, my friends, or you.

"I figured if I just stayed away from everyone for a bit and hid out at Elektra's something would come to me. But, I realize now that it was foolish to think that way. Oh, and remind me to tell you later about my Fan Club, and how they came through for me. I had no idea they were keeping tabs on me. I'll have to thank those special ladies. Will, thank you, too, for being there for me."

We hugged, even though he was wet from the rain and golden from the paint.

"I really would like to accept that phone message invitation for another date, if it's not too late?" I asked. "But I have an idea. Have you ever painted a picture of a sand dune?"

THE PRODIGAL
By Mike Owens

He wasn't sure exactly why, maybe just a need to change his daily routine, maybe some feedback from the Mexican food he'd eaten the night before, but Lou Ballantine begged off the third round of beers and pushed his chair away from the table.

"That's it for me, guys. Gotta run."

"What? You late for a nap?" Bernie, a retired stockbroker and a regular with their golfing foursome, was just getting started. Most likely he'd spend the rest of the day, his fat butt parked at that same table, dealing cards, knocking back beers, interrupted only by trips to the bathroom. Lou had wondered why the guy didn't move into the clubhouse permanently, he spent so much time there, until he met Bernie's wife at a cocktail party. Then he understood perfectly.

"A nap sounds like just the thing." Lou stood and stretched, a little stiff after the morning's eighteen holes, even though he'd driven the course in his cart. He ran his hand through his thinning hair. He'd left his hat on the peg by the door. The others still wore their baseball caps with the East Beach logo, two golf clubs crossed beneath a bright yellow sun, but Lou wore a hat, and he took it off inside the clubhouse, always.

"Hey, great round today, Lou. You keep hitting them like that and we'll have to make you play left-handed." Morrie, his closest friend, gave him a gentle nudge with his elbow as Lou walked past his chair. "Everything okay?"

"Oh, sure. No problem." At least, no problem he could put his finger on. Was he coming down with something? He'd skipped his flu shot this year, but there had been no flu cases in the area, and it was the wrong time of year anyway. It was more like a sense of foreboding, like when you feel a change in the weather coming before it actually happens. Maybe he just needed a little change, like he'd thought earlier. Of course, his group didn't take change lightly; after a certain age, most change wasn't likely to be good. They never discussed it, just agreed without saying so. But the routine, sometimes it got to be a bit much. Try as he might, Lou still couldn't get used to chugging down beer before noon. It took him half the day to recover and by then it was cocktail hour and it started all over again. That was one routine he'd pass up.

So he left his golfing buddies in the cool dark recess of the clubhouse then stepped out into the noonday sun. He'd learned to keep his eyes almost shut at first, until the blindness resolved and he could see where he was going. He picked his way up the path to where his golf cart was parked, partially shaded by the overhang of the clubhouse roof.

This time of day, when the sun seemed to launch an all-out assault on anything and everything moving beneath it, he sometimes wondered whether his choice of retirement spots was really right for him. When he'd left his two-bedroom apartment in Darien, Connecticut, five years ago, his initial goal was to get as far away as possible. Where he went mattered little, it was all about distance. There had been a brief stay on Florida's gulf coast, a few miles north of Tampa, but the bugs and humidity drove him crazy, so he packed up again and wound up in East Beach. Since he no longer had any active family commitments, he was able to reduce his location requirements to three: warm, relatively quiet, and a golf course nearby. East Beach had those in abundance.

It didn't have Carolyn, of course. Carolyn, caught up in the Darien art scene with her artsy ideas, all the motivation in the world but no talent. It didn't take a genius to see that. The paintings she'd insisted on hanging in their house gave Lou headaches.

Then, one October afternoon when he'd just finished raking the leaves off the front lawn, his artsy wife of twenty-six years announced that she'd filed for divorce. Just like that, no warning, nothing. Found herself a younger man, an art student, of course, someone who could appreciate her talent. But six months into her new life she discovered that her new boy toy was a switch-hitter, caught him in the act with their neighbor's kid, a scholarship football player, home from college.

Ah, Carolyn. Of course, she'd called several times, distraught: "Can't we try again?" No way. Keep it simple, words he lived by. And Carolyn wasn't simple.

The intensity of the heat made him rush from one shady spot to another lest he desiccate in the sun. He'd learned that much from watching the little striped skinks that darted about seeking shelter from the direct sunlight. Mornings weren't so bad, though; he hadn't had to miss a golf date yet because of rain. And the convenience of everything was hard to beat. He hadn't taken his Mercedes out of the garage in weeks; wherever he needed to go, he got there by golf cart. Yeah, keep it simple.

"Don't you get bored?" an old friend, visiting from Connecticut, had asked him once. It wasn't a question, not really. Lou watched envy spread over the man's face like a greenish glow as he took in the striking architecture of the East Beach homes. "I mean, nothing but golf and sunshine and horny widows?"

Lou just winked, grinned at him. Yeah, it was pretty basic, his life. But that's what he wanted. People who walked around with high expectations, always looking for something new, they were just asking for trouble. He was old enough to know better.

He made a left turn into the narrow alley that led to the garage on the back of his house. He'd only driven a short distance when Brewster, the huge boxer that lived one street over, climbed halfway into his golf cart and shoved his massive head into Lou's lap.

"Hey, Brewster, how's the world treating you?" Lou said, and began scratching the dog's ears. Almost as an afterthought he greeted Brewster's owner, Charlotte, who had just been dragged across the street.

"Three months of obedience classes, and this is what happens. You know, he only behaves this way when you're around," she said.

"Could be worse," Lou said. He couldn't deny that he and Brewster had some special affinity. From his first encounter with the dog, when Charlotte was taking him for a walk one crisp fall afternoon, Brewster had taken to him immediately, and so it had been ever since.

"I think you have visitors," Charlotte said. "There's a van parked in front of your house." She raised an eyebrow, like there was more than she was saying.

"Not expecting anybody," Lou said. "I'd better go check it out."

It took both of them to pry Brewster off Lou's lap.

The monstrosity parked in front of his house, blocking his driveway, was like something out of the sixties—some kind of van with collision marks fore and aft. Whoever had repainted it apparently ran out of the color they started with and just continued with whatever else they could find, leaving the vehicle silver on one end and orange on the other. Neither could possibly have been the original color.

Lou wheeled up behind the van. Someone was waving to him from his front doorstep.

"Hey, Dad."

No, it couldn't be. Amy? The last time he'd seen his daughter was at his fiftieth birthday party. There had been the usual argument followed by the usual result; she'd called him a fascist pig and stormed out of the house. Nothing now for what, fifteen, sixteen years?

Two women in his adult life, disasters, both of them. Carolyn had cycled in a different orbit, of course, but Amy—

Lou and his daughter had butted heads almost from the moment she was able to stand upright. Later on, most of their fights, he couldn't even remember what started them. They weren't really about anything, just winning and losing. Usually he lost.

"She's a girl, for God's sakes," Carolyn had said. "Can't you understand that?"

No, he couldn't. Where was all the sweetness, the sugar and spice? This one, as soon as she'd grown upper and lower teeth, bit him. An irresistible force and an immovable object, Carolyn had called them, but she never said which was which.

Biology? He'd wondered about that. Was she really his daughter? He never had the courage to ask Carolyn, but one of his sisters, up visiting from South Carolina, had remarked that the only resemblance between Lou and Amy was they both had arms and legs. But that wasn't it. Their animosity was something more basic, fundamental. Something he couldn't grasp. He doubted Amy could either. As the years passed he expected things between them to get better; they got worse, to the point that the home address in Darien was all they had in common.

Earlier on, before he'd simply closed the door on their relationship and walked away, (Walked? He'd run like hell!) he'd wondered why things had gone so badly. Was there blame to be laid at someone's feet? If he followed the assumption of childhood innocence—although in Amy's case he was never sure about that—then the burden of proof fell on him. He was the adult, after all. And yes, he'd been the classic absentee father, so much a stereotype that it was laughable. Every weekday morning for what, thirty years, he'd stood on the Amtrak platform in southern Connecticut, crammed there alongside so many other nameless, faceless, overcoat-clad, briefcase-lugging, morning paper-folded-beneath-the-arm men going off to a job he hated, as probably did most of the herd to which he belonged.

How many of the cattle who surrounded him on that platform were abject failures as fathers? How many had daughters who hated them? How many of them, like Lou, staggered home late at night, poured a scotch, then hid away. "I've got work to do," was the nightly lament, when, in truth, as soon as the door to his study closed, the briefcase got tossed into a chair, unopened, and he flopped into his recliner trying to blot out the thought that tomorrow would be just another day at the office.

Okay, so he'd been a provider, not really a father. Provider was a simple role, something he understood. Something all the other guys on the platform understood, too. When he stepped outside the provider role, that's when things turned to crap.

When Amy was ten, she brought home a kitten, a skinny little calico. "Her name is Button." That's as far as the conversation got, no explanation of how she came to possess the cat or where it came from. They didn't find out until later about the fleas, or that Amy was mistaken about the cat's gender. As Button grew, he took on some of the more obnoxious tomcat qualities. He became territorial and marked his spots in the house by backing up to whatever and spraying. The "whatever" might be a wall, a chair, or, once, Lou's briefcase.

"What the hell is that smell?" The man next to Lou turned up his nose and edged away, as did others on the platform. When he got to the office he tried to wipe the odor off his bag with wet paper towels, but it still smelled like three-day-old fish. "Damned cat," he muttered.

When he got home, he looked around for Amy; something had to go and that something was the damned cat. He couldn't find his daughter, but he did find Button, curled up on his desk. "Get outta here, damn you." The cat raised its head, gave Lou that look of total disdain that must be hard-wired into cat brains, and went back to sleep. He rolled his newspaper tightly and swatted the cat, harder than he'd intended. Button leapt with a loud hiss, knocked Lou's favorite pen set—the one he got after fifteen years with the company—onto the floor where it broke into six pieces.

He threw the city phone directory at the cat just as it

dashed for the door. Must have hit it, because the cat turned up limping.

"What did you do?" Amy stood in front of him, cradling the cat in her arms.

"What? I didn't do anything." Lou looked away. He never could meet her gaze directly. It was like she could see straight through him.

"You hurt Button." The cat lay curled in her arms, the picture of contentment. Mission accomplished.

"I don't know what you're talking about, but I have work to do." He retreated to his desk, made a show of rummaging through his briefcase.

She didn't move, didn't flinch, just stood looking at him. Her eyes bored through him like laser points, and the kid never blinked. "Don't you ever hurt my cat again." What was it, a threat, a warning? Certainly not a request. After a moment that seemed so very, very long, she turned and walked away.

Lou jerked at his tie, tore the button off his collar, had to get air, had to breathe. Now he understood why Carolyn was such a poor excuse for a mother; the same reason he was such a poor excuse for a father; this kid scared the piss out of him.

Now, there she stood in front of his East Beach house, his refuge, smiling at him. And kids. She had kids with her now, one in her arms and two clinging to her skirt.

"Long time no see," she said gaily, as if her absence had been for a couple of weeks instead of all those years. "Aren't you going to invite us in? Hot out here."

Lou stumbled getting out of his cart. He opened his mouth but nothing came out, stood there gaping like one of the air-hungry skinks. But there were practical matters to attend to. He unlocked his front door and hurried them all inside. Explaining Amy and the kids and that godawful van to his East Beach neighbors would be hard, if not impossible.

"How did you find me?" he asked.

"It wasn't easy." Outwardly she hadn't changed much, maybe a few more pounds, same close-cropped mousy brown hair. Carolyn's eyes, of course, eyes that constantly darted about, looking for an opening. Eyes that swept over him like he wasn't even there.

"Great," Lou whispered. He trailed behind Amy at what he considered to be a safe distance. An observer, unaware of their history, might consider his behavior absurd, paranoid, but Lou, like a dog that had once too often been lured close by the promise of a treat only to get kicked in the ribs, knew better than to get too close.

His daughter toured the living room, rocking one child in her arms while the other two trailed close behind. "This is nice. Kinda small, but nice."

The little boy closest to Lou screamed and dug his fingers into his mother's thigh. "Ouch." She tried to dislodge his tiny talons with her free hand. "What's wrong with you?"

"A rat. A big one." He pointed to the sofa where a furry tail disappeared behind the armrest.

"Oh, God, rats." Amy backed across the room, the kids clinging to her like a brood of baby opossums.

"That's not a rat." Louis raised his voice above the tumult. "That's just Clyde. He's my ferret." Clyde was Lou's own little secret, and he planned to keep it that way.

"You keep rats?" Amy wailed. "Mom always said you were weird."

"Ferret...ferret. Not a rat. A ferret."

"Get it out of here, whatever it is."

"He won't come out now. He's frightened."

"For God's sake, Dad. Think of your grandchildren. Rats in your house—I can't believe this."

"Come on into the kitchen. He won't follow us. He's scared to death." As was Lou himself. And why did she keep calling him Dad? She'd never called him that before. He'd even stopped using the word himself. All the cards he sent her, he signed Lou, never Dad. Whatever was going on, he didn't get it, not at all. Right about now he'd love to join Clyde beneath the sofa.

"How is it you know the name of that rat but can't name your own grandchildren?"

"How in hell was I to know I had grandchildren?"

"Don't swear in front of the kids."

"Who are their…their fathers?"

"How dare you." Amy shot him her "I'm painfully injured" look. He had to hand it to her. The girl still had it. Her repertoire of facial expressions would rival that of any seasoned screen actress.

"Well, look at them," Lou said. "Are you telling me all three of them came from the same two gene pools?"

"Never mind that now." Another of her favorite expressions—disdain—reduced his comment to ashes, not worth consideration. "Where do we sleep?"

"What?"

"Sleep. The children are exhausted. They've been on the road all day and the air conditioning on the van is busted. Why on earth you had to pick such a hot place to live is beyond me."

"I only have one bedroom."

"Don't give me that. No house has just one bedroom."

"These houses, they're called patio homes. They're very small—one or two people at most."

"Great. Thanks a lot, Dad." She plopped into a chair beside the kitchen table. Lou could almost see the wheels of her mind spinning. What tact should she try next? The blond kid wiped his nose on her blouse leaving a trail of green slime.

"Is he sick?" Lou asked.

"Would you care?"

Lou took a couple of deep breaths, trying to calm the tide of bile rising in his gut. The onslaught overwhelmed him, but that was the whole idea, wasn't it? Nothing subtle about Amy. He called it her Chinese Army tactics, full frontal assault with everything she had. As soon as he thought he had one issue covered she hit him with a half dozen more. For a moment he closed his eyes. Maybe it was all just a bad dream.

"What, you're going to sleep now?" Her voice rose. "Pretend I'm not here? Not gonna work this time, Dad." She said the word "Dad" like she was rubbing it into an open wound.

"How long has it been, Amy? How many years without one damned word from you?"

"I asked you not to swear in front of the children."

"I'm sure these kids—if they're really yours—have heard, and seen, far worse than anything I could come up with. What do you want from me?" He couldn't stand it any longer. Maybe she could play this game all day, but he certainly could not. He had to know.

"What a question. I'm your daughter, remember?" Her eyebrows shot up, then down again, as if she'd asked and answered her own question. God, the girl could do more with eyebrows than most people could do with an entire face. "Most fathers would be happy to see their daughter. All I want from you is to act like a regular dad. Is that too much to ask?"

Regular dad, regular daughter, regular family unit—they hadn't been anything like that for years, probably never had. Now what? The prodigal returns, wanting reconciliation? Not the Amy he knew. The first agenda she showed was always a smoke screen, never the real thing. Lou turned to the little blond boy, half-hidden behind Amy's chair. "How old are you?"

The boy held up four fingers, then shook his head and added a thumb.

"Five?"

Next the swarthy boy with the dark, sparkling eyes. He also held up a hand with all five fingers extended.

Lou leaned back, making a show of counting backward on his fingertips. "2015… '14…'13….So, you got all maternal around 2010 or so? What happened? Suddenly realize the joys of motherhood were passing you by?"

Now the tears. Silent, no sobs, no wails, just a quiet cascade that soon drenched the front of her dress. She made no attempt to wipe them away; that would ruin the effect.

"Must you hate me so much? How can you treat me this way?" She sat erect, a wounded and wronged heroine.

The two older boys milled about, apparently unimpressed by the water show. The child on her lap watched Lou closely.

For a moment, just a moment, the kid reminded him a bit of Carolyn, especially the eyes.

There was a time when Lou would have bitten on the "hate me" question, protested. No real father could hate his only daughter. Yeah, he'd have embraced her, opened himself up, and probably got his ass kicked for the trouble. A younger, more resilient man might risk it, but not Lou. If he chased every trial balloon Amy sent up he'd be running around in circles forever. "What are your plans?"

"What's wrong with just a visit? Why can't I simply visit my father, introduce him to his grandchildren?"

He let that one slide, too. Grandchildren? He wasn't sure where she got the kids, or where she was taking them. Yeah, they were probably somebody's grandkids, not his though. "Ah, a visit. Now we're getting somewhere. First, we have to get you situated. Obviously there's no room here, but there's a nice Econo Lodge a couple of miles east. They have a pool. They should have plenty of vacancies this time of year."

"But—"

"And I'll start working on an itinerary, so you can see the sights. Maybe a trip to the beach. The kids would love that. Of course, you'll have to get an early start. You don't want to be poking around in the heat of the day." Lou warmed to the task, a bit proud of himself. Two could play this game.

"Dad—"

"I'd love to come along but my doctor says I have to avoid the heat—heart's not as strong as it used to be—and I wouldn't want to slow you down." He didn't mention playing golf almost every day. She didn't need to know about that.

The tears had stopped flowing right after he mentioned the Econo Lodge. Now her shoulders slumped. She dragged the child off her lap and plopped him on the floor, shedding her maternal cloak like—dare he even think it?—a snake shedding its skin.

"Look, here's the thing." She laid her palms flat on the table. "I need money."

"I'm sure I can stake you to a few nights at the motel. No

problem."

"More than that."

"Meals included. Think of it like a paid vacation." So, the dance went on, but at least he was holding his own.

"I need a thousand dollars."

"Hey, you're planning to stay awhile." There, now he knew. He could have guessed as much. No real need to drag things out, but he couldn't help himself.

"I'm not planning to stay at all. Can I have the money or not?"

He shrugged. "Of course. But I don't keep much cash in the house. I'll have to give you a check."

"Where can I get a check cashed around here, for God's sake?"

"We have a little branch bank right here, two blocks down on Shore Drive. They know me. I'll call them and tell them you're coming." He left the room and returned with his checkbook. Getting out of this mess for a thousand bucks looked like a real bargain. But as he started to write in the amount, he hesitated. "I can make it for more if you need it."

"Whatever you can spare. These kids are really expensive."

"I can imagine." He made out the check for five thousand and slid it across the table.

For just a moment, when she reached for the check, their fingertips touched. He almost lost it then as a deep burn crept up his arm and settled somewhere in the center of his chest. He stared at the tabletop, not daring to look at her face. Was she looking back? Even a glimmer of tenderness from her and he'd fold like an old tent. So, he never knew.

She took the check, then picked up the toddler. "I guess we'll be going then." She turned to the blond boy. "Come on, Ronnie."

"I'm not Ronnie." The blond kid pointed to his swarthy counterpart. "He is."

Later, Lou would speculate on the evil that overcame him at that moment. He wasn't a bad guy, not really. It just slipped out. "You know, you never really introduced me to the grandchildren. What are their names?"

"You go to hell." She grabbed the blond kid's shoulder and the other one trotted behind her. Halfway to the door she stopped short. The kid following her plowed into the backs of her legs. "You're really dying to know, aren't you? You want to know if any of them is really your grandson."

"I guess I would, yeah."

"Well, one is, but I'm not going to tell you which one. And don't forget to call your damned bank."

Lou called the bank like he said he would, after he'd listened to the van sputter, die, then finally start. He didn't watch them drive away, just sat slumped in the chair Amy had vacated, still warm from her body. Clyde reappeared from beneath the sofa and crawled into Lou's lap, then rolled onto his back, presenting his abdomen for scratching. "All clear now, boy. Things are back to normal." Normal? Yeah, as close as he'd probably ever get.

He walked to the window, cradling Clyde under his arm. He looked to where the hideous van had been parked shortly before. Somehow the elation he should have felt at surviving Amy's latest charade was lacking. Not much to be proud of, after all, a meaningless victory in the ongoing war with his only daughter. In truth, he'd won nothing, a skirmish, maybe. But the war? He'd lost that long ago.

THE PROPOSAL

By Gina Buzby, Jayne Ormerod and Jenny F. Sparks

"You'll never find the answer in the bottom of that Guinness, Danny Boy."

Daniel Callahan lifted his pint glass and downed the dregs of the smooth ale before lifting his gaze to the bartender, his brother Liam. "Can't a guy at least look?"

"If nobody looked, I'd be outta business." Liam tossed a white towel over his shoulder, propped his elbows on the bar, and leaned in real close. "I'm guessing Ellie dumped you."

"I never said that."

"Don't need to say it. Your eyes tell me all I need to know. "

"Then you need glasses, old man. Ellie did not dump me."

"Well, something's up. Wanna talk about it?" Liam asked.

"What, me take advice from someone who's been divorced three times?"

"Two divorces. One annulment."

"Who's counting though, right?" Daniel dragged his hand back and forth across his mouth as he weighed the pros and cons of pouring his heart out to his big brother, at great risk of being laughed out of the place. "Pour me another Guinness and we'll talk."

Liam did, then slid it across the bar. "Let me take care of my customers and I'll be right back."

Daniel watched as Liam made his way toward the two tables of guys watching the lopsided Duke/UNC game on the large-screen TV. Through hard work and savvy marketing, his brother had managed to turn a run-down watering hole on the shores of Pretty Lake into a thriving drinking establishment. On slow nights like tonight, Liam ran the bar while Skippy, the cook, turned out chicken wings and pizza that had won Best of Norfolk three years running. They did a great take-out business lately, thanks to the high-end neighborhood building up around them. Called East Beach, the community was based on the concept of New Urbanism, whatever the heck that was. Daniel just hoped Liam stayed true to his fried-food roots and didn't upscale to tapas and lettuce wraps. If that happened, Daniel would have to find a new place to stop by for a cold one on the way home.

Liam came back with a basket of taquitos, fresh from the deep fryer. "I'm thinking of adding these to the menu. Let me know what you think."

Daniel snatched one of the tightly rolled corn tortillas, ran it through a side cup of sour cream and took a bite. It was hot, both in temperature and taste, with a strong flavor of taco meat. He gave it a thumbs up while chewing.

Liam crossed his arms, rocked back on his heels and looked Daniel in the eyes. "So, what's eatin' you, little bro?"

Daniel thought about his problem with Ellie Kerrigan. They'd met three months ago, at a Tides game. Baseball was his passion, especially the AAA level. A foul ball was coming his way and he'd stretched his arm out to snag it, but in the process spilled his beer on the woman in front of him. It turned out to be Ellie. He thought he'd died and gone to heaven. He was a sucker for the chestnut hair/chocolate eyes combination, but it was her smile that made him weak in the knees. And if that wasn't good enough, he'd met her at the ballfield. Three dates later he learned that she hated the sport—all sports, really—and had only been there as part of her company's mandatory fun day. But by the time Daniel learned that about her, he'd been in love long enough to overlook that small defect.

"I'm gonna ask Ellie to marry me." Daniel reached into his pocket and pulled out the blue velvet box he'd been carrying around for two weeks now. He opened it to reveal an antique two-karat square-cut diamond bordered by a row of smaller diamonds. For six weeks Ellie had left a magazine on her coffee table, opened to a page showcasing that style of ring. He'd hunted high and low to find one just like it. Set him back one entire paycheck, but the look on Ellie's face when he presented it to her would be worth it.

For the first time that Daniel could ever remember, Liam was speechless.

Daniel set the box on the bar and reached for another taquito. "Say something. Anything. Talk me out of it, if you can."

"What's the problem, bro?" Liam asked.

"The problem?"

"You've got the girl, and you've got one helluva ring. You drop to one knee and ask her. Then tell me when to put on my monkey suit, and I'll be there for the ceremony."

Daniel shook his head. How to put this in words? After a long draw on his Guinness, he confessed. "I'm afraid she'll say no."

"Come on, I've seen you two together. She loves you, dude. Way more than any of my exes ever loved me."

"According to her sister, Ellie's turned down three guys in the past ten years."

"Why?"

Daniel shrugged his shoulders. "She was married once, so it's not like she's against the concept."

"She's gotta be over husband number one by now."

Daniel didn't know much about the fiery crash that had taken Ben, Ellie's first husband, more than ten years ago. That was one thing she didn't talk about. Ever. And by all accounts she should be over him. So why turn down so many offers of marriage?

Liam leaned over and wiped down the bar with his towel. "Maybe it's all in the proposal. Super romantic is the way to go."

Daniel laughed and shook his head. "You'd think, right? But Ellie's turned down some of the most romantic proposals on record. Get this, the first guy arranged for a plane to fly up the coast, trailing a 'Marry me, Ellie' banner."

"Chicks love that stuff."

"She said 'no.' " Daniel took a sip of Guinness. "You know that song 'Marry Me' by Train?"

Liam nodded.

"A choir of eighteen serenaded them. On the boardwalk while the sun set and the waves crashed behind them. He takes a knee, she cries, the crowd and choir applaud…."

"But she says 'no.' "

"Correct."

Liam looked in the direction of his customers. "Gotta take care of business. Be right back."

Daniel stared into the bottom of his empty pint glass, but still couldn't find any answers to his problem.

Liam returned a few minutes later, all smiles. "Oh, have I got an idea for you!" He tapped out a few beats on the bar. "Are you ready to hear the most romantic proposal ever? You both love New York City. You arrange for dinner at a five-star restaurant, and you somehow, someway slip that gorgeous ring you bought into her glass of champagne."

"Sounds great, but it's already been done."

"Offer number three?"

"Yup."

Liam stared up at the ceiling of the dark restaurant, deep in thought. He shook his head. "Danny Boy, maybe you should quit playing Can You Top This. Ellie doesn't seem to be impressed by that overly romantic stuff."

"Easier said than done." Daniel tipped up his beer glass and waited for the last few drops to dribble down to his mouth.

"Did Ellie have any childhood dreams you could tap

into?"

"She wanted to be an artist."

Silence hung between the two brothers. Daniel had been the only person to ever fail eighth grade art class, despite turning in every assignment on time. Other students at least had received a C for effort. The F in art had kept him off the honor roll. His brother and sisters had teased him about it mercilessly. Those failures led him to an extreme dislike for all things art, and hence, he now led an art-less life.

Liam tapped him on the head with his bar towel. "You, my brother, are screwed." He left to deliver five bottles of O'Connor's Norfolk Canyon to table six.

As he polished off the rest of the taquitos in what would count for dinner, Daniel thought about Liam's advice. How could he tie Ellie's love of art to a romantic, heartfelt proposal?

Daniel slid off the bar stool and headed out into the night to wait for his Uber ride. There had to be a solution, he'd just need to find it.

❖❖❖

Lizzy Warren had more paint on her fingers than on the canvas, and class hadn't even started yet. She wiped her hands on the black artist's apron she wore that displayed a collection of monthly paint stains. Setting up for the evening's paint night always proved to be a bit messy. Preparing twelve foam plate palettes with eight colors each and then finding room on the tables for them, plus table easels, brushes, water cups, etc. Somebody, somewhere, at some time, was going to find a small, stray blob of paint.

And usually it's me.

Lizzy was a professional artist and gallery employee who also taught a paint night at the local sandwich shop once a month. Paint nights were the trend right now. One of the top five fastest growing franchises in the U.S. was a woman-owned paint-night company called Art with a Twist. It replaced the generic happy hour with a purpose-filled evening, in addition to the drinking. And it was satisfying in that it got everyone away from their cell phones and reconnected with a fun childhood pastime.

Her set-up routine was interrupted when a man at the counter spoke to her. "Hi, my name is Daniel. What's this you're setting up?" he asked.

Ooh, he's cute, Lizzy thought. "Hi, Daniel. I'm Lizzy, the instructor for tonight's Van Gogh and Vino social paint night. Are you joining us?"

"No, but thanks. So, a bunch of people get together to paint a canvas and drink wine?"

"That's pretty much it, yes. It's a new nation-wide craze. Paint and drink."

"What if you can't paint?" he asked as he gathered his sandwich and chips from the counter.

"It's fun art, not fine art! That's one of the many mottos of paint night. You're supposed to just come, relax with a glass of wine and your friends in order to break away from work, the cell phone, the routine. And have a great time."

Daniel looked to be deep in thought as his gaze flitted over all of the paint night paintings on the wall. His brow furrowed as he got a little closer to inspect the one painting of the mermaid in the ocean wave.

"One of your students did this?" he asked.

"Yes. A first-timer. We all do the same painting. I walk you through each step and you go home with a beautiful, colorful, eleven-inch by fourteen-inch canvas souvenir."

"I have this girlfriend," he said, then added, "and she's always wanted to be an artist."

Of course he has a girlfriend. Too cute not to.

"You should bring her sometime. We do several classes geared toward couples. You could come and work on your own painting and at the end of the night the two paintings go together to make one."

"Hmmm. I really like that idea. Would you mind if I met you here tomorrow to tell you about my plan? I am trying to formulate a unique way to propose and I think your class might just be ideal."

"Gosh. A proposal? Well, sure. Let's meet here at one o'clock tomorrow and we can discuss it," Lizzy offered.

Daniel arrived on time the next day.

The Sandwich Shoppe was a central meeting place for everyone in the East Beach neighborhood. One o'clock was a busy time. They grabbed a table next to the window in the Wine Room, where sunlight glinted off the cubbies filled with merlots, cabs and chardonnays. Daniel purchased two cheesesteak sandwiches based on Lizzy's recommendation. While they waited for their sandwiches to be delivered, they sat and talked.

"So, how did you meet Ellie?" Lizzy asked.

"At a Tides Baseball game after I spilled a beer all over her. Thankfully, she forgave me and let me take her out to dinner."

"She sounds very special."

"Yes, but she's been proposed to three times already. And she's turned each suitor away," he said

"Wow. Three times!" Lizzy exclaimed. *I'd just like to have one! What is this gal's secret?*

"Yeah. That's why I'm trying to make this one extra special. A stand-out." He opened his chips and looked at Lizzy. "How about you? Are you married?" he asked.

"No. I thought by now I would be. I just haven't met the right guy, I guess. But I just started dating a really great guy. His name is Will Addison. He's sweet and very old-fashioned, but he's always so busy. I never get to see him. He's with the Norfolk Police Department."

Lizzy munched on her sweet potato chips and sipped some sweet tea. She noticed a silver Camry slowing to a crawl as it passed by the shop. The woman driver seemed to be staring at the two of them. When she caught Lizzy's eye, she sped up and disappeared from sight.

Hmmm. Maybe she's lost.

Lizzy and Daniel talked about a way to incorporate a proposal with the Van Gogh and Vino paint night. Between the two of them, a great plan came together.

Yes, they can make this work and it will be lots of fun for everyone.

"Daniel, I have to ask...are you sure she's going to say 'yes?'"

"No."

"What do you mean, no?"

"She's turned down three guys in the past decade. I'm sure I love her. She says she loves me, and we talk about a future together all of the time. I can only hope."

I'm worried for him...

"Do you have any guy friends who can support you that night?"

"None of them would want to do this, and if they were there, Ellie would know something was up."

"Okay. If we are going to make this a couple's event, let me ask my boyfriend, Will, if he can participate. We'll want at least one guy there who knows what's going on."

Will could use a little push in the romance department anyway, and this just might be the key!

❖❖❖

"Do you believe in one true, forever love?" Ellie Kerrigan asked her best friend, Sara.

"What do you mean?"

"I mean, do you think there is one and only one true love for everyone? Or is it possible to fall in love more than one time in your life?"

Sara pondered this as the two friends walked along Chic's Beach one evening. They often walked the sands of Chic's, solving world problems and problems of their own. Chic's was a quiet beach where the locals came to get away from the tourist part of Virginia Beach. Dogs ran freely in and out of the waves. Children were scattered about building sand castles and flying kites while their parents sat and enjoyed the sun.

"Are you asking this because of Daniel?" Sara inquired.

"Yes. I can feel that he's getting serious, and I know that he is a wonderful guy."

"And how do you feel about him?"

Ellie stopped and turned toward the water. "I think I'm in love with him."

"That's wonderful news, Ellie."

"Is it?"

For several days now Ellie had been thinking about her husband, Ben. They had met as sophomores at Old Dominion University in Norfolk and had instantly fallen for one another. From that point on they had been inseparable. Ellie had always been fascinated by words and language, so it had seemed natural to become a speech pathologist. She particularly enjoyed working with children. Ben had studied criminal justice and had gone to the police academy right out of college. As soon as Ben had been accepted into the Norfolk Police Department they'd married and settled into a small beach bungalow in Chic's. Their big plan had been to save a little money and then start their family.

But, that plan was not meant to be. One rainy night Ben was in a high-speed chase on Shore Drive. The driver of the car being chased lost control of his vehicle. Ben didn't have time to avoid the ensuing collision. There were no survivors.

Over the past fifteen years, with the help of good friends like Sara, Ellie had learned to move on with her life. Ellie had never wanted for a date. She had even reluctantly let three relationships get as far as proposals. But she had turned them all down. Even the one from one of Ben's friends from the force. None of the men were Ben. She knew that was unfair. How could anyone compete with a ghost? Now with Daniel, her allegiance with the ghost of Ben seemed to be fading. Ellie was still trying to decide if she was okay with that.

"Yes, Ellie, it is a good thing. It's time to let yourself have a life."

Ellie put her arm around her friend. "I need wine."

The next day found Ellie driving through the East Beach neighborhood. Part of her job was to make home visits with her clients. Seeing someone in their home gave her some clues on their lifestyle and support system, which was helpful in treating them. And the travel in between clients gave her time to detox and prepare for the next visit. It also gave her time to stop and get lunch at some yummy local restaurants.

Her client this morning was an elderly woman living with her son and daughter-in-law in East Beach. Ellie loved this neighborhood. She could picture herself rocking away an evening on one of the front porches. But, at that moment she was hungry. She remembered seeing a sandwich shop as she drove in and thought she would give it a try.

As she slowed her car down to park she looked in the window to see if it was crowded. What she saw was a familiar profile. Daniel! And he was sitting with a pretty blonde woman. They were leaning in to one another and appeared to be having a very serious conversation.

Ellie's heart sank. How could this be? Was he really seeing another woman? Maybe they were friends. Maybe they were more than friends, but it was none of her business. She jammed the car into second gear, popped the clutch, and sped on down the road. She wasn't hungry any more.

That evening Ellie found herself at Sara's house. There was always something going on there. Sara's husband was doing his best "airplane" imitation, trying to get their toddler to eat his dinner. The dog was trying to edge his way under the dinner table so he could poach the toddler's rejects. Ellie and Sarah were on the couch dissecting the day's events. The conversation ran the gamut from all men are evil to Ellie was just overreacting.

Finally, Sara said, "You know, El, Daniel's really a nice guy. Why don't you give him the benefit of the doubt?"

Just then Ellie's phone binged. It was a text from Daniel.
Hello, beautiful. I have a great idea for our date on Friday.

❖ ❖ ❖

Daniel could not remember ever having experienced this feeling of sweaty palms, weak knees, and a rolling stomach that seemed to have been invaded by construction men all trying to jackhammer their way out. Not even the flu or the worst hangover on record (after Liam's bachelor party three years ago) had left him feeling this way. He didn't like it, not one bit. He considered getting up and walking out while he could. But then he caught the instructor's eyes, smiling encouragement at him.

How had he let Lizzy encourage his crazy idea? And with a glass of wine, no less? He was a beer man, through and through. But the event wasn't called Van Gogh and Guinness, so he'd play along.

Ellie had texted she was running late. That was two vinos ago. He stepped up to the counter to order another cabernet. Out of the corner of his eye he saw the front door open. He turned his head, and there was Ellie. And she looked as if someone had pissed in her Cheerios that morning.

His gut told him the answer would be "no," and he hadn't even asked the question yet.

❖❖❖

Ellie walked into the sandwich company ready for combat. Her past few days had been long and her clients had been difficult. Now she had to face Daniel and the possibility that he had been seeing someone else. She had been shocked when he'd suggested they meet here. It took a lot of nerve for him to ask her to the same place where he'd met the other woman. In fact, the same pretty blonde was here, too!

Ellie scanned the restaurant and her gaze locked with Daniel's. She took a deep breath and wove her way through the tables covered with easels and paint palettes, finally stopping in front of Daniel. He stood to greet her and leaned down to give her a kiss.

"What's the matter, sweetheart? Did you have a bad day?"

"You could say that," Ellie said. "What's all of this?"

The blonde woman walked over to them. "Hi, I'm Lizzy. Welcome to Van Gogh and Vino."

"I'm Ellie. Van Gogh and Vino? Oh, it's a paint night. I've heard of these. It's nice to meet you. So you're the teacher for the class?"

"Well, I can't say the title should be teacher...it's more like rodeo cowgirl in that I just try to keep everyone corralled and focused. Once you incorporate alcohol into the mix you can't really call it teaching." Lizzy laughed as she finished the statement.

Ellie laughed, too, and started to wonder why Daniel would have been meeting with her at lunch. The green monster was still alive. "I used to paint a little when I was younger," Ellie said. "But those skills just never got honed. I really loved it and always wanted to be an artist."

"Oh, no worries there. This class is meant to be fun art, not fine art. Just relax and have some fun." Lizzy smiled as she walked away. But it seemed to Ellie that her smile was directed at Daniel.

Daniel handed Ellie the glass of cabernet he'd just picked up from the register. "Here, looks like you could use this. I'll go get myself another one."

Ellie settled in and sipped her wine as she looked around the restaurant. She realized she was staring at Lizzy, who was kissing the man who had just walked in the door. Wait, what was going on? Now Ellie was really confused.

The man pulled back from the kiss and his gaze met Ellie's. She nearly dropped her wine when she recognized him...Will Addison. He had worked with Ben on the force. And he had been the first man she had dated after Ben died. They had gotten serious quickly. But the relationship had ended after she'd turned down Will's proposal. She had always felt guilty about hurting him. He had gone to so much effort with the airplane and banner. They had tried to remain friends, but it just hadn't worked out.

Will whispered something in Lizzy's ear and then started walking toward Ellie. He reached her and bent down to kiss her cheek.

"Who's this?" Daniel interrupted the reunion, and by the look on his face the green-eyed monster was haunting him, too.

"Daniel, this is Will Addison. We used to date a long time ago. Will, this is Daniel Callahan. We're dating now." Ellie took an uncomfortable sip of wine. She forgot that she was angry and began to feel awkward instead. She remembered Sara telling her to give Daniel a chance.

❖❖❖

"Okay everybody, let's get started," Lizzy called out.

It was a small but fun crowd of ten people. Lizzy had asked Will along for moral support, and yet five other couples had shown, including Ellie and Daniel. The restaurant was warm and inviting, and everyone had had appetizers or sandwiches earlier and then settled into their seats for their painting night. The men were seated on one side of the long tables and the women opposite them. Their table easels were back to back so the couples could not see each other's paintings.

Lizzy thought it was very interesting that Will knew Ellie, but she couldn't focus on it as she had so much to prepare for before class began. She'd decided to seat Daniel and Ellie in the first row across from each other so that when the big moment arrived, everyone would be able to watch. Lizzy was painting both sides of the painting, two different canvases, and the class would follow her step by step. The women would copy the scene on the left and the guys would paint the image on the right. At the end of the evening, the couples would join their paintings side by side to create a diptych, or a two-part painting that goes together. It was going to be fun to compare the talents—or lack thereof. Lizzy reiterated, several times, that this was fun art, not fine art, in hopes there would be no competition among the couples. There were several couples that were ignoring this motto. They asked multiple, detailed questions throughout the demonstration, and teased each other as they painted.

Chatter and giggles filled the room. Everyone seemed to be enjoying the painting and wine drinking. Lizzy noticed Will seemed preoccupied. He had such a sad, dark face. And it seemed he kept staring at Ellie with a somber look.

It came time for the paintings to be finished and then

displayed, two by two, in a pair of golden frames Lizzy had situated on easels in the front of the room. She started at the opposite end of the table with Will. Lizzy removed the right hand demo painting and he came up and replaced it with his beach scene painting. She then pushed the two together to show how they continued the sunset beach image from one canvas to another.

"Will, you did a wonderful job!" Her compliment was sincere. The two paintings melded in style and textures. *A good sign for our future.* "Thanks for helping me out. Everyone, this is my boyfriend, Will, and this is his first time participating in Van Gogh and Vino. Let's give Will a bit of applause, please."

Will smiled and bowed ever so slightly and quickly removed his painting from the frame to return to his seat and a new glass of wine.

Lizzy watched as Will purposefully glanced at Ellie while she applauded. A storm cloud descended over his features. It was then she realized. Will must have been one of Ellie's three rejected proposals!

❖❖❖

Ellie had really enjoyed the night. She had relaxed after realizing Lizzy wasn't after Daniel. Seeing Will had been a little awkward, but he and Lizzy made a cute couple. Plus, she was ready to see how her painting looked when joined with Daniel's.

After seeing and applauding the efforts of the other couples, it was time for Daniel's and Ellie's paintings to be displayed. Ellie had just figured that, with all of Daniel's attention to her that evening, he must have just been reserving their seats for this event when she saw him with Lizzy earlier in the week. As they walked up to the stage, Lizzy stepped down to allow them to share the spotlight together. Ellie placed her painting in the frame while Daniel slowly placed his in the one on the right. They stepped back to look. There was a collective gasp from the group. Ellie looked, fully prepared to be embarrassed because one night Daniel had explained to her, with much laughter, that he had failed art class. Not just a slight fail, but an epic fail. She took a deep breath and prepared for the worst.

She glanced at Daniel's painting.

She didn't see a beach scene. Instead, she saw in big red letters, "Ellie, will you marry me? Love, Daniel," displayed beautifully in the gilded frame. Out of the corner of her eye, she saw him bend down on one knee and open a small box.

❖❖❖

What's it gonna be, Ellie? Yes or no? He dared to glance up for a hint of what she was thinking.

Her face softened as she reached to touch his cheek.

"Well?" he asked.

Ellie smiled. "That was so romantic, Daniel. I love you, too. And yes! I will marry you!" She pulled Daniel to his feet, hugged him tightly, and kissed his lips.

Their classmates applauded. Daniel looked over Ellie's head to a sea of smiling faces. He gave a thumbs up to Lizzy. "Thanks, everyone, for celebrating this moment with us. If you'd like to join us at my brother's bar across the street, the first round of Guinness is on me."

TAG! YOU'RE DEAD
BY MICHELLE DAVENPORT

There's nothing better than a weekend with your best friends. Especially when it's a three-day holiday and you are helping one of your best friends move into a great new neighborhood.

Everything had started out great. My best friends, Melinda, Adina, Rachel, and I had gathered at Melinda's new house in East Beach to help her unpack, watch movies, eat junk food, and consume adult beverages. What could be better, right?

With the four of us working together, the unpacking only took a day. Melinda then took us on a walking tour of her new neighborhood, so we could admire the beautiful homes and cozy ambiance of the area. East Beach had the feel of a small coastal village, and Melinda told me that was exactly what the community was going for. It worked. I admit I was a bit jealous of those lovely homes with the porches so close to the sidewalks. Everywhere I looked I saw neighbors walking their dogs and chatting with other neighbors. I must have stopped to pet at least a dozen adorable pooches along the way to East Beach Sandwich Company, where we enjoyed a quick bite to eat and a few drinks before heading back to Melinda's place.

When we finally did get back, we started a marathon of cheesy zombie movies and catching up. Well, I thought the movies were cheesy and said as much on numerous occasions, but my friends were fixated. They were completely into the zombie craze and huge fans of that *Walking Dead* show. I'd seen a season or two of it, but I was only watching it for the cute actor in it. I just didn't get the whole zombie craze. In fact, I wasn't much for scary stuff in general.

"Have you guys taken that online quiz?" Rachel asked.

I rolled my eyes. Rachel was always taking whatever quiz popped up on Facebook.

Melinda sent a wink my way, as if to say she completely understood my thoughts. "Which one?" she asked. Sometimes we were completely in sync with each other. I love that about her.

"The one about how long you would survive if there's a zombie apocalypse?" Rachel went on, oblivious to the faces Melinda and I were making.

"Oh!" Adina piped in. "I've taken that quiz. I didn't do so well." She shrugged slightly but quickly perked up. "Have you seen that there's a Zombie 5K going on next month? We should all enter that one!"

Melinda laughed and pointed at me. "You did say that the only way you'd ever run is if a zombie was chasing you."

I threw popcorn at her and stuck out my tongue as everyone laughed. Running was not something I thought of as fun. And yes, I had said that exact thing when they'd tried to get me to participate in a 5K before. I'd have to be more creative to get out of this "fun run."

❖❖❖

That's the last thing I remember before waking up on the beach. I had no idea where I was or where my friends were. I'll admit that I truly started to freak out, but then I took a deep calming breath and noticed how quiet it was. I could hear waves lapping at the shore. It was a soothing sound, but I heard nothing else. Was that normal? I glanced around and even though I didn't see anyone else, I felt like I was being watched. That creepy feeling was enough to get me moving.

Fortunately, I discovered the beach wasn't far from a paved road. That was a good start. My grandfather always said that as long as you could see paved roads and telephone wires, you weren't lost. I took that as a good sign.

I noted with relief that I was still in East Beach. The only reason I knew that was because Rachel had pointed out the East Beach clubhouse when we'd passed it the other day and I remembered the tower. Sadly, I had a terrible sense of direction and couldn't remember how to get to Melinda's place. Did I turn left on Pleasant Avenue? Or was it Coventry? How did I even get to that road? What road was I even on? I thought it was East Beach Drive, but I wasn't sure. I felt a hand on my shoulder and let out a strangled cry. I whirled around to find Adina staring at me like I was the only other person in the world.

"Geez, Adina!" I clutched my chest. "You nearly gave me a heart attack."

Adina squeezed me in a tight hug. Normally this wasn't an odd thing, but she was acting as if I was a long lost relative or something, and she was squeezing a bit too tightly for my comfort.

"I'm so glad you're okay!" She pulled away slightly to look me over. "You are okay, right?"

I shook my head. "Define okay. I'm a bit freaked out, but—" I narrowed my eyes at her. "Why wouldn't I be okay?"

Adina squirmed.

"What's going on here?" Pushing myself farther from Adina, I continued, "I don't remember going to the beach this evening. How'd I get there? And where is everyone?" Glancing up the street at the darkened homes, I tried to remember how colorful and cheerful the neighborhood had felt, but could not get past the eerie quiet and darkness that had settled over the area.

Adina gave a half-hearted chuckle. "You're messing with me, right?" She stared, as if waiting for me to admit I was joking with her. "Right?"

All I could do was shake my head. "No, I'm not. The last

thing I remember is the talk about the zombie 5K. What happened?"

Adina grabbed my hand and started to head up the street. I wrenched my hand away, forcing her to turn and glance nervously about. "I need answers, Dino!" I figured using her high school nickname would show her I was serious, and possibly even calm her down. That didn't seem to work.

"I'll explain on the way to Melinda's. Come on!"

I nearly fell over at the tug Adina gave my arm. This was not like Adina. She was the most docile one of our group. Something was definitely wrong.

❖❖❖

We walked for nearly two blocks in silence. I was losing patience and Adina's behavior was making me feel really on-edge when I had just started to calm down. Where were the other girls? Where were all the people and dogs from earlier today? And why did the neighborhood seem so dark and quiet? Why did I feel so creeped out?

Adina spoke excitedly as we walked. "One of Melinda's neighbors stopped by and invited us to a party on the beach this evening. We thought it sounded like a great way to meet new people and for Melinda to meet her new neighbors." Adina turned to me as if she could sense that I'd lost all of my patience. "We were having a great time when this person showed up, went nuts and attacked another guest." She held up her hand when I gasped. "It gets stranger! He was biting him!"

"You're kidding me! No one goes around biting people." I shook my head in disbelief.

"No, seriously! And pretty soon the people he bit..." Adina bit her lip and gave me an odd look.

"Well?" I tried to hurry the story along. Adina liked drama and I figured she was playing this up because she noticed I was unnerved.

"They started acting weird." She looked everywhere but at me. "They started attacking the other partygoers. I think—" She shuddered slightly. "I think they became zombies."

I threw my hands in the air. "Really! This zombie thing has gone too far. Stop messing with me and just tell me what really happened, Adina."

Before Adina could answer, a rustling came from the bushes to the right of us and a person lurched into view. I moved toward the person to offer help, but Adina grabbed my arm to stop me.

"Zombie," she whispered.

I shook my head in disgust at what I thought was Adina playing things up. Then the person started staggering toward us. That's when I knew Adina hadn't been overly dramatic or trying to put one over on me. The person ambling toward us was white as a sheet, a very hungry look in his eyes. And I don't mean he was looking for a love connection.

I don't think I screamed, but cannot swear that I didn't. I did grab Adina's hand and started to run like my life depended on it. And in that moment, I'm pretty sure it did.

❖ ❖ ❖

After a few blind turns, we slowed to catch our breath. "What the…" I said before I stopped to pant, not being able to finish the thought. I looked to Adina, hoping she'd have an explanation, and thinking that I definitely needed to get in better shape. I shouldn't be out of breath after running only a few blocks. I silently promised myself to start going to the gym tomorrow. That is if I made it to tomorrow.

"I told you. Zombies!"

I could only shake my head at Adina. I was not yet ready to declare this the zombie apocalypse.

"We need to call for help." I patted myself down in search of my cell phone. "Do you have your cell on you?" Adina shook her head. "Why don't we have our cell phones? We always carry our cell phones!" I could hear the hysteria creeping into my voice and made myself take another deep breath. I was not going to freak out. Adina would never let me live it down.

"Rachel said we should leave them at Melinda's because

you and I," she said, pointing to me and then herself, "are on our phones way too much and this was a chance to meet people."

I nodded. That sounded like something Rachel would say. I did tend to spend too much time on my phone. "So, what's the plan?"

"Plan?" Adina looked at me like I'd lost my mind. "I thought you'd have a plan. I'm just happy to have found someone who doesn't want to munch on me like I'm a snack or something. You're the one who comes up with the plans. I just follow along. That's how it's always worked. You lead and the rest of us follow."

I glowered, but I doubted she could see my expression, since it was quite dark. "Okay," I hedged. I didn't believe that statement but wasn't about to start an argument over it. "We need to get back to Melinda's place. From there we can call for help and barricade ourselves inside until help arrives."

"Great!" Adina looked around. "So which way do we go?"

I groaned, only to hear multiple moans echo back in reply. My head snapped up as the moans continued and seemed to be coming closer. Grabbing Adina's hand, I ran. The fight or flight reflex kicked in. And, being a big old chicken, flight was the correct answer.

Adina suddenly became helpful, telling me when to turn. It didn't stop me from running into another person. We went down in a tangle of arms and legs. I'm sure my language was foul enough to make a sailor blush, but I think under the circumstances it was allowed.

"Mindy!" Adina cried in relief. She threw her arms around Melinda and I thought she was going to strangle her.

Melinda may have thought the same thing as she gently pushed Adina away. "What on earth is going on?"

Adina and I stared at her, unable to truly process her question. She didn't look like she'd been running for her life. She looked as fresh as a daisy. It kinda ticked me off. I mean, here I was running in fear for my life and looking like it. I was sweaty and I felt nasty. Not a good look.

"Are you kidding me?" I nearly screamed. I had enough sense to realize I didn't want to draw the attention of those people we had run from. I still couldn't bring myself to call them zombies, not yet anyway.

"What?" Melinda looked from Adina to me. "I got chilly, so I went back home to get a sweater. When I got to the beach, everyone was gone and the place looked trashed, so I decided to go back to the house. What happened to you two?"

Adina glanced around before whispering, "Zombies."

Melinda chuckled but stopped when she saw I wasn't smirking. "Seriously?"

"I don't know if it's zombies, but something bad is going down." I felt horrible that I couldn't reassure her, but brightened slightly at a new thought. "Do you have your cell phone on you?"

Melinda shook her head. "No, we promised not to. Remember?"

My shoulders fell.

"Missy can't remember anything since our talk about the Zombie 5K." Adina chose that moment to be helpful.

"Really?" Melinda asked. I could tell that Melinda thought Adina had finally lost her mind.

I shot Adina a look that promised retribution, not that she was paying any attention to me or my face. "Yeah. No clue how I got to the beach or what happened."

"Holy cow!" Melinda turned to Adina. "So, what did happen?"

"You wouldn't believe it, Mindy! It was zombies!" Adina's voice crept higher and louder as she warmed to the topic. "A guy came to the party and started biting people." Adina took a deep breath, only to be interrupted by several moans that seemed to be coming closer.

We all looked around, panicked. "We need to move!" Adina pushed Melinda and ran in front of us. Out of all of us, Adina was in the best shape and I momentarily hated her for that, but the safety of Melinda's house spurred me on.

We ran across an open area and as I looked around, I

pictured how beautiful this place must be during the day. I imagined art festivals, children playing, family picnics. I think my mind was trying to find a happy place instead of focusing on the current situation. It was how I dealt with stress. Think of something else. Anything else. And right now I did not want to think about zombies.

"Melinda, we gotta get back to your place," Adina shouted as we ran in what I hoped was the right direction. "We'll call for help from there."

She said it like she was the one who'd come up with the plan, which normally would have ticked me off, but I was too busy trying not to throw up. I focused on trying to keep pace with them and didn't notice anyone lurking in the shadows until it was too late. I tripped over Adina as she was tackled. I heard Adina scream just as Melinda pulled me to my feet.

"Run!" Melinda screamed as she pulled me along. I glanced over my shoulder and really wished I hadn't. Adina lay on the ground, struggling with four people who seemed to be pulling at her. And one of them had red hair that was very familiar to me.

"Melinda, that was Rachel." I stumbled, but Melinda pulled me up and kept running. "Rachel attacked Adina. Why would she do that?"

"We can't think about that now, Missy." Melinda kept a blank face as we ran.

My jaw dropped. "Oh, my gawd! She's a zombie!" That's right. I could finally call them that as I witnessed one friend attack another. Tonight was not my night.

The closer we got to Melinda's house the more moans and shuffling we heard. I refused to look back for fear of what I would see. Turns out I was right not to do that. I swear I'm not normally a clumsy person, but as freaked out as I was I didn't have an iota of gracefulness in me.

"Run, Mindy!" I screamed as she scrambled up her front steps and headed for the front door. I tripped on the last step as Melinda fumbled with the doorknob. "Open it!"

"I'm trying!" Mindy fumbled with the door some more.

"It's locked." She frantically pulled on the doorknob.
I swear my friends and I are smart, but fear really does a number on you. Especially if you think you're going to die.
"Use your key!"
Melinda frantically searched her pockets. "I don't have it," she sobbed. That's when I saw her go completely still and the blood seemed to drain from her face. She looked around, as if for an exit or hiding place.
"What..." I didn't even manage to finish my question when I felt a hand clamp on my ankle and pull me backwards. I screamed like a banshee as I was dragged down the stairs. I screwed up my eyes knowing that this was the end for me. All my regrets flashed through my mind. Like, why hadn't I bought those shoes that I thought were so cute last week? Or told my last boss what a jerk he really is? And why wasn't I fighting back?
That's when I noticed the hand was no longer on my ankle and I wasn't moving. I cracked an eye open to see what was going on, and saw a pale face grinning in front of me.
"Tag. You're dead," came a soft voice. This was not the voice of a zombie. I don't think zombies can actually talk.
"What?" I looked around in confusion, only to see a number of zombies grinning at me and my three best friends doubled over laughing. I was offered a hand up and tentatively took it. "What's going on?" I looked around, hoping someone would answer me. I knew it wouldn't be my supposed friends, as they were laughing too hard.
"Didn't Melinda tell you?" asked the zombie, who helped me to my feet. This is when I got a really good look at him and discovered he was pretty cute under all that white makeup. All I could do was shake my head and wish that I looked a little more presentable. He glanced in Melinda's direction and she stopped laughing.
As Melinda headed toward me, someone sounded an air horn twice and slowly porch lights started coming on one by one. As the darkness receded and the zombies started socializing, the creepy vibe I felt earlier disappeared.

"I'm so sorry, Missy." Melinda reached for my hand, but I wasn't feeling very friendly toward her so she dropped her hand back to her side. "The community had posted a flyer for a game of Zombie Tag and we decided to try it out this weekend. I thought it would be really fun for all of us. But the way you were trashing the zombie movies and claiming how people wouldn't react the way they did, made me, well it made me want to see if you would react that way. So I didn't tell you and well, you know the rest."

My jaw dropped. "You what?" I couldn't believe my supposed friends would put me through that. I'd thought two of my friends were dead and now they were just a few feet away. That's when it all clicked into place for me. I knew exactly how they'd pulled it off. Tequila. I tended to get extremely sleepy when I drank too much tequila. That also explained why they kept bringing me drinks all afternoon. They'd sweetened them up so I wouldn't notice what was in them. I was betting that after I nodded off they took me to the beach and just waited for me to wake up. It didn't take much tequila to make me sleepy and my naps were really short. Needless to say, this really ticked me off. Rachel and Adina had stopped laughing. And I think they were starting to feel pretty guilty.

Rachel started toward me, pulling Adina along. "We didn't mean to scare you so badly."

"It was all in fun," Adina added quietly.

"Fun?" The tone of my voice must have freaked them out, as they both took a step back. "Did it look like I was having fun?"

Just then the cute zombie touched my arm. "You look like you could use something to drink. One of the couples just a few houses down is opening up their house for a get-together. Would you care to join me? We are honestly a fun bunch."

I smiled back at him. I mean, how many neighborhoods do you know of that could pull something like this off? Maybe this evening wasn't a total bust after all. "I'd love to." I took his arm and shot a look over my shoulder at my friends.

I'll probably look back on this night and laugh at myself,

but not right now.

"You don't think she's really mad at us, do you?" I heard Rachel ask as she watched me walk off without them.

"Nah," Melinda said as she hurried to catch up to us. "Missy never holds a grudge."

I smirked at that comment. Oh, I would forgive them, but I wasn't about to forget this little episode any time soon. And I would definitely be getting them back.

But that's a story for another time.

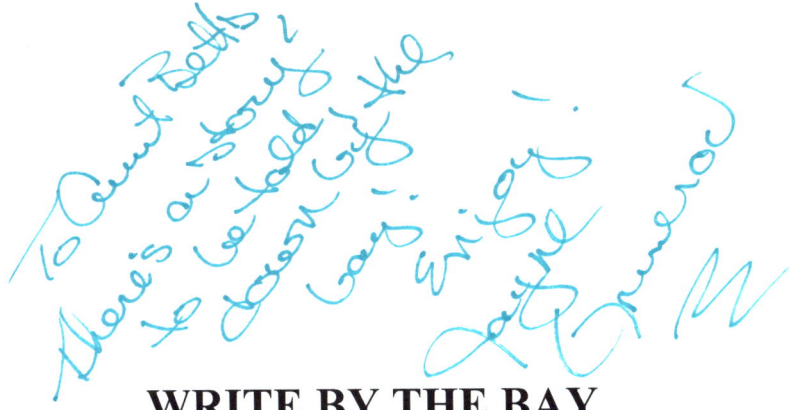

WRITE BY THE BAY
By Jayne Ormerod

"Cassie, I need your help." My landlady, Mrs. Williamson, stood on her small but meticulously landscaped back patio, wringing her hands in that nervous way she had. I lived in the carriage house apartment over her detached two-car garage, but it was a rare occasion when we crossed paths.

"What's wrong?" I'd just come back from a run along the shores of the Chesapeake Bay. I'd run extra distance and extra hard as I'd mentally worked out a tricky plot twist for the latest cozy mystery I was writing. *Write by the Bay.* Yep, that's me, Cassandra M. Hanover, author of thirteen Life's a Beach mysteries, which have brought me a modicum of fame but little fortune. You've (hopefully) seen my website, blog, Facebook page, Twitter handle, or license plate.

But right now I was sweaty, stinky, and wanted nothing more than a cool shower and a glass of chilled chardonnay—not necessarily in that order—before setting my fingers to keyboard and getting my current musings down on paper.

A chat with my sometimes-scatterbrained landlady was not on the agenda.

"My diamond and sapphire necklace is missing," she said.

Mrs. Williamson was always reporting something missing. Usually her reading glasses, which were invariably perched atop her dyed blonde curls, or her car keys, often found dangling from the ignition of her Volvo XC90. One time I'd discovered them with the car still running, and she'd been home from the Food Lion three hours by the time we'd begun our search.

I wasn't the least bit worried about the misplaced necklace. We'd find it. Chances were, someplace obvious. Speaking of which...I dropped my gaze to her neckline. Nope, no sign of the treasured jewelry. That would have been too easy.

"I think it's been stolen." Mrs. Williamson sank onto the wicker chair as if the mere thought was too much for her to bear.

"I'm sure it's just been misplaced," I said. If I were a betting woman, which I'm not, I'd lay odds we'd find it in her freezer under a Gladware bowl of last Christmas's leftover turkey gravy. That's where she hides her rubies and pearls. Calls them her "frozen assets." She'd read in a woman's magazine that thieves never think to look in the freezer for valuables. Any bandit who'd read that article looked there, and I'd told her on more than one occasion that the necklace—a gift to her great-great-grandmother from a crowned European prince—belonged in a safe-deposit box. But did she listen? Nope.

"When did you last see it?" I asked.

"About an hour ago. I took it out to show it to the girls."

"The girls?"

"My granddaughter and two grand-nieces are here."

It was news to me that Mrs. Williamson had any family. Although I'd been her tenant for six months, she'd never mentioned any relatives, near or far. Her husband had died three years ago, after forty-two years of marriage. Somehow I'd gotten the feeling she was the last of the line. I guess I was wrong.

Mrs. Williamson rubbed her eyes with the tips of her fingers, another indication of her frazzled state of mind. After a few good scrubs, she stopped, hands still resting on her cheeks, and looked at me. "I invited them over today to discuss which of them would inherit the necklace. I took it out of the freezer and placed it on my nightstand while we enjoyed some refreshments and chatted a bit. It's been over a year since we were all together. When I went to show them, I discovered it was missing." She dropped her hands to her lap and let her shoulders droop, reminding me of a deflated balloon. She drew a deep, quivery breath then said, "I've looked everywhere. I just know it's gone forever."

"Come with me," I said, taking the woman by the hand, tugging her up off the chair and herding her toward her back door. "We're calling the police."

"No, you don't understand," she said, pulling away. The first tear appeared on her cheek and she brushed it away with the back of her hand. She dipped her head and softly whispered, "I have a feeling one of the girls took it."

It went unspoken that she didn't want the Williamson address printed in the weekly crime statistics, or for it to get around the neighborhood that one of her relatives was a thief. In a tight-knit neighborhood such as East Beach, appearances were very important, especially for Mrs. Williamson.

"You're so very clever, writing those mystery novels," she said, laying her hand on my arm. "I want you to find out what you can. And I trust you to keep this our little secret."

I wasn't sure if that was a request, or a threat.

❖❖❖

Mrs. Williamson led me to her living room, which was filled with sunlight and offered breath-taking views of the Chesapeake Bay. I'd joined my landlady a few times for cocktails (the woman made a mean basil martini!) during my brief tenancy. A girl could dream, and every time I walked into this room I fantasized maybe someday, if I sold about two million more of my cozy mysteries, I'd be able to move to a Grand House on the Water instead of renting out a 500-square-foot carriage house over the garage.

Three women stood near the window, talking and sipping Mrs. Williamson's signature basil martinis, a slurpee-like drink made with muddled basil, tangy lime juice and vodka. Lots and lots of vodka.

Discarded glass plates and linen napkins lay on the coffee table. I'm not a detective (I only play one in the books I write), but based on the shrimp tails and half-eaten mini quiches left on the plates, I deduced that while Mrs. Williamson had fished her jewels out of her freezer she had grabbed the first boxes of wholesale food items she'd found there. A gourmet chef she was not.

"Girls," Mrs. Williamson said, "I'd like you to meet my new tenant, Cassie Hanover."

The ladies turned to greet me.

Mrs. Williamson introduced them one at a time. "This is my sister's granddaughter, Amy Sullivan," she said. If Amy were a character in one of my books, I would describe her as follows: a thirty-something mousy woman with thin brown hair pulled into a ponytail. She wore a mauve-toned sweater set, black capris, and ballet slippers. No makeup, no jewelry. Her smile seemed forced, her nod of acknowledgement barely discernable. I would cast her in the role of small-town librarian. But looks can be deceiving, and it would be ever so much more interesting if she were a pole dancer down at the Cheetah's Men's Club.

"This is Janet Mallardi, my brother's granddaughter," Mrs. Williamson said.

I'd slap an "Aging Starlet" label on Janet and call it a day. She was a tall, fiftyish woman dressed in a black-and-white designer outfit. Her blonde hair was piled in an elegant chignon and her extreme makeup seemed more suitable for an appearance on stage than a day at the beach. Diamonds dripped from her wrists, fingers, and ears. All that for a snack of mini-quiches and frozen shrimp with her Great-Aunt Martha? Something fishy about that.

"Nice to meet you," she said, holding out her long-fingered, exquisitely-manicured hand to me.

"Nice to meet you, as well." Her handshake was as fishy as her overdressed state.

"And this is Staci, my granddaughter," Mrs. Williamson said. "Pardon her appearance. She's just returning from a dip in the bay."

Mrs. Williamson's statement was redundant, since Staci sported a jewel-toned beach cover-up from which stretched long, tanned legs. I noticed her flip-flops were designer, as were the sunglasses perched atop her curly red hair. She sent off a 1960s Bond-Girl vibe. I half expected her to light up a long cigarette and blow smoke circles toward the ceiling.

Staci gave me the once-over, then asked, "She's not some long-lost offspring who also has claim to the necklace, is she?"

"Cassie is not in any way related to you," Mrs. Williamson said, her back up a little bit, as if the mere suggestion of an illegitimate child in their lineage was offensive. "But right now nobody is going to get the necklace because it's been stolen!"

Amy, the librarian/pole dancer, gasped. "When?"

"This afternoon," Mrs. Williamson said, her voice full of despair as she collapsed back onto an exquisite, white wing-backed chair.

"Aha!" Staci said. "I saw a couple of young thugs running across the common area in front of the house when I was coming back from the beach. They looked very suspicious, wearing dark sweatshirts and heavy jeans. I bet they snatched the necklace. I'm going to call the police. Don't worry, Grandma. We'll have it back before sundown. Where's my phone? Damn, it's in the car." Staci raced out of the room, her flip-flops slip-slapping as she left.

Mrs. Williamson struggled out of the chair, then raced off in pursuit of Staci, begging her not to call just yet.

Janet and Amy exchanged puzzled glances, then turned toward the window, whispering amongst themselves.

I felt sufficiently dismissed and turned to admire the artwork hanging on the wall. While trying to decide if the Picasso-style beach scene "spoke" to me, my thoughts turned to the missing necklace. Mrs. Williamson felt certain one of the girls had taken it. I channeled my inner fictional detective, and that got me to wondering if the necklace truly had been stolen or just mislaid. Especially considering Mrs. Williamson's penchant for losing things. There was only one way to find out.

I wandered off to take a peek at the scene of the crime. I'd been tasked with taking care of Mrs. Williamson's two cats, Uncle Fester and Sneaky Pete, one weekend. They liked to hide from me, so every time I visited I had to get eyes-on to be sure they hadn't escaped, as Mrs. Williamson warned me they are wont to do. So I'd been in the house and knew the lay of the land. One of the many, many, many things I loved about the floor plan was the first floor master, also offering magnificent views of the bay. Since that was the last place Mrs. Williamson had seen the necklace, it seemed the most logical place to begin the search.

Decorated in a soft color pallet inspired by the sea, this was absolutely my dream room. The door was open, so I walked right in. After all, Mrs. Williamson had asked me to help locate the necklace.

I approached the off-white chalk-painted nightstand, but there was nothing to see. Not a lamp or a book or even a speck of dust. I got down on my hands and knees and peered under the bed. Other than a few grains of sand—which is all part and parcel of a beach lifestyle—the space was clean. I ran my hand under the low-set nightstand into the places that bugs go to die, bracing myself for the worst. My hand brushed across something and I yanked it back. I maneuvered myself into a reverse supine twist yoga pose to try to see what was under there. The shape was not a small, dead mouse silhouette, as I had feared, but large and possibly jewelry shaped. I reached all the way back, grabbed it and pulled it out.

I held in my hand the missing diamond and sapphire necklace. Now that I got a good look at it, I had to admit, it was stunning. Two dozen sparkling sapphires, each surrounded by two circles of glittering diamonds, were clipped side by side to form a choker that was nothing short of magnificent.

"Found it," I called as I returned to the living room.

The girls and Mrs. Williamson gathered round, oohing and ahhing over the exquisite piece of jewelry. Everyone was relieved that it had not been stolen.

We toasted with a round of basil martinis. Shortly thereafter, I made my excuses and climbed the stairs to my carriage house for a much needed shower.

An hour later, as I curled up with a glass of chilled chardonnay and my laptop, I felt relieved the crisis had been averted. I typed up some notes, thinking I could use the storyline in a future novel, but the only way it would work was if I added conflict. A lot more of it. A huge heapin' dose of it. Maybe I could—

Before I could finish that thought there came a loud banging on my door. I answered it to find Mrs. Williamson standing on the landing. The antique jeweled necklace gifted from a crowned European prince dangled from her finger.

"Cassie, this necklace you found is a fake."

❖❖❖

Detective Walt Oliver taught me everything I needed to know about paste jewelry but had never been interested enough to ask. Come to find out, paste stones—so named because of the way it looks like pasta when being made—is simply high lead content glass which is ground with silica and set in a foil backing. Once polished, it shimmers like the real thing, maybe more. Its popularity from the 1700s through the 1940s had to do with its flexibility in design; you could make it any shape you wanted, whereas diamonds required you to work the jewelry around the cut of the stone. But the fake stuff also made it affordable to the middle class. Suddenly everyone and their sister was sporting sparkly bling.

Care of paste jewelry requires it not get wet. The problem arose when Mrs. Williamson had knocked the dregs of her basil martini over and it splashed onto the necklace. She did what any goodly woman would do and had rushed to the sink to wash off the stickiness. When the foil back of one of the jewels fell off, Mrs. Williamson realized something was wrong. She made a quick phone call to her jeweler in New York City, who had explained that's what happens to the fake stuff.

At some point, someone had switched the fake for the real. The questions now were, who and when?

"I don't know, Mrs. Williamson," Detective Oliver replied when asked his theory. "The art of making paste stones died out about the 1940s. It's now valuable for historic significance and rarity because it doesn't last forever like the real thing, but the value isn't close to what diamonds and sapphires in a white-gold setting would fetch. This necklace, before it disintegrated, would have probably been worth about five hundred bucks."

In other words, Detective Oliver suspected they had been fake since the prince had given them to Mrs. Williamson's great-great-grandmother in 1902.

To say Mrs. Williamson was heartbroken was an understatement. She slumped back in the white chair, put her arm over her eyes, and dismissed us with a wave of her hand.

The detective and I made for the door, but a thought occurred to me. I stopped and turned toward the living room. "Mrs. Williamson, did you ever have the necklace appraised, for insurance purposes maybe?"

There was silence for a brief moment before she popped up from the chair and looked at us. "I did. Right after my husband died. It was valued at over a million dollars." She paused for a brief moment, as the dots connected in her mind. "The jeweler would have told me then if it had been a fake, right?"

Detective Oliver and I returned to our seats.

Mrs. Williamson set her gaze on me as she resumed her hand wringing, this time at a frenetic pace. "Cassie, remember Staci said she saw someone running in front of the house when she came back from the beach this afternoon? I bet they stole it."

I shook my head. "Staci said they looked like teens, and why would they go to the trouble of replacing the real necklace with a fake one? That doesn't make sense. Those kind of thieves would have scooped up everything of value and hightailed it to the nearest pawn shop."

Detective Oliver agreed.

So if we could figure out when the fake necklace had been substituted for the real one, we'd have our thief. Mrs. Williamson had had it valued three years ago, so anytime between then and today. The suspect pool included everyone who had ever been in her house in that time, and anyone who may have snuck in while she was away. In other words, a whole lotta people.

The way I figured it, the chances of Detective Oliver solving this case were slim to none.

On second thought, forget the slim part, there was no chance at all Mrs. Williamson would ever see her necklace again.

❖❖❖

Dusk settled on our beach community as I made my way from the Grand House to my small living space above Mrs. Williamson's two-car garage. The wind had picked up and I could hear the waves crashing against the breakwater from the other side of the dunes that buttressed Mrs. Williamson's property. The briny scent of the bay usually calmed me, but not tonight. I shivered, despite the seventy-three degree temperature, and scurried up the stairs to my accommodations.

I fixed a plate of nachos, heavy on the jalapeños, then went into mystery-writer mode and began formulating a list of suspects.

Each of the three cousins had opportunity to switch the heirloom necklace. Mrs. Williamson admitted to having shown it to the girls many times over the years, promising them someday it would be theirs. *One* of theirs.

The demurely dressed Amy didn't seem like the type who would ever have occasion to wear a jeweled necklace, but she might benefit from selling it.

The overdressed Janet appeared to have plenty of money at her disposal, but there were some things—like heirloom necklaces with familial ties to a crowned European prince—

that money couldn't buy.

Bond-girl Staci might feel entitled to it since her mother owned it, but would she go so far as to steal it to keep it out of the hands of her cousins?

All three had possible motives, and all three had access to the property—and the freezer—over the years. The thing is, would they have gone to all the trouble to have a paste substitute made? Especially one of such high a quality that even Mrs. Williamson didn't notice the switch.

A thought popped into my mind and I pushed it aside. But it kept tap-tap-tapping at my consciousness until I brought it out and examined it, and I didn't like the path my thoughts were taking. Not one bit. But if I were to be honest, Mrs. Williamson should be on the short list of suspects. It appeared to me she might be experiencing cash-flow problems or she wouldn't have rented out her carriage house apartment to me, a total stranger, after it had sat empty for five years. Could she be trying to pull the old fake-theft insurance scam? Oh, lordy, I couldn't imagine that dear sweet lady with a propensity for hand wringing doing anything illegal.

I pushed the thoughts away and forced myself to look at things from another angle. There must be someone else. There had to be. Anyone but Mrs. Williamson and her family. Think! Think!

And then another thought popped into my head. What had the relationship been between the prince and the great-great-grandmother? Serious enough that she received a very expensive diamond and sapphire necklace. So just what had great-great-grandma done to earn such a valuable gift? Could there be a long-lost heir? One who felt the jewels should have been kept in the bloodline? Inquiring minds wanted to know.

After pouring myself a goblet of Flip Flop Chardonnay, I grabbed my computer and googled the gift-giving prince. Interesting guy. He'd been labeled "a rogue," what we call "players" nowadays, and not inclined to settle down as the king and queen had decreed. He was famous for bestowing family heirlooms upon his current ladyloves, giving away a dozen of them in a ten-year span.

Sadly, he never did make it to king, having died in a horrible carriage accident at the age of twenty-nine. The article hinted at foul play, but no mention of any heirs, legal or otherwise. That didn't mean they didn't exist, though.

When I hit a wall while writing, I turned my attention elsewhere and let my subconscious process the scenarios. Maybe it would work for this puzzle.

I flopped onto my futon and clicked over to the Hallmark Movie and Mystery channel, to lose myself in the fictional crime-solving world. But something Mrs. Williamson had said about wearing the necklace to the New York Philharmonic when she and her husband had lived in the city nagged at me. After twenty minutes of staring at the television screen without absorbing what was going on, I reached for my laptop and flipped through the New York City society page archives. Sure enough, I found a much younger Mrs. Williamson wearing the stunning necklace. I zoomed in, and had to admit the fake I saw today looked identical to the real one of twenty-two years ago.

Many people had seen the necklace in person, and just about everyone in the world with Internet access could have viewed the online image. And any one of them could have concocted the plan to have a reasonable facsimile made and switch the two. And it seemed like a sure-fire scam. For a $500 investment in a paste necklace you could parlay that into a million dollars. That's a really good rate of return.

Heck, I might have done it myself, had I thought of it.

❖ ❖ ❖

With so many thoughts running through my head, I knew sleep would be impossible. I needed someone to talk to, and the only person I knew who might possibly still be up at 10:47 on a Sunday evening was Lauren Nelson. She was a free spirit by every definition. We'd met in fourth grade as we'd sat on the bench outside Principal Baxter's office. My teacher had caught me with the latest Nancy Drew tucked inside my math book. (The intrepid girl detective's adventures were ever so much more interesting than multiplication tables.) Lauren was there because she'd socked a boy who'd dared to pull her ponytail. We'd remained friends through school, but our paths had drifted apart after graduation. She'd had a trust fund begging to be spent while I had gone off to Virginia Commonwealth University to earn a business degree, waitressing at Applebee's while doing so. Neither of us had had time for maintaining a long-distance friendship.

Lauren had run through her never-have-to-work-a-day-in-her-life inheritance in less than seven years. This summer found her living—rent free—aboard her father's 32-foot sailboat docked at the Bay Point Marina at the south end of East Beach. So after years with oceans separating us, we ended up only four-and-a-half blocks apart.

I sent a quick text: **R U awake?**
Yup. What's up?
Need to chat. Heading your way.
Will have Riunite on ice.

A running joke between us, I replied, **That's nice.**

Not bothering to change out of my yoga pants and hooded sweatshirt, I arrived at the marina in ten minutes. Six floating docks were home to over a hundred boats of all shapes, sizes, types, and conditions. Some didn't even look seaworthy, but they still floated. *A metaphor for how some people went through life.*

Lauren's father's boat was at the far end of A-dock. I trip-tropped down the pier. The sound of my sandals slapping against the wood was swallowed up in the halyard-against-mast cacophony conducted by the strong breeze.

Movement on the deck of a large trawler caught my eye. A woman dressed in a gauzy beach cover-up danced, arms out to her sides as she twirled and dipped. Not quite *Dancing with the Stars* level, but still a lovely, albeit a lonely, waltz.

At that moment, moonlight caught her face as she twirled my way. The face…OH MY GAWD! It was Mrs. Williamson's granddaughter Staci, and she was wearing the heirloom necklace!

I knew for a fact that the fake necklace was in the hands of the police. So either Staci was wearing another fake—but really what were the odds of that?—or she was wearing the real thing.

I ducked behind a large dock box and leaned my back against it as the puzzle pieces snapped into place with satisfying clicks.

Staci certainly had had opportunity to swap necklaces. Mrs. Williamson's parting words to Staci this afternoon had been, "Don't forget the key on the table. I had the locks changed last week and the key you have won't work anymore." *Click.*

Staci had been defensive, and dare I say proprietary, when she thought I might be a rival in the necklace lottery. *Click.*

Staci had been the one to spot hooded youths running across the common green space in front of Mrs. Williamson's house. She said they'd been wearing dark clothes and heavy sweatshirts. It had been 87 degrees out this afternoon. Nobody wears a dark hooded sweatshirt in 87-degree weather, not even thieves. Seems to me Staci had been lying, perhaps to throw suspicion away from her and on to them. *Click.*

Staci had just returned from the beach and had sand on her feet. And there had been sand under the bed while the rest of the room had been spotless. Had she gone in there to swap the real for the fake? *Click.*

I slipped my phone from my pocket with the intent to send a text to Detective Oliver. Or should I call 9-1-1? Both, I decided, but not from here. I stood to sneak down the dock toward land, where I could sound the alarm and yet keep an eye on Staci, but I didn't get far. My toe caught on a cleat and I went down with a clunk and a yelp. Crap. Had Staci heard me?

"Who's there?" Staci called out.

I didn't want to confront her without benefit of police backup, so I hoped she would dismiss the noise as coming from a feral cat. Curling up in a tight ball, I played possum. It was very dark out, so if I stayed still maybe she would think I was a discarded tarp or something.

Footsteps approached then stopped within inches from my head. Her toe poked my arm. "Who are you and why were you spying on me?"

I looked up.

Staci gasped. "You!" Her heel smashed into my thigh. Hard. Then she stomped on my head. It smacked against the pier. *Holy crap!* Pain shot from the side of my head down my neck.

I scrambled to my feet as my flight instinct warred with my fight side, facing Staci to assess my success with either option.

Staci, her face contorted with rage and hatred, took menacing steps in my direction.

Get out of here! the little voice of reason in my head screamed. But before I could turn tail and run, Staci's shoulder slammed into my gut, sending me sprawling into Pretty Lake inlet.

I resurfaced, spitting nasty water out of my mouth and yelling as if my life depended on it. Which it did, because I was not a strong swimmer, especially dressed in a heavy hooded sweatshirt. "Help! Help! Someone help me!"

A metal pole appeared, a lifeline, with Staci holding the end. I grabbed it.

But instead of pulling me in, the pole pushed down, and I went along with it.

What the hell?

I let go, but before I could swim away the pole caught me in the small of my back and pushed me under.

Oh, my God. Staci is trying to drown me.

I twisted away and resurfaced, gasping for air.

SMACK! The pole hit me on top of my head. *Damn, that hurts!* Again and again she hit me, each time landing a blow that had me cussing.

I managed to grab the pole and a tug of war ensued. Staci had leverage on the dock, while I had nothing but cold, deep water beneath my feet.

"Help!" I yelled again and again and again, each plea

weaker than the last. My lungs burned and my muscles ached, fighting to keep my head above water while Staci tried to send me under.

Why hadn't anyone heard me?

Just then the fight went out of the pole and I had it in the water with me. I tucked it under my armpits and used it as a floatation device as I kicked away from the dock and toward the channel.

I didn't need to dip into my adrenaline reserves, because help had arrived.

"Hey, you, in the water. You okay?"

I looked up and saw Staci trapped in a headlock. By Lauren.

"Lauren, you angel!" I called. "You saved my life!"

"Cassie, is that you?"

"Yes, it's me!"

"What's going on?"

By now I noticed other boat people had arrived to see what all the commotion was about.

"I'll explain later," I yelled. "First you need to call the police. Staci is wearing a stolen necklace worth a million dollars, and she just tried to kill me."

❖❖❖

It would be three days before Lauren and I had opportunity to crack open the Riunite and pour it over crackling ice. Detective Walt Oliver joined us, off duty, of course (the romantic spark between Lauren and the detective was obvious to everyone...except them...) and he had a lot of information to share.

"Staci found the paste duplicate for sale on an antiques website," Walt told us, "The royal families often had paste copies made of the family jewels, and this one had recently been discovered and come on the market. Staci recognized it as an exact match to her grandmother's and hatched a plan to switch out the fake for the real one stored in the freezer. She didn't think her grandmother would ever be the wiser."

"Motive?" Lauren asked.

"I think I know," I said. Walt nodded for me to continue. "I googled Staci Williamson and found she'd been arrested for cocaine possession with intent to sell, and had done some hard time. Tough to get back on your financial feet with a felony conviction, so she pulled the old swindle-the-addle-brained-grandmother trick. And almost got away with it."

"Got it in one," Walt said. "And while I can't comment on an open case, let's just say she's made a lot of trips south on that boat of hers."

"She's trafficking?" I asked.

"Big time," Walt replied. "And thanks to you, we got all the evidence we need, once we got a search warrant for her boat."

I sat back in my seat and let my mind wrap around that tidbit of information. Mrs. Williamson had been worried one of the three women might be a thief. A granddaughter trafficking narcotics might send the dear old woman into an apoplectic fit.

Walt rested his arms on the table and leaned in. "Something's bugging me. How did you figure out Staci had made the switch that afternoon?"

I smiled. "Sand."

The puzzled looks on Walt's and Lauren's faces were priceless. I smiled.

"Sand?" Lauren asked.

"Yup, sand. Mrs. Williamson's room was spotless except for a few grains of sand under the bed. Staci had just returned from the beach. It was a guess, but it turned out to be correct."

Walt held his red solo cup of wine up to me and we toasted my excellent deductive abilities.

"Well done," he said. Then without me even asking, he filled in a few of the missing pieces. "It seems Staci had been in the middle of the switch when she heard Mrs. Williamson coming down the hall. The fake necklace had slipped through her fingers and fallen behind the nightstand. She was waiting for her grandmother to notice it missing before she went in and found the fake, and no one would be the wiser. However, when the announcement was made that it had been stolen, Staci saw a way out and made up the story about the fleeing youths. But we wouldn't have even known they were fake if not for you."

"The real credit goes to Mrs. Williamson," I said. "If she hadn't washed the basil martini off the jewels, they never would have disintegrated."

Lauren laughed. "Hate to see good vodka get washed down the drain, though." She shot a flirtations glance in Walt's direction. "Maybe you should book Mrs. Williamson on alcohol abuse."

Walt and Lauren looked at each other and laughed.

Feeling like the proverbial third wheel, I finished my wine, made my excuses and headed home.

❖❖❖

If I had written the ending to this story, then no one would have inherited the necklace. Instead, Mrs. Williamson would have sold it to the highest bidder and used the money to do good things like build a no-kill animal shelter or save endangered koala bear habitats or something. I'm a sucker for a Disney ending.

But in real life, the necklace was sold to pay off gambling debts. Seems that after a few rounds of basil martinis, Mrs. Williamson would run up quite a tab betting on the ponies down in Sarasota. Her system relied on picking those which sported green racing silks.

You think you know your landlady, then you learn something like that. She'd told me many times her favorite color was purple.

But it's all worked out nicely for me. She relies on my rent check to help make ends meet. That allows me to continue to create stories of murder and intrigue from the safety and security of my carriage house, where I write, by the bay.

ABOUT THE AUTHORS

GINA WARREN BUZBY is originally from Columbia, South Carolina. She has a B.A. in Art and Advertising from Columbia College (SC) and a Masters of Education from Clemson University. Currently, Gina serves on many boards, including Columbia College Board of Visitors, Armed Services YMCA of Hampton Roads, East Beach Writers Guild, and the Tidewater Collection at Norfolk Naval Base.

Gina is also a proud member of P.E.O. – Philanthropic Educational Organization, Chapter AK. She works as a Professional Fine Artist from her carriage house studio in East Beach. She enjoys leading the "Van Gogh and Vino" classes through private bookings. View her paintings and *plein air* pieces on her website.

Website: www.GinaWarrenBuzby.com

PATRICK CLARK was born in Milwaukee, Wisconsin. He is a graduate of the School of Journalism at the University of Wisconsin – Milwaukee and holds a Master of Arts degree in National Security and Strategic Studies from the U.S. Naval War College.

After twenty years as a Surface Warfare Officer in the U.S. Navy, Patrick retired and went into industry as a Vice President of Operations.

His writing themes leverage his knowledge of the

ABOUT THE AUTHORS

military and government to develop stories with suspense and intrigue. He currently lives in Norfolk, Virginia.
His debut novel, *The Monroe Decision*, is scheduled for publication in summer 2017.
Website: www.patrick-clark.com

MICHELLE DAVENPORT is a Midwestern girl who spent a majority of her adult life in the Norfolk, Virginia, area. She recently moved out to the west coast, because home is where the Navy sends your spouse. When not taking care of her little family (two cats, a dog, a bird and loving husband), she volunteers on the Homecoming Committee of the Surface Officer Spouses of San Diego and Anchor Scholarship Foundation.
Blog: www.michelleddavenport.blogspot.com

KAREN HARRIS is a writer and editor from San Francisco, California. A graduate of the University of California, Davis, she is the coordinator for the Virginia Beach Master Gardeners' Annual Trial Garden and sings with Bellissima Women's Chorus. Her first short story, "I Have a Dress" was published in the first *By The Bay: East Beach Stories*.

WILL HOPKINS lives in East Beach. He is the author of three police mysteries set in mid-century Norfolk: *Willowood, Full Fathom Five* and *Miss Nike Ajax*. His most recent book is *The Lights*, a collection of short stories set against the great flying-saucer scare of 1952.
Website: www.willhopkins4.com

ELIZABETH KIMBALL is a Florida attorney, Navy wife, and East Beach mom to two girls who love the Chesapeake Bay. She actively serves her community by volunteering with The Tidewater Officer Spouse Association, The Federalist Society, and other organizations.

ABOUT THE AUTHORS

JAMIE MCALLISTER works as a freelance writer. In addition to writing for businesses and agencies, her work has also appeared in several Hampton Roads publications, including *Coastal Virginia Magazine*, *The Health Journal*, *Coastal Virginia Business Magazine*, and *Tidewater Women*. This is her first published short story. She and her husband, James, live with their two rescue cats in Virginia Beach, Virginia.

Website: www.mcallisterwe.com
Twitter: @jmcallisterwe

L.W. "SKIP" MCLAMB was born and raised in High Point, North Carolina. He earned degrees from North Carolina State University, The College of William & Mary, and Old Dominion University that lead to a career in teaching. He has resided in Hampton Roads for over forty years.

Currently retired, Skip worked for four decades in the Virginia Beach Public Schools in a variety of teaching and administrative positions. He is active in a variety of environmental organizations.

His interests include camping, hiking, kayaking, fishing, and visiting his children and grandchildren. He hopes that writing will provide a new avenue to extend his teaching career.

MARY JAC O'DANIEL is originally from Richardson, Texas. She has a Bachelor of Science in Education from Baylor University and is currently pursuing a Master's Degree in Speech Pathology from Old Dominion University. Mary Jac has been published in the *Elephant Journal*. A former high school English teacher and track coach, she has also taught in California and China. An avid traveler, Mary Jac has been able to visit every continent except Africa and Antarctica. She enjoys running, swimming, and competitive sailing. Mary Jac is a

ABOUT THE AUTHORS

military spouse and lives in East Beach with her husband, Paul.

JAYNE ORMEROD grew up in a small Ohio town then went on to a small-town Ohio college. Upon earning her degree in accountancy she became a CIA (that's not a sexy spy thing, but a Certified Internal Auditor.) She married a naval officer and off they sailed to see the world. After fifteen moves she realized she needed a more transportable vocation, so turned to writing cozy mysteries. In addition to two short stories in the first anthology, *By the Bay: East Beach Stories*, Jayne's publication credits include four additional short mysteries in various anthologies, two full-length cozy mysteries, and one novella.
Website: www.JayneOrmerod.com
Blog: www.JayneOrmerod.blogspot.com

MIKE OWENS, a retired physician, has undergraduate and medical degrees from the University of North Carolina in Chapel Hill. He obtained his MFA degree in creative writing from Old Dominion University in Norfolk, VA in 2011. His nonfiction works include: *Care of the Terminally Ill Cancer Patient* (2002) *and Primary Care Issues for End-of-Life Care* (2003). His first novel, *The End of Free Will*, was published in January, 2014, followed by a second novel, *The Threshold*, in September 2014. His latest work, *Screwed*, a retelling of the steamy eighteenth century saga, *Moll Flanders*, will be released by The Wild Rose Press in 2017.
Website: www.mikeowens42.com

JENNY F. SPARKS was born and raised in South Carolina. She graduated from the College of Charleston with a BS in Sociology and a minor in Health and Gerontology.

Married for 28 years to a career Naval Officer, she has lived throughout the United States and raised two sons.

ABOUT THE AUTHORS

Jenny has volunteered in various positions in her children's schools and with the Navy in jobs ranging from PTA president to ombudsman. She has been employed as a preschool teacher, vocational education teacher, vocational consultant, and senior center director.

Jenny lives in Virginia with her husband and their dogs, Millie and Twyla.

ABOUT THE AUTHORS

FOR MORE INFORMATION ABOUT THE AUTHORS

There's more to our stories! We've posted interviews and photos of our authors having fun on our blog: www.BytheBayStories.blogspot.com

And be sure to join the discussion on our By the Bay Facebook group. On Wednesdays, the authors answer whimsical questions offered up by family, friends and fans.

(One last thing…)
THE BOOK REVIEW
BY MIKE OWENS

We hope you enjoyed *By the Bay 2: More East Beach Stories*. Please consider writing a brief review on Amazon.

What is it? Just a few lines about the book, setting, characters writing style, things like that. Whatever strikes your fancy. Nothing elaborate, unless you're feeling inspired. If you are, that's okay, too.

How do I do it? Turn on your computer (sometimes I forget this step…) and ring up Amazon Books. Enter our title, *By the Bay 2: More East Beach Stories*. Click on the book cover and you'll see our starred rating along with how many reviews have been posted this far. Click on that to read what other readers have said. On that page you will see a gray box that says "Write a Customer Review." Click there, rate by stars (5 highest/1 lowest), and maybe a sentence or two about what you enjoyed about the book.

Why should I do it? Amazon is the Grand Poobah of book ratings and sales, and reviews make them smile. Our book can rise in the Amazon ratings as more reviews come in. This can boost sales, and, since all of our revenues go to local charities, the more sales the bigger our charitable contribution. Write on! And thanks!

Made in the USA
Middletown, DE
24 November 2018